The Commitment Test

AMANDA ⋆ AKSEL

Cover Design by Amanda Aksel & Mona Lin

Edited by Lauran Strait
http://www.linkedin.com/in/lauranstrait

For Joe

Acknowledgments

A special thank you to my husband, Joe, who was a tremendous help during the creation of this story. I could not have done this without his support and encouragement.

Producing a novel takes a village and I would like to thank Heather, Julie, Jessica, Danielle, Lauran, Steph, Nicole, and my wonderful mother, Lorraine.

I am truly grateful to all my friends, family, and readers who kept asking when they could read the next book. I wrote this for you and I hope you enjoy it.

CONTENTS

Chapter One- Love in San Francisco   1

Chapter Two- Marin in Montana   9

Chapter Three- Happy Birthday   25

Chapter Four- The Proposal   32

Chapter Five- Girls Night Out   41

Chapter Six- The Market   57

Chapter Seven- The Other Book   69

Chapter Eight- Happy Couples   81

Chapter Nine- Family Matters   93

Chapter Ten- Surprise from Thailand   105

Chapter Eleven- Miss Independent   113

Chapter Twelve- Play House   119

Chapter Thirteen- Fell Street   127

Chapter Fourteen- St. Patrick's Day   139

Chapter Fifteen- Mother Material   149

Chapter Sixteen- South of the Border   164

Chapter Seventeen- Sexy Getaway   170

CONTENTS

Chapter Eighteen- Office Space   176

Chapter Nineteen- My Taste   184

Chapter Twenty- Jack is Back   190

Chapter Twenty One- Sentimental or Just Mental   202

Chapter Twenty Two- Will or Won't   210

Chapter Twenty Three- San Jose   216

Chapter Twenty Four- Just Say Yes   225

Chapter Twenty Five- Friendly Advice   234

Chapter Twenty Six- Are You Positive?   247

Chapter Twenty Seven- Threes a Crowd   253

Chapter Twenty Eight- An Affair to Forget   269

Chapter Twenty Nine- The Commitment Test   281

Chapter Thirty- Breakups and Makeups   288

Chapter Thirty One- Mr. and Mrs. Cash   296

Chapter Thirty Two- The Decision   302

Chapter Thirty Three- Coming Home   307

Chapter Thirty Four- Moving On   316

Epilogue- Our Special Day   324

The Commitment Test

1

Love and San Francisco

COMMITMENT BEGINS WITH THE BEST of intentions. That's what I thought as I sat across from the couple in their early thirties. Both were dressed to perfection in expensive suits.

They looked perfect for each other. But looks could be deceiving.

Silence hung between them in a reflective moment. Tick, tock, tick, tock. It was like the two were playing a game of honesty chicken, each hoping the other would speak first. I was tempted to break the silence, but held on a moment longer.

Finally, she opened her mouth, but before she could summon the words, her husband jumped in.

"I'm just going to say it," he said. "I think marriage ruined our relationship."

Dun, dun, dun—Now we were getting somewhere.

She scoffed. "How can you say that? Marriage doesn't ruin relationships."

"Of course it does, we've seen it over and over again. Remember when we first got married? All of our friends were getting married too. How many couples did we hang out with? Five? Five other couples. It's been eight years, and how many of them are now divorced?"

"That's different!" she said.

"Three. Half of us couldn't even make it to ten years. Remember Janet and Danny? Those two were crazy about each other until they got married. And now they're divorced."

"Why don't you just say what you really mean? You want out. Stop using our friends' failed marriages as an excuse for why ours isn't working." Tears slid down her cheeks.

"Then you tell me, why isn't it working?" He raised his voice.

"I don't know. That's why we're here!"

"Okay, okay," I interrupted. "He's right. Some relationships fail after marriage. However, marriage doesn't ruin relationships, people ruin them and sometimes relationships ruin themselves."

She sniffled with sorrow filled eyes, and he pulled a tissue from the floral box on the table. His eyes harbored something else. Something that looked an awful lot like regret. No husband wants to be the bad guy, hurting his wife with words and feelings he couldn't help but let go of, if only to unhinge the chains enough to breathe a little more.

I caught the wife's gaze. "You really don't know why you're here, do you?" I asked.

She shook her head. "I thought everything was fine."

"I thought so too," he said and dropped his head.

"What are we going to do now?" she asked.

"You two did the right thing by seeking help," I said. "This is your opportunity to find out what's really going on. Is that what you both want?"

They nodded.

"Good," I continued. "We're going to work on your communication and get to the root of the problem. And trust me, what's in the best interest of each of you, is the best interest of both of you. Okay?"

The broken lovers agreed, and I sighed, anticipating an arduous journey. Then, he gently took her hand in his.

I smiled at the sweet gesture. There was hope for this couple.

By the time they left, it was the end of the day. I pulled my dark hair back into a neat ponytail and finished some office odds and ends. Just as I was packing up to leave, I noticed a missed call from James. That's right, my boyfriend, James.

Almost a year and a half ago, he'd rescued me for the second time from yet another preventable tumble. That was the day he gave me a second chance, and I promised myself in that moment that I wouldn't screw it up. Or at least I wouldn't repeat any of my same mistakes, which included being cunningly deceitful and setting him up to cheat. As the saying goes, I turned a new leaf that day.

"You're still here?" Andy popped in.

"Yeah, what's up?"

"You and James wanna meet me for a drink in a bit?"

Andy was one of the partners in our three-therapist practice. Somehow after years of my contempt for him and the stint in which he was my emotional drill sergeant, a.k.a. my therapist, I started to see him as a human being and not just an egotistical, know-it-all prick who only cared about himself. Andy was actually a nice guy with a big heart, but I was sure I was sworn to secrecy. He had a reputation to protect.

In fact, we became the kind of friends that met for drinks with our significant others. Though, Andy never really had a significant other. They were more like insignificant others. We became so friendly that I even suggested a date with Telly. They went out, of course. Once . . . that I knew of anyway. Neither of them would tell me what happened that night. In fact, they get a little weird whenever I mention it. Both use the same answer as if they were contracted to do so. "It could never work between us." Sure. . .

After asking a dozen more times, I let it go.

"I wish we could, but we've got to get ready to leave tomorrow. I'm still not packed."

He snapped his fingers. "That's right, you're going to Montana."

I confirmed with a smile.

"Are you nervous about meeting the parents?" Andy asked.

"No, I've video chatted with them lots of times."

"They have internet in Montana?"

I smirked and swatted his shoulder. Truthfully, the question had crossed my mind before too.

"Well, enjoy it. I'll see you next week."

"I will. Ciao!" I swung my five-pound purse over my shoulder.

Downstairs, pairs of run-of-the-mill push and pull doors had replaced the untrustworthy revolving door during the remodel. As I made my way out of the building, a chilly breeze brushed my cheeks. All winter long, I never got used to slightly freezing while walking the six blocks home in the evenings. Though the city lights illuminated the street, I couldn't wait for daylight savings time and warmer San Francisco air.

I dug my leather gloves and phone out of my tote purse and called James.

"Hey, baby doll," James' voice crooned on the line. I blushed.

"Hey, you," I said, slipping on my gloves. Much better.

"I just dropped Marvin off at David and Rachel's. You wanna sleep at my place or yours tonight?"

Hmm . . . his place or mine . . . our favorite dilemma. We hadn't moved in together, but we spent enough time at each other's places to be considered cohabiters. At least that's what I told myself to ease the pain that it had been over a year and we hadn't yet made the move.

To be honest, I feared a Chad repeat, or at least a version of it, if James moved in. Chad, my ex-fiancé, hadn't even unpacked his boxes when I caught him in bed with another woman. Most of the time, I strongly advised couples to live together before marriage, but in my case with James, I wanted to wait. In case I was cursed.

"My place is closer to the airport, and my bed is nicer," I said.

"So you say."

"It's a fact, James. MapQuest it." I covered my nose with my hand and breathed out hot air to warm my face.

"I was referring to your insult about my bed."

"Babe, you can't argue with a Tempur-Pedic and Vera Wang sheets." I could use those cozy sheets right about now.

"Uh, I only understood half of that."

Men.

"It doesn't matter," I said. "My place it is."

He chuckled. "I'll pick up dinner and be there in an hour."

"See ya then, love you."

"Love you too."

Later, I discovered that expensive bedding did not always result in luxurious sleep. I usually fell asleep on my left side, but I couldn't get comfortable so I switched to the right. Same thing. I flattened on my back and glanced at the clock. Only four more hours before the alarm would go off. James breathed wispy sleep sounds next to me. His warm body heated the bed like an oven. I kicked off the covers and stirred him in the process.

"You okay?" James mumbled.

"I can't sleep." I shoved my pillow deeper into the pillowcase.

"How come?"

I sighed. "I'm anxious."

"About what?" James rubbed the sleep out of his blue eyes.

"About meeting your family. Your entire family."

James' cousin, Emily, was getting married and all of the Young clan were gathering in Montana for the event.

"Why?" he asked.

"I'm a half-Chinese girl from California. I don't know anything about life in the mountains."

He scrunched his face and scratched the stubble on his cheek. "Mar, it's Montana, not the old west."

"I know. I just want to fit in. I want them to know I'm Young material, ya know?"

"Shhh . . . you're over thinking it." He pulled me in and swaddled me with his strong arms. They were like a protective shield; nothing physical, emotional or other-wise could hurt me. "My family adores you, and the rest are gonna love you because I love you."

"Okay," I said and snuggled into him even though it was too warm. Within minutes, he fell asleep. Eventually, I did too.

2

Marin In Montana

IT WAS ALMOST FIVE O'CLOCK in the afternoon when we reached the resort in Big Sky, Montana. Clouds covered the atmosphere, and I couldn't tell if it was snowing or if the wind was picking up flakes and whirling them around. It was a picturesque winter wonderland, and I imagined every night in that town was spent near a warm log fireplace. At least in the cold month of February. San Francisco never saw much snow, and I had forgotten how much it brightened the scenery, even with the overcast.

Between the lack of sleep, an early flight, and a long drive to the hotel, I was spent. But I had no other choice than to get my ass in the shower and show up. It took a moderate amount of moisturizer, multiple coats of under eye concealer, and extra blush before I was ready to meet the family.

My palms perspired as we made our way down to the reception hall for the rehearsal dinner, despite the fact that it was thirty degrees outside. We barely stepped foot in the room when I heard, "James!" James' mom, Gloria, rushed over and embraced him like she hadn't seen him in years.

"Hi, Mom," he said and kissed the top of her head. The height difference was significant. She pulled away and looked up at him. A second later, she turned to me. Her smile creased all the lines on her face, but she beamed bright like the sun, spilling her warmth over us.

"Marin," she said softly.

"Hi, Gloria," I said. That's right, first name basis.

She pulled me in for a hug, and for a moment, I was engulfed in the scent of her White Diamonds perfume. "You're even more beautiful in person," Gloria said.

Her comment was not only flattering, but relaxing. If I was in with Gloria, the rest would be easy.

"Hey there, son," Frank said as he shook James' hand and brought him in for a manly embrace.

"It's good to see you, Pop," James said.

Frank shook my hand, his rough callouses scratching my skin. His face was warm, but weathered from his outdoor work. "Thanks for comin' all this way to keep James company."

"I'm happy to be here." I smiled.

"Isn't she just the sweetest?" Gloria said, embracing me as we walked into the family gathering. James' sister, Amanda, and her husband, Evan, greeted us warmly at the table. Their daughter, Addison, barely six, jumped in to James' arms, blonde curls covering his face as he held her. I had met Amanda and her family on several occasions. They loved to visit California. Their familiar faces soothed my nerves.

"Did you get her?" Gloria asked Evan.

Evan held an iPad with a live video of James' sister Andrea, who was still stationed in Australia.

"Hi, honey," Gloria bent down to face the iPad-Andrea.

"Hi, Mom," she replied in her silvery voice. Andrea was like the female version of James, sandy blonde hair and Big Sky blue eyes.

"Hey, Sis." James leaned in. "You're lookin' good. Glad you were able to make it digitally."

"Yeah, I wish I was really there, but then again, it's summer here." Andrea seemed to laugh at this, but her video stream disrupted and froze her face, mouth crooked and eyes drooping. It was the only thing I didn't like about video chatting.

Jacob, the groom, called for everyone's attention with a clink of his wine glass. The room silenced, accept for Andrea, who continued to talk, unaware of the toast that was about to take place. The crowd turned to our table and Evan silenced the iPad.

While Jacob gave a brief but sincere toast, my eyes wandered around the dimly lit room at all the smiling faces witnessing the happy occasion of love and family. James rested his arm around me, tickling my shoulder with his fingers. I leaned in and nuzzled myself underneath his chin, and he squeezed me tighter.

Small talk persisted during dinner, but by the time dessert reached our table, James and I were mingling with the crowd. Emily, the twenty-six-year-old bride, spotted us and made her way over seconds later. She gave James an adoring look—the kind a little sister gives to her brother.

"It's so great that you came. We've all heard so much about you," Emily said, after greeting me with a hug.

"I'm happy to be here to celebrate your special day."

"Have you met Grandma?" Emily asked, pulling over a frail old lady who couldn't take her eyes off James.

"James Christopher, is that you?" The loose skin around Grandma's neck jiggled as she spoke.

"Grandma!" James bent forward, carefully wrapping his arms around her. She couldn't have been taller than five feet.

"Have you moved back yet?" she asked.

"No. I live in San Francisco now, remember?" James said, as if it were the hundredth time he'd told her.

"Yes, I remember. I'm old, not senile. I'm also sentimental and want you to come home."

"Okay, Grandma. I want you to meet my girlfriend, Marin." James diverted the conversation.

"Oh, yes, yes. Nice to meet you. You're very pretty, aren't you?"

I shook her fragile hand. It was soft and wrinkly, like an aged piece of fruit. "It's nice to meet you too."

Amanda tapped James on the shoulder. "You got a second?" she asked.

"I'll be right back," he said and took off to another corner of the room.

"So . . ." I said. Emily and Grandma smiled and

stared, waiting for me to say something interesting. "I love your dress," I told Emily.

"Thanks."

"How long have you and Jacob been together?"

"Two and a half years," she said as if annoyed they weren't married sooner. "It took him over a year and a half to propose. You've been with James for about two years now, right?"

"Almost a year and a half," I answered. Technically, we started dating almost two years ago, but we don't really consider the first five months of our "relationship" dating since, at the time, I was using him to prove a point. James and I had dubbed that time the *summer façade*. I plead insanity.

"When are you and James getting married?" Grandma asked.

"Well, we're not engaged yet, but hopefully soon."

"Hopefully soon is right. You're no spring chicken." She pointed her feebly finger at me.

"Grandma!" Emily scolded.

"Well, you'll have to start having children soon. Otherwise it'll be too late." Grandma snapped her fingers while simultaneously zapping my fertility. "When I was your age, I already had four children."

I was at a loss for words. Ten minutes earlier, I didn't know Emily or Grandma and now we were discussing my familial future. "Exactly how old do you think I am?" I asked.

Grandma gave me a once over. "Thirty-four, thirty-five." I was thirty-two. Okay, I'd be turning thirty-three in a week, but still. Thirty-five?

"Hey, Grandma. I think there's more bread pudding. Why don't we get some?" Emily ushered her away, while giving me an apologetic look. Grandma was right. James and I were of a certain age, and we weren't getting any younger. Her calling me thirty-five made it all the more real that I was running out of time.

I found James across the room, talking and laughing with more of his family members. He had one of those big smiles you could see from afar and the sweetest wrinkles around his eyes when he laughed. I imagined that over time they would crease more and more until they became a permanent reminder of his happy life . . . with me.

"You look tired. Do you want to head back to the room soon?" he asked.

"I look tired?" I asked, touching my fingers to the skin under my eyes, feeling for bags and lines.

"Yeah, you've been yawning all night."

I hadn't noticed. How could I be yawning with all the excitement going on? But I agreed that it was time for bed, and we wished everyone a good night.

"Did you have a good time?" he asked, taking my hand as we walked to our room.

"Yeah, it was nice to finally meet everyone. You?"

"Yeah. It feels good to be back." He smiled and squeezed my hand.

I remembered what Grandma asked him. "Do you miss it?"

"Sometimes."

"But you don't want to move back, do you?" I held my breath for a moment.

He chuckled. "No, I love San Fran."

"Good," I said, wrapping my arms around his waist. "Hey, do I look thirty-five?"

He looked down at me with a questionable expression and no answer.

"Do I?" I asked.

"You don't look a day over twenty-five," he said.

Liar. I looked at least twenty-seven.

The next morning, I awoke refreshed and excited, and I wasn't the only one. James and I spent the morning fooling around in bed, working up an appetite for our forty-dollar room service breakfast. But the fun didn't stop there. I fed him pieces of bacon and he licked syrup off my body, leaving my legs and chest sticky. We were having so much fun that I almost wanted to skip the wedding. And I love weddings, a ceremony of hope, romantic and full of beautiful intentions of love. Maybe a year from now, James and I could have our own ceremony of hope, if not sooner.

James warmed the car while I bundled up. The brief walk outside was almost painful. The cold air seemed to pierce through all of my outerwear and snow stuck to the sides of my suede booties. Inside, the car was much warmer.

"Why did they want to get married in February? It's freezing," I told James and rubbed my gloved hands briskly against my legs that were protected with only my thin tights.

"I dunno. I guess they couldn't wait until summer."

"That's sweet. What about you? Would you want to get married in the winter like this?"

He shrugged. "I dunno. Maybe. Guys don't really think about that stuff."

"I guess that's true. That's why you need us girls." I pinched his cheek, which grew pink. He rolled his eyes.

At the chapel, the seats were almost full. We found Gloria and Frank and scooted next to them on the wooden bench. I turned to the large triangular window that framed the beautiful outdoor mountains. Timber, branch-like beams adorned the ceiling and white flowers hung on the edge of the pews.

"Did you get enough sleep, Marin?" Gloria asked.

"Yes, I feel very rested." When really I was feeling a little sleepy after the morning's events.

"That's good. You had a long day yesterday. And you have to go back tomorrow?"

I nodded.

"Well, that's a shame. I was hoping we'd have more time together." Gloria pouted her lip. I was touched by her effort to get close to me. She'd make the best mother-in-law. Poor James wouldn't be so lucky. Then again, my mom was nicer to James than to any other guy I'd ever been with. At least he had that going for him.

"It would be great if you could visit us in California," I told her.

"I'm sure we will one day. Maybe if there were a wedding or a baby we could visit sooner."

Maybe Gloria and my mother weren't so different after all, though I liked the idea too. I looked up at James, hoping his response would shed a little light on his thoughts. He seemed to be rendered speechless.

"That's enough, Gloria," Frank said, and I smirked. James cleared his throat and began glancing around the room, waving every second or so.

"Who's that?" I'd ask and he'd give the name and relation of each of them. There must have been at least a hundred and fifty people there and most were relatives. My family was so much smaller in comparison. My father's parents had passed and my Uncle Al never had children. Not to mention that he lived on the opposite coast in D.C. My mother's family, on the other hand, was still across the Pacific Ocean. I'd only met them a couple of times and staying in touch wasn't much of an option since I didn't speak Mandarin.

The music began, an unfamiliar but beautiful song. Emily and her bridesmaids strolled down the aisle. It was a beautiful ceremony, tearful for me, as usual. Emily and Jacob gazed into each other's eyes as if telling each other *I love you* over and over again. My perspective on relationships and romance had been restored over the last year and a half with James. His cousin's wedding only fueled my sense of hope about my future with him. I knew our happily-ever-after would come soon.

Later at the reception, we watched the bride and groom's first dance and clinked our forks against our glasses to get them to kiss, the same as every other wedding I'd ever been to, but entertaining and sweet nonetheless. James' family migrated to the dance floor, while we stayed behind to feed each other slices of vanilla wedding cake.

"Well, aren't you two just adorable," Emily said as she approached with a grin. Her cheeks were flushed. No doubt it was all the happiness going to her head.

"There's the beautiful bride," James said and stood to give her a congratulatory hug.

"I'm so glad you and Marin are here. I hope you two are coming to brunch in the morning."

"I have to take Marin to the airport first thing. She has to head back," James said.

Emily frowned. "You're gonna let this beautiful woman go home without you?"

James shrugged. "I won't be far behind her."

"Well, thanks for coming, Marin. I hope you have a safe trip home."

"Thank you and congratulations." I gave her a big smile and she returned it, one girl in love to another.

"She's a keeper, James," Emily sang with a wink and moved on to her next adoring guest.

"You are a keeper. You know that, right?" James kissed me softly. I looked into his sweet blue eyes and had to catch my breath. "And you were worried my family wouldn't like you," he said.

"Can you blame me? Remember how nervous you were to meet my family?"

"Yes, but it turned out great. Just like this."

"I still can't believe how well that went. They love you," I said, remembering how my parents never seemed to like my serious boyfriends like Chad or even my med school boyfriend, Jack, who was from a good family and a future doctor. One thing we could all agree on was that James was wonderfully different.

He pushed my hair behind my ear, then put another piece of cake in front of my mouth. I shook my hand to dismiss the sweet sponge, and he stuffed it in his own mouth. A tiny vanilla crumb sat on his bottom lip. His look turned serious as if he wanted to tell me something, something that had been on his mind. My heart raced as he took my hands in his. I held my breath.

"Do you wanna dance?" he asked.

I exhaled and wiped the crumb off his perfect mouth. "I'd love to."

James spun me around the dance floor until I was dizzy with his touch, his smell, and his warmth. He pulled me in close and my hand rested softly on his chest as he led. Emily and Jacob swayed slowly to the song, staring into each other's eyes as she ran her fingers through his hair. A picture perfect newlywed couple. James noticed them too.

"Do you think that'll be us someday?" I asked. He looked at me again with that same serious look, like he wanted to say something. He opened his mouth to speak.

"Okay, all you single gents!" The DJ announced, deterring his attention. "It's time for the garter toss."

"I guess I better go," James said and began walking with the crowd. I pulled him back.

"Wait, were you going to say something?" I asked, searching for something in his eyes. Maybe it was the wedding, the champagne, or the closeness I felt toward him since going to Montana, but I had a strong feeling our relationship was about to rise to a new level.

He smiled and brushed his hand along my cheek. "I was going to say that I love you." He took my hand and kissed it, then ran off to catch the garter that Jacob was seductively slipping off of Emily's leg. Jacob twirled the garter around his finger and I watched about twenty un-married men huddle near him, laughing and shoving each other a bit. Why were men so competitive?

The groom flung the satin garter in the air. All the guys reached out for it like a football, but James was the one to catch it.

Was it a sign? Was my proposal finally coming?

He swaggered back to the table with his prize like some kind of hotshot.

"What happened?" Andrea called from the iPad.

"James caught the garter," Amanda told her.

"That's hilarious," she said. "Why did you go out there anyway?"

James sat down and took the iPad from its propped position at the table. "Because, I like to make a fool of myself sometimes."

"Are you going out there too, Marin?" Amanda asked.

"Of course!" I said, and thought that catching the bouquet would be a sure sign that James and I would be married next.

"You better go. They're calling for the toss."

Beyoncé's single girl anthem rang throughout the re-ception hall as I made my way to the dance floor, where a smaller, but livelier group of ladies, all with hands held up, had gathered.

Emily threw the flower bunch into the air.

I propelled my whole body forward.

As my fingers grazed the soft petals, I could almost feel the weight of gold and diamonds on my left ring finger. But I had thrown myself too hard, because I lost my balance and fell flat on the floor. Ouch!

James rushed over, concern covering his face, and helped me up. When I had finished wiping the dust off of my black tights, I saw that James' nineteen-year-old cousin, Grace, had the bouquet along with my hopes of a perfect ending and a sure sign of my soon-to-be engagement. She cried with glee, almost smug in her smile.

Fine, she could have it. It was a stupid superstition anyway.

"Are you okay?" James asked.

My face felt hot and I swallowed a lump in my throat before speaking. "Yeah, I banged my knee of course."

He examined my leg. "Well, it's not bleeding, but you've got a tear in your stockings." I looked down and saw the wide snag. Another pair of tights ruined. "Oh wait," he said. "You've got something right here." James tickled the back of my leg and I flinched, giggling like a little girl. He laughed.

"See, all better." He smiled, and I blushed back at him. "You ready to call it a night?"

I looked down at my torn tights and the emptying chairs. "Do you think everyone saw what happened?" I asked.

"Everyone who's here." He gave me a sympathetic look.

"Yeah, let's go."

We congratulated the bride and groom, and his family wished me a safe trip back in the morning, but not after asking me if I was all right. James kept a hold on my waist to keep me from any more accidents as we headed back to our room.

The next day I returned alone to warmer weather. It would have been nice if James could have come back with me, but his family was important to him and he rarely saw them.

None of that stopped me from calling him as soon as I got back to my apartment.

"How was the flight?" he asked.

"Not too bad. It's good to be home, but I miss you."

"I miss you too. I'll be back on your birthday." I remembered when birthdays were a great excuse to get gifts and have too many cocktails. Now that I was turning thirty-three, it was only a reminder that time was running out and I still hadn't accomplished what I'd set out to. "I'm taking you to Masa's for dinner," he said.

"Really?" Okay, so it was still a good excuse to let my boyfriend take me to a nice place.

"Of course. My special girl deserves a special dinner."

"Don't forget, it's Valentine's Day too."

"I didn't forget. Actually, I've been thinking and there's something important I want to talk to you about."

I paused and felt my cheeks warm. "Talk about

good? Or talk about bad?"

"It's good. I promise." Whew!

"Can't you tell me now?"

"How 'bout we wait for your special day, okay?"

Hmm, good news that he wanted to save for my "special day." I knew it! It seemed as if my waiting would soon end.

3

Happy Birthday

"I'M GETTING ENGAGED!" I yelled out, leaving Holly and Telly struggling to swallow their sandwiches without choking. The news bubbled up inside me until I couldn't contain it any longer.

Telly sat across from me, lightly covering her full mouth. "What do you mean you're getting engaged?"

"James is going to propose tomorrow night."

Telly and Holly looked at me awkwardly, but I remained steadfast in my brilliant smile.

"How do you know?" Holly asked with a half smile as if it took all she had to produce that much. It wasn't the reaction I was expecting from them.

I brushed the crumbs from my hands and leaned forward, looking intently at my friends. "Well," I began like I had a juicy piece of gossip, "James is coming back tomorrow from Montana and he said he wants to talk to me about something important. He made reservations tomorrow night at Masa's. Plus you know what tomorrow is?" I dragged out the "is" for emphasis.

"Your birthday." Holly said, adjusting her newsboy cap.

I beamed. "And?"

"Valentine's Day." Telly grimaced suggesting the holiday left a bad taste in her mouth.

"Exactly, it's the perfect day for a proposal," I told them in that giddy girl sort of way.

"That sounds really nice and all, but what if he just wants to take you somewhere nice for your birthday and Valentine's Day. That doesn't exactly mean a proposal is coming." Telly pursed her lips.

How could I blame Telly for trying to talk me down? Especially since I had a habit of getting a little zealous from these types of notions. Sometimes they were real and sometimes they were not. When I added the wedding, meeting the family, his words, our relationship, and the significance of the day, it all summed up to one conclusion. A proposal.

"I know it sounds like I'm getting my hopes up, but I can feel it. Something big is going to happen soon. It's just one of those gut feelings." My words must've fallen flat on the persuasion scale, because by the look on Telly's gorgeously tanned face, she wasn't buying it. Surprisingly, neither was Holly.

"That's great, Marin," Holly said, almost with a sympathetic smile. At least she was pretending to be happy for me. We looked at Telly, waiting for her to join us. Instead, she gazed off and chewed her sandwich slowly. I would never understand how she made chewing look sexy, but that was Telly for you.

"So what are you going to wear for the occasion?" Telly finally asked.

I paused for a moment and did a mental run through of my entire closet. And of course it was water, water everywhere and not a drop to drink. I shrugged and told her I didn't have anything that I deemed appropriate for the evening. This news sparked a light in her dark eyes. "I know just the dress," she said.

Later that day, Telly took me to a boutique on Haight Street and introduced me to a dress she'd been ogling in the window for the past week.

"I was going to buy this for myself this weekend, but I think it would be perfect for your date with James." Telly admired the ivory one-shoulder dress with the loose top and cinched-in waist. She was almost half a foot taller than me in her three-inch nude stilettos.

"You're right," I said. "It's the perfect dress."

She put her arm around me as we walked into the store. "You'll let me borrow it sometime, right?" I gave her a playfully reluctant smile and agreed.

I purposely left my morning appointments free so I could get enough rest for my big night with James. That was wishful thinking because I spent most of those hours tossing and turning and thinking about how he would propose, what he would say, when we'd get married, where we'd live, our family. Basically, I imagined our entire life together.

The morning light woke me up earlier than expected.

Even with the lack of sleep, I couldn't wait to get out of bed. My stomach fluttered with butterflies of anticipation. Twelve more hours before I would see James, and I prayed that they would fly by. I grabbed my phone from the nightstand. I had three *Happy Birthday* text messages, one from Telly, one from Holly, and one from my beloved, James. His flight home would leave soon, and I was dying to hear his voice. I avoided the urge to dial and sent a quick text.

Happy Valentine's Day, my love. I can't wait to see you tonight!!

After two cups of coffee, a few bites of undesired toast, and a completed "difficult" Sudoku puzzle, I headed to work. It was just before ten when I entered the office suite. Diana greeted me as normal. Slowly but surely. Only this time it was even slower because she added *Happy Birthday* to her greeting. I thanked her and headed back to my office, which was flooded with sunlight of the mid-morning. I was used to being greeted by a much subtler morning light in the earlier hours. The noticeable change in the light reminded me that there were only nine more hours to go. Before I could adjust the window blinds, I noticed a beautiful bouquet of white orchids sitting on my desk. My favorite! I rushed over to see the card.

To my beautiful Birthday girl and Valentine. Love, James.

My cheeks flushed and I held the card to my chest, almost hugging it. How could I not gush over James' sweet gift? I did a little dance before sitting down at my desk to admire the flowers some more. My heartbeat seemed to increase as if it were following along to a feel-good love song. In that moment, I was so happy I could have cried, but before I decided whether or not to let the tears through, I heard it. It was like a singing waitstaff at Applebee's.

Happy birthday to you
Happy birthday to you

Katie, Andy, and Diana walked into my office wearing birthday hats and carrying a small cake with one burning candle instead of thirty-three, which would probably have been a fire hazard.

Happy birthday, dear Marin
Happy birthday to you.

Diana sat the cake on my desk.

I covered my face shyly but then smiled. "Oh, you guys, you didn't have to do this."

Andy placed a cardboard, cone-shaped birthday hat on my head. "Make a wish."

I rolled my eyes at him, knowing that he was thinking the same thing I was . . . I was too old for such a childish tradition, but in the spirit of fun and my birthday, I made a wish and blew out the candle. They applauded and wished me happy birthday again. Diana left to cut the cake in the kitchen, Katie followed, licking the icing off the single candle, and Andy stayed behind.

"So what'd you wish for?" he asked, sitting on the edge of my desk.

I took my birthday hat off, careful not to smack myself with the elastic band. "I can't tell you or it won't come true."

"Can I guess?" he asked.

"Sure."

Then, in a tiny, girly voice he said, "I wish that James and I will get married and have a big house on a vineyard with lots and lots of children and lots and lots of wine to help subdue the pain of my boring predictable life."

I gave him a little shove and he snickered.

"I'm joking!" he said.

"Well, as a matter of fact, James and I are getting engaged."

He stopped laughing and his eyebrows stretched high on his forehead. "You are?"

I nodded. "Tonight. He's going to ask me to marry him tonight!" I wanted to scream the words.

"Congratulations," he said and gave me a congratulatory hug.

"Thank you!"

"How do you know he's gonna ask you tonight? It's supposed to be a surprise, right?"

"I have my ways," I said.

"Your ways?" he asked with a suspicious tone.

"Yes, my intuitive ways."

"Oh, because for a second I thought you were spying on him again. Now I don't know which of your ways is more perverse."

I gave him another playful shove and he chuckled again.

"Seriously, I'm happy for you. I'll text him a congrats too."

"No, don't say anything. I don't want him to know that I know."

"Okay, I'll wait 'til tomorrow when you tell me all about it."

"Good."

4

The Proposal

THE HOURS DRAGGED ON, one after the other, patient after patient, until it was finally time to head home and ready myself for the evening. As soon as I walked in the door, I stripped off my clothes and ran a hot bubble bath. My Pandora station played my favorite love songs, while I shaved my skin smooth. The ivory satin-like dress hung on my closet door as if it floated from my dreams. I slipped on my nude undergarments and laid the sexy lingerie I bought for the evening on my bed. Twenty minutes of curling my long, thick hair resulted in a pinned, side up-do. And just in time since it was nearly seven.

I slipped on my metallic pumps and practiced surprised looks in the full-length mirror. "What took you so long?" I asked in a Marilyn Monroe voice with a matching pout. I'd make a terrible actress.

What if I cried? I faked a cry, pretending to dry tears by waving my hand. I let out a sniffle. "Yes, yes, a thousand times yes!" Cute, but a little too dramatic.

I straightened myself out, cleared my throat, and rehearsed a genuine surprise. "Yes, of course I will." Classic.

At that moment, the doorbell rang and startled me off my balance. Finally, James had arrived! My poor little heart raced with the anticipation of seeing him again, kissing him and holding him in my arms. I hurried to the door careful not to trip over my heels. James let himself inside. There he stood in my living room, all six feet of him, and handsome as ever. We had only been separated a few days, but I felt like I had missed him for years.

"Hey, beautiful," he said, sweeping me up in his arms right away. Our lips joined like magnets for a gentle kiss, the kind that could only be articulated as *I love you.*

"I'm so glad you're back," I whispered as he held me tightly.

"Me too. I missed you so much," he replied, leaving a kiss on the top of my head. I pulled away just enough to look up at him.

"Happy Valentine's Day," I said.

"Happy Valentine's and Birthday." He took my hand and spun me around slowly.

"You look . . ."

"What?" I asked.

He ran his eyes over me without blinking. "Like a dream."

I smiled shyly, almost too giddy to say the words *thank you*, but they seemed to come out okay.

"This is for you," he said, handing me a bottle of champagne.

"What's this for?" I took it from him.

"It's for later. We're celebrating."

"Celebrating what?"

"You'll see." He teased.

He took my hand and we headed out.

In the restaurant, candlelight glistened off of faces of couples having romantic Valentine's Day dinners. Champagne bottles seemed to adorn every table next to tiny fine dining portions of decadent chocolate desserts. James and I were torn between the same two-entrée choices, so we ordered one of each to split. Before the waitress stepped away, James asked for a bottle of their best cabernet. James and I loved to drink wine during dinner, but we very rarely ordered a bottle for just us.

During dinner, James brought me up to speed on what I missed while he was in Montana, though I was only half paying attention. All I could think about was what he wanted to talk to me about. The food was delicious, but my nerves inhibited my appetite. I cut my food into tiny, squirrel-sized bites. Instead of eating, I continued to drink the red wine that my nerves were begging for. The waitress cleared our plates, and there was still no ring and no proposal. What was the hold up?

"So, you said you had something important to tell me," I said.

James smiled and looked down as if I had caught him being cute. "Yes, there is something I wanted to ask you." He put his hand on mine, and I leaned forward batting my eyelashes at him hoping my eyes sparkled in the restaurant's romantic candlelight. He leaned in and kissed my hand.

"I've been thinking . . ."

"Uh-huh?" I urged on, hoping I wasn't being too obvious.

"I love you, Marin. I love being with you. We've always taken everything slowly, and that's cool, but I think it's time we took the next step. Don't you?"

I took a deep breath in. "Yes, I do." I do, I do, I really do!

"Good, because I think we should move in together," he said.

"Okay, and what else did you want to ask me?"

This was it! He was about to pop the question.

"That's it."

That was it? I stopped breathing for a moment. I couldn't even imagine the utter shock on my face. Live together? That's what he wanted to ask me on Valentine's Day and my birthday! The pride of triumph suddenly turned to the sulk of defeat. Would I never get my husband, my kids, and my house in the suburbs? Before I could respond, the restaurant broke out into a polite applause. James and I turned in each direction to see what the praise was for. The couple two tables over from ours had just gotten engaged. The woman gazed at her shiny, new engagement ring, while I would be getting a dingy old apartment key. Talk about salt in the wound. Why couldn't I be the one people were clapping for? Was I not engagement worthy? How much longer would I have to wait to be a bride?

"Wow, look at those two." James applauded as the

newly engaged couple embraced in a sweet kiss. "A Valentine's Day engagement too." He looked really happy for them.

Was he kidding?

"So what do you think?" James asked.

I wanted to tell him 'not without a ring' but thought better of it.

"Yes, of course."

He kissed my hand and smiled.

"Good, there's something else," he said. My stomach tightened and I held my breath again. Maybe this wasn't over yet.

James reached into his jacket pocket and pulled out a small navy box tied with a white ribbon. It wasn't a ring box, but a ring could still be inside. James had a habit of fooling me with my gifts. Last year for my birthday, he gave me the impression that he bought a pair earrings that I'd been eyeing for months. But, I was immediately disappointed when I felt the heavy weight of the bag. Then, I reached inside and pulled out a small box. It was the earrings. He had filled the bag with pebbles to weigh it down. "You should've seen your face. Gotcha, didn't I?" He laughed.

Yes he had.

It all made sense, waiting until the end, throwing me off with the "moving in" question and the bigger box. Yeah, my man was clever. He slid the gift across the table.

"Is this what I think it is?" I asked.

"Only one way to find out."

My fingers trembled as I pulled the white ribbon

loose. My heartbeat was so loud, I could hear it reverberate throughout the room. Slowly, I pulled the top off.

A watch?

"Do you like it?" he asked, obviously proud of his gift.

I wanted to cry and scream and tell him to take it back and exchange it for a ring, a diamond engagement ring that I could wear on my finger forever and ever and ever! Instead, I sucked back my disappointment. "I love it." I gritted my teeth and forced a smile.

"I'm glad. Happy birthday, baby," he said and held up his wine glass.

After dinner, James and I went back to my place for champagne and chocolate birthday cake. I'd already had a couple glasses of wine, but I continued to shoot the champagne down my throat. In truth, the night had been a total disappointment, knocking the wind out of my sails. Getting drunk was, in my opinion, the best way to surmount the disappointment. And, for the most part, it worked. James and I had very sexy, intoxicated birthday sex. But even in the midst of our sweaty bodies grinding against each other, I still couldn't shake the massive let down.

I lay in bed still sipping what was left of the champagne, while James stood in my doorway brushing his teeth.

"So what do you think, you move in with me or I move in with you?" I asked.

"I was thinking we could find a new place, build a new life together," he said with a mouth full of sudsy toothpaste. That sounded promising. He walked away and there was a lapse in conversation as the water ran in the bathroom sink. I glanced down at my left ring finger, mourning the loss that even a new apartment couldn't fill. The faucet stopped. "Were you thinking of renting or buying?" I hollered. Subtext; committed or open-ended?

He reappeared in the bedroom and slid into bed next to me.

"Um, I guess rent," he said, the smell of minty fluoride lingering on his breath. I was still drunk, and now I was sad. The combination could only result in one thing . . . a crying spell. Tears escaped my eyes faster than I knew what was happening. I covered my face quickly, but couldn't control the sobbing.

"Oh, no. What's the matter?" he asked, now facing me on his knees. He rubbed my shoulders lightly, and I looked up at him. How had this special night come to this?

"It's this whole moving in thing," I said, trying to regain my composure.

"What do you mean? You don't want to move in together?" He looked somewhat desperate, like he expected me to break it off.

"No, baby, I do." I took his hand. "I'm just . . ." I couldn't get the words out. Like if I admitted them to James he'd think I was being insecure, and no one likes to be with someone who's insecure.

"What?" His voice was quiet and he tried to make eye contact.

"I'm afraid," I said, looking down at his hand in mine.

"Afraid of what?"

"I'm afraid once we move in together, you'll find some annoying flaw and want to break up or find someone new."

"Aw, Marin, that's not gonna happen," he said softly, shushing me. He wasn't taking it seriously.

"You don't know that." I folded my arms against my chest.

"Yes, I do."

He swept me up and rocked me like a baby. I could feel the love and certainty radiate from his body like a beam of sunlight. "It's gonna be great."

"I was kinda hoping we could get married first." I uttered and just like that, he dropped his arms.

"Really? I didn't know you wanted to get married."

Had he lost his damn mind?

"Of course, I want to get married. Don't you?" I could sense his body tensing. Was he really that surprised?

"Eventually, I guess. We've never talked about it before."

"What do you mean? We've talked about it plenty of times."

He looked dumbfounded. "No, we haven't."

Sure, I knew men had selective hearing, but shit. I paused, thinking back to our previous conversations about marriage or getting married, but I couldn't remember a single one. We talked about our life together, where we'd live, and children we'd have. Marriage goes without saying in those conversations, right?

"We've talked about having kids," I said.

"Yeah, eventually."

"Eventually? James, I'm thirty-three years old. It's not like we have all the time in the world." My boiling blood pulsed through my veins and my cheeks felt hot. He was acting like we were having a casual relationship, like we weren't in love, like we didn't want to be together for the rest of our lives. He was silent longer than I would have liked. I hated that I was forced to ask, but it was now or never. "So what, you don't want to marry me?"

"No, it's not that," he blurted.

"Then, what?" This conversation had turned me into one of those crazy, clinging women. Ugh.

"I just don't know if we're ready to get married yet . . . we've only known each other for a couple of years."

"And that's not enough?" How much more time did he need? I was ready. I knew he was the one.

"Why don't we move in together first and go from there?" He danced around the words, careful not to disturb the hive.

It was the old try-it-before-you-commit-to-it proposal, saying no by saying yes. What was he really saying? Since, apparently, this was our first discussion on the topic, it was probably best to drop it for now, even though I was tempted to bully him into proposing. Like Grandma had said, I was no spring chicken.

5

Girls Night Out

"WELL, LET'S SEE IT!" Andy stood in the doorway of my office. I looked over the piles of files on my desk and saw his smiling face through the stacks. I regretted saying anything about the engagement. Why did I rely on a hunch instead of concrete proof like say, a ring? Now I'd have to explain that there was no engagement, and I was wrong. Both of which were easier said than done.

"There's nothing to see," I answered quietly, hoping he'd suddenly develop a case of amnesia and forget that I ever mentioned it. But, no such luck.

"That's weird. There is usually a ring that comes with a marriage proposal." Now he was being condescending.

"There was no proposal, Andy. I'm not engaged." He sat down in one of the chairs and I braced myself for his reaction. Surely, he would go into one of his "I told you so" speeches and explain why I still had so much to learn about love and marriage, blah, blah, blah.

"I know what you're going to say," I told him.

"And what's that?"

"You're going to say, 'Marin, after everything you've been through, you shouldn't have been so naïve, getting your hopes up like a little girl. You should know better. You're thirty-three now. You need to have more realistic expectations instead of getting hung up on dreams and fairytales.' Or something like that."

He blinked incredulously for a moment. "Wow, you're thirty-three?"

I opened my mouth to speak, but nothing came out.

"Actually, I was going to say that sucks. You seemed so happy yesterday."

I sighed in frustration. Of course, he would choose this moment to be kind. Now he was going to think that I believed everything I said that I thought he was going to say. And I didn't believe it. At least I didn't think I did. Did I?

"So what happened?" he asked.

"He asked me to move in," I said still frowning.

"That's good." He rubbed his finger against his chin, which made a slight scratching noise. It reminded me of James and how I loved to stroke his five o'clock shadow when I cuddled with him at night. I wanted those moments to last forever.

I nodded, giving another long sigh of defeat.

"Don't you want to move in with James?" he asked.

"Yeah, after we're married, if we ever get married."

"What's that supposed to mean?" he asked.

I rolled my eyes, hating that I had to say it aloud. "He says he's not ready to get married."

Andy chuckled. "Yeah, that's because guys are never ready to get married."

"That's not true."

"Yeah, it's true. I hate to break it to you now that you're not engaged, but guys never want to get married, they're just eventually forced into it."

"Whatever. How much longer do I have to wait?"

"Just be patient, Marin. Put in the time, be a good girlfriend, and one day you'll be Mrs. James Young."

"But what if it doesn't happen?"

"It will. Besides, he's asked you to get a place together. That's a step in the marriage direction. Trust me it's better to live together first."

"Not for me. Chad moved in before we were to be married and it scared him into an affair. If James and I are married before we live together, he's more committed and less likely to do something damaging."

"First of all, that isn't true. If James is a cheater, he is going to cheat regardless. But we've already established that he's a dad, not a cad, right?" Andy argued, referencing our therapy sessions. "And second, I thought we worked through your issues with Chad. You're starting to make me second guess my work."

I shrugged at this notion. I didn't know it was an issue, but apparently it had been there in the background all along.

"Don't worry about it, Andy. I'm going to move in

with him despite my so-called issues. It's not ideal, but I'll take it."

"Good."

"Why do you know it's better to move in first?" I asked.

"Because, I got married before we lived together. That wasn't the reason for my divorce, but if I had lived with my ex for a year before the wedding there probably wouldn't have been a wedding. That's all I'm saying."

He made a valid point, which I agreed with for everyone else. Now, I'd have to convince myself it was the right thing for my relationship too. Then I had another thought. "Do you think he wants to wait because he's divorced?" I asked.

"That's a possibility," he said and glanced down at his cell phone, commented on the time, and quickly left my office.

That Friday evening, James and I met at a pizza place in my neighborhood. My mouth watered as he chomped on a greasy piece of pizza and I nibbled on my salad. I recalled the days that I could pound pizza, burgers and fries, and chocolate cake without gaining an ounce, but sometime around thirty, that luxury had disappeared. I got lucky, some of my friends had to stop the junk food binge at twenty-five.

"We're all set with Jared for tomorrow afternoon," James said.

"Jared?" I asked.

"My realtor friend, remember?"

"Oh, right."

James was quick to start the process, which was a good sign. The thought of apartment hunting for a new place with James was kind of exciting, and I tried to relish in that feeling, reminding myself that moving in with the man I loved wasn't the worst consolation prize for a non-marriage proposal. "Do you mind if I bring Telly? She's my sound real estate advisor."

"Telly's a divorce lawyer," he said.

"She owns three places."

He nodded. "Then bring her along."

"Can you pick me up in the morning?" I asked.

He nodded with his mouth full of pizza. I checked the time.

"Are you almost done?" I asked. "Holly's picking me up in an hour." He swallowed his bite and took a swig from his iced tea.

"Yep, we can go," he said. I hopped off of my chair and planted a kiss on his mouth. He really was a great boyfriend.

Later, I met Holly, Telly, and a few of our friends for a belated birthday celebration at Parlor, a lounge bar near the Marina district.

"Happy birthday, Marin!" Holly shouted when I walked in. She greeted me with a warm hug and a kiss on the cheek. Holly was my oldest friend and I had spent all my birthdays with her.

"Your hair looks good and your boots are so cute," I told her. She was clearly trying to dress up her casual look by taming her wild and wavy brown locks.

Rachel, her younger sister, embraced me in another

birthday hug. "You know, I can never get her to put on a skirt." Rachel's smile was brighter against her unseasonably tanned skin.

"You're glowing," I said.

She blushed and waved her hand around her face. "This is from St. Barts."

Next to Holly stood a woman with a full head of tight curls and dark luminous skin. Holly pulled her in.

"Marin, this is Corrine, from work."

"Nice to meet you, Corrine," I said.

Corrine greeted me with a firm handshake and friendly eyes. "Happy birthday. I hope you don't mind that I tagged along."

"The more the merrier."

"Hey, birthday girl!" Telly announced as she arrived with a small tray of shots.

"That better not be tequila," I told her.

"Relax, it's SoCo and lime."

Yeah, like whiskey was any better. I sighed.

We each took a full glass from the tray. Telly leaned over. "Too bad you're committed, because there are some hotties here tonight."

I looked around the room. She was right. There were some cuties. But like she said, I was committed. Well, soon-to-be-living-together committed.

"I'm gonna get me some," Telly sang and shook her hips like a true Latina.

"You can't be hungover tomorrow. I need you to come with us to look at apartments."

"What time?" she asked.

"Noon."

She rolled her eyes. "Marin, it's your twenty-ninth birthday. Let's have a good time tonight, noon tomorrow is hours away."

If Telly wanted to pretend I was turning twenty-nine, then I could stand to have a few drinks with her. Telly lifted her shot, and we rose our glasses to meet hers.

"To Marin on her birthday!" she said.

The rest of the group shouted, "Happy birthday!" before sucking down the tasty shot.

"Sorry, I'm late." The voice behind me was familiar, but I couldn't place it.

"Ginger!" Holly shouted and moved passed me to greet her. Ginger was our next-door neighbor when Holly and I first moved to San Francisco about six years ago. She'd trap us in the hallway with mindless gossip for what seemed like hours. Probably the reason I hadn't kept in touch.

"Happy birthday, Marin," Ginger said, handing me a silver gift bag stuffed with red tissue paper.

"Ginger, what are you doing here? We haven't seen you in—"

"Ages, I know. I ran into Holly at lunch yesterday, and she told me about this little birthday bash, and I said 'I have to go to this thing and see my girl, Marin.'" Ginger crinkled her nose and pinched my shoulder.

"Great!" I stretched my smile out as far as it could go and I still couldn't catch up to hers. Her stare became impatient and she batted her lashes a few times.

"Well, open your gift, birthday girl."

"Oh." I broke from the trance of her bubbliness and investigated the gift bag. I pushed the tissue aside and pulled out Nars mascara and duo eye shadow pallet in Charade, Bobbi Brown lipstick in Ballerina Shimmer, and a beautiful plum Laura Mercier nail polish called Temptation. It was about a hundred dollars' worth of makeup.

"This is really generous, Ginger. You didn't have to get me anything, especially all this," I gave her a grateful smile followed by a hug.

"You're an incredible girl and you deserve to have incredible makeup. It's nothing, really."

It may really have been nothing. Ginger started at the cosmetics counter at Neiman Marcus and later became a buyer for the department. My guess, she was still a buyer with the eye of a makeup artist. Her color choices were spot on. Then again, Ginger and I had similar coloring and features, so maybe it wasn't a stretch. Still, I couldn't wait to try the Ballerina Shimmer.

"I'm glad you're here," I told her.

As we slid into the lounge, I stared at Ginger. She'd made a few changes since I'd last seen her. Her hair had been lightened from black to golden brown, and her cup size was increased by about two and disproportioned to her tiny Korean frame.

"I love your watch," she said and pulled my wrist toward her to examine the clock. I couldn't admit it on my birthday, but it was a nice watch. Still, I would've much rather been showing off an engagement ring.

"Thanks, it's a birthday gift from my boyfriend." Then, I glanced down and saw it. The one thing I wanted

to avoid from everyone—a brilliant cut diamond ring.
An engagement ring.

"Are you getting married?" I asked. Her big smile grew larger and she threw her hands up in a dramatic dance sorta way.

"Yes! Isn't it incredible!"

I had no choice but to mirror her enthusiasm. "That's great news!" Even though it really wasn't.

"Thanks! You know what? You should totally come. Yes, I have to have you at the wedding." She squeezed my hands and bounced them in my lap.

"When is it?"

"May 15th. Five, fifteen!" She whipped out her phone and began texting something. "Let me get your address and I'll send you an invitation."

I began reciting my address when Rachel swooped in. "Not so fast," she said. "You're address is changing soon. Didn't you tell her the good news?"

Word travels fast. Ginger looked at me seriously for an explanation.

I nodded slowly and was almost embarrassed about what I had to confess. "My boyfriend and I are getting a place together."

"That's incredible," Ginger said with what seemed like the slightest twinge of pity. I continued to nod. Ginger had a diamond ring and I was getting a joint lease . . . incredible. As a matter of fact, I was feeling incredulous. Was it really so unthinkable to expect an engagement ring by now? I knew we both wanted to take it slow, but I was done taking it slow. I wanted to speed this ship up!

"I'm gonna get a cocktail. You want one? What do you want?" Ginger asked.

"Whatever goes down easy and clouds my judgment," I said.

"Like Telly's date over there," Rachel commented, gesturing to the bar where Telly was flirting dangerously with the scruffy bartender.

"Rachel." Ginger gave her a friendly swat on her shoulder. "I don't remember you being so naughty."

"I'm married now, which means I rarely get to do and say very bad things."

"Rachel!" Holly reprimanded.

"I'm kidding." Rachel smirked.

"No, I like it. You're like a cheeky little kitten." Ginger clawed her hands in the air as she stood and made a purring sound before she started giggling. No doubt at her own ridiculousness. "You girls are fun!"

Rachel and Ginger scooted to the bar, leaving me with Corrine and Holly.

"You okay?" Holly asked.

"I'm great, why?"

"The whole no-engagement thing's still fresh. I'm sure Ginger's wedding stings a little."

"I'm fine." An insincere smile spread across my face. I wasn't fine and Holly knew it. I just had to get through the night.

"Okay," she said. "I'll be right back."

The second Holly walked away she pulled her phone from her back pocket and began texting.

I turned to Corrine who was sipping a Mojito. "Have you noticed Holly on her phone a lot at work?"

"No more than usual. Does she text a lot in the evening?" Corrine asked.

"Seems like it." I watched Holly walk out the front door and put her phone to her ear. "Who's she talking to?"

Corrine leaned in as if to tell me a secret. "I think she's talking to Noom again."

"No!" I gasped. Corrine nodded slowly. She seemed convinced.

Noom was a guy that Holly met during her first expedition to Thailand. The two fell in love over drain mats and roof soil. Since then she'd made several shorter trips to Southeast Asia and every time they'd argued about her leaving and him not wanting to come to the states.

"I don't know what she sees in him," I said. "He's too short for her, he won't even come to the states to see her, and he barely speaks English. I don't even know how they communicate."

"Can't help who you love," Corrine said with a shrug, and I mentally shrugged it off too. "She talks about you a lot."

"Oh, yeah?"

"She said you've had a rough couple of days, but didn't say why."

I sighed. "It's nothing. I was just expecting to get engaged the other night."

Corrine raised her brows and nodded. It seemed to

scream of judgment.

"What?" I asked.

She hesitated for a moment. "I probably shouldn't say this to a marriage counselor, but I don't understand why women are in such a hurry to get married."

"You do know it's my thirty-third birthday, right?"

She sneered. "Yes, and you're a young woman. How long have you been with your boyfriend?"

"Almost two years."

"Think about it, do you really want to be stuck with someone or something you've only known for two years?"

I didn't know what to say. Lots of couples got engaged after two years. Many of my clients were engaged well before two years. Which, I suppose, isn't the greatest argument since I don't work with happy, healthy couples.

"Okay, when I was in high school," she started. "I became obsessed with David Bowie."

"David Bowie?"

She shrugged. "Yeah, I was kinda a lone wolf on that one since I was born about ten years too late."

"Right . . ."

"I really wanted to get a tattoo of his face on my lower back, like on the *Aladdin Sane* album cover. I begged my mom for it, and of course, she said no. After a couple of years, my obsession subsided, and I thank my mother for not allowing me to get that ridiculous tattoo. I love David Bowie, but I don't want his face plastered near my ass. You know what I'm saying?"

I knew what she was saying, but I couldn't believe

she was comparing my situation to a story about an al-most-David-Bowie-tattoo.

"What I mean is, if you and your boyfriend are happy with the way things are, then why change? As you know—very well I might add—there are a lot of married people who don't have a tenth of the happiness that you and your boyfriend share. Don't feel disappointed, just be grateful that you found him."

I nodded. "You're right." And she was. I should've just appreciated the fact that he even took me back after everything I'd put him through eighteen months earlier. He'd made me feel like the luckiest girl in the world. Why couldn't that be enough?

Ginger returned with a Long Island iced tea and I guzzled it like lemonade on a hot summer day.

"Slow down, sister," Telly said, taking the glass from me, and shooting Holly a knowing glance. I looked around at my group of friends and took stock of my life. I had a great job, a wonderful boyfriend, amazing friends, and fabulous new makeup, but still, something was missing and I had a hard time admitting it. Even admitting it to myself. I was, for the most part, a free woman and I celebrated that freedom with a few more Long Island iced teas.

By the end of the night I was pretty hammered.

"Who's taking Marin home?" Telly asked.

"Holly!" I shouted and threw my arms in the air. They landed over her shoulders and I nuzzled into her. "Let's have a slumber party like the old days."

"I guess I will," Holly said and walked me over to a

cab.

"Telly!" I called out. "Let me know if that bartender goes down easy." I raised my eyebrows suggestively.

"Okay, we're going," Holly said and ushered me into the cab.

When we got back to my place, Holly helped me out of my dress and into bed.

"Whew! I haven't been this drunk in a long time," I said as Holly turned me on my side and pointed at the small trash bin to use in case I got sick. "You're my best friend. You know that, right?" I was feeling sentimental, another symptom of too much alcohol.

"I know," she said softly and smiled.

"Holly, if you were a lesbian, would you marry me?" I asked, slurring my words through my lazy lips.

"Of course, you'd be the love of my life."

"Do you think you'll ever get married?" I closed my eyes and listened.

"I dunno. If it happens, it happens. I'll probably never have children so I'm not in a rush." Her comments were sobering. While growing up, Holly never talked much about having a family. She was a free spirit, but her ability to nurture was so strong, I believed one day she'd want a baby of her own, a mini environmental warrior to help heal the world.

Holly was only fifteen when she found out that her chances of ever getting pregnant were less than ten percent. I wanted to cry with her, but she wouldn't cry. I wanted to comfort her, but she insisted she was fine. I wanted to tell her that they were wrong and she'd have a baby one day, but she said she had already accepted the news.

When you know someone as well as I knew Holly, then you know when it's not okay. It wasn't until a year later that Holly's despair resurfaced after our classmate made a joke about her own abortion. I remember following Holly off of school grounds. Her tears were uncontrollable, so I held her, for what seemed like an eternity, as we stood on the sidewalk in one of the many cookie-cutter housing divisions.

I cried with her. I comforted her. And I told her that the doctors were wrong. That's when she said, "I never wanted to have a baby more than the moment I found out I'd never have one."

I looked into Holly's brown eyes with all the focus I could muster after so many cocktails. The pain seemed to linger there, as it probably always would. Holly covered my shoulders with my blanket and tucked it under my chin, just the way I liked it. It was too bad about her fertility. She'd make the best mom.

6

The Market

"BABE, ARE YOU HERE?" a faint voice called from the living room. It took everything I had to lift my heavy lids.

"You're still sleeping?" my soon-to-be roomie asked.

I focused on his face then glanced at the clock.

"It's eleven!" I said. Ugh, my head. What had I been thinking, celebrating my birthday with lethal cocktails?

"Yep." James handed me a glass of water and some aspirin.

"I partied like it was my twenty-second birthday," I mumbled with the pills on my tongue.

"Holly told me. I called you three times this morning. You okay?"

"I will be." I grabbed my phone from the nightstand. Six missed calls, three from James, two from Holly, and one from Telly. I slid back into my sheets.

"Oh, no you don't," James said, pulling the covers off.

I tugged them back and whined like a child. "What? It's Saturday."

"Marin, we have to meet Jared in an hour. Remember?"

"Shit, that's today. I need to tell Telly where to meet us."

"I already called her. She's good." He sat on the bed and pulled me into him.

"You did?" What a terrible girlfriend I was, hungover, forgetful, and running late, while he took care of everything. No wonder he didn't ask me to marry him.

"Uh-huh. Go take a shower. I'm gonna get you coffee and some breakfast, okay? We can still make it on time."

I looked up at him, pouting my lip, and smelling the remnants of Irish Spring soap on his skin. "Are you mad?"

"About you having a good time with your friends for your birthday?"

I nodded, exposing my puppy-dog eyes.

He kissed my forehead. "No, I'm glad you had a good time."

Whew. He didn't think I was a terrible person. Besides, I probably wouldn't have had so much to drink if I hadn't been trying to drown my sorrows after the no-engagement blow. But, in that moment, as he held me and helped me overcome my Long Island hangover, Corrine's words about appreciating what we had now returned to me. James could be holding any woman, making coffee for someone else, looking for a new place with a better person, but he was doing it with me. Ring or no ring, marriage or no marriage, James was mine.

Only five minutes late, we met Jared in the Mission District for the first set of apartments.

"Jared, this is my girlfriend, Marin."

Jared shook my hand and handed me his business card. "Good to meet you finally. You ready to see some apartments?"

"Yeah."

"Great, then let's get started." Jared motioned us to his car.

"Wait," I said. "My girlfriend's coming with us. She should be here any minute."

"Sounds good," Jared offered before beginning small talk with James. Jared was handsome and had a certain, easy confidence about him. A no pressure attitude, like he'd be just as happy showing apartments to anyone else. He kinda reminded me of Telly's on again, off again boy-friend, Will.

"There she is," I said a moment later, watching Telly as she hurried across the street. Speak of the devil and she will appear. I greeted her with a friendly hug, which she accepted hesitantly. She wasn't much for affection unless it was a special occasion or before sex with a man, but I imagined not after. Since this was neither, her reaction was quite Tellyish.

James introduced her, and I could feel her temperature rise when she shook his hand. Jared didn't seem to notice. That was sure to pique her interest. She bit her lip, eyeing Jared, and I knew she was fantasizing about the two of them having a little romp in one of the empty apartments. I just hoped it wasn't too much of a distraction. She was here to be my real estate expert not to hook up.

The first apartment we viewed was in the Haight-Ashbury neighborhood on Page Street. I was already rooting for it because it was near my current place and in a super cool area. We walked up the stairs to the second floor apartment. The maple colored wood floors and sunlight from the bay window warmed the white walls, creating a golden hue.

I breathed in, exploring the main room. "Ahh, smells like fresh paint."

"What's the story with this one?" Telly asked, scrutinizing the place.

Jared consulted the listing on his iPad. "It's fifteen hundred square feet, three bedrooms, one bath, granite countertops—"

"No fireplace?" I asked. Strike one for the apartment.

"No, but it's close to Panhandle and Golden Gate Park, not to mention Whole Foods." Jared's attempt to steer me back worked. I loved those parks and Whole Foods.

As I explored the apartment, I tried to imagine my life there with James, a combination of his taste and mine, evening walks in the park, Saturday afternoons spent at a café on Haight Street. Just a cozy life, in a cozy apartment. It was definitely in the running until I saw the unimpressed expression on James' face.

"What's the parking situation here?" James asked.

"Street only," Jared replied.

James looked out the window. "The street looks a little crowded."

"It's Saturday, baby," I said.

"Yeah, and we're going to live here on Saturdays too."

I pursed my lips at him. Smart-ass. "What do you think, Telly?" I asked.

She shrugged and asked about the monthly rent. "A little steep if you ask me," she said. "I think you can get a better value in another neighborhood.

"What about you, James?" I asked.

"It's all right." He shrugged. "The park proximity is cool, but I'd really like to have a driveway or parking garage."

"I've got some of those to show you too," Jared said and motioned us to leave. We viewed several more properties, but found something terribly wrong with all of them. Jared and Telly agreed that many of our objections were a bit nitpicky and it's not as if we were buying a place. So far none of the places inspired me to move, even if I was moving in with James.

For the last viewing of the afternoon, Jared took us to see a top floor condo in the Marina District. No crowded street there. We parked in front of the garage. Two front doors stood side by side, and Jared unlocked the one on the left. We climbed the glossy wooden stairs, every step raising my hopes until we reached the top and I was overcome with excitement. Beautiful crown molding lined the ceiling around the living room. The window took up almost the entire wall, illuminating the room with gorgeous natural light. I could see myself snuggled with James on the couch and reading a magazine on a sunny Sunday afternoon and enjoying a glass of wine by the fireplace on a cold evening.

"This is gorgeous!" I said, running my hands along the crisp white molding.

"Yeah, it's nice," James said with his hands resting on his hips, surveying the room.

I walked through French doors into the large dining room. My heart raced as I imagined dinner parties with friends and family. The dining room led into the stark white kitchen with a breakfast nook. I was in love.

"This has to be the best use of fifteen hundred square feet I've ever seen." Telly seemed impressed.

Jared winked at her. "Glad you like it."

I pulled Telly into the master bedroom where we could have some privacy. "What do you think?"

"I fucking love this place. I almost want to make an offer to buy it myself."

I grinned and bounced around, pulling Telly along with me.

"This is great! I hope James likes it." Telly and I peeked out of the room and watched the guys discuss logistics.

"I don't know, but I definitely see something I like," Telly said.

"Are we still talking about the apartment?" I asked.

Telly ran her fingers through her hair and shook it

out, giving it more volume. "I think I'm gonna ask him out."

"Who? Jared?"

She nodded.

"No, Tell. He's our realtor."

"And?" She drew out the word.

"And, if it goes bad then you won't come on any more of these showings, and I need you here."

"C'mon," she whined. "I haven't been out with a cute guy in so long."

"Didn't you go home with the bartender last night?" I asked.

"No." She seemed appalled that I would even suggest such a thing. "We just made out on the street for a little bit."

I rolled my eyes and shook my head. In the world of romance, Telly and I never saw eye to eye. And believe me, we'd tried.

"Look, if you really don't want me to, I'll back off," she offered, but I knew it was just a reverse psychology ploy. It worked too.

"Do what you want. I wouldn't want to get in the way of true love or anything," I said.

"I wouldn't worry about that. I just want to have a good time."

James peeked his head in. "You girls hungry?"

The four of us sat at the bar at Chez Maman, drinking cocktails, browsing listings on Jared's iPad, and snacking on beef tartare. Telly giggled and nudged Jared with her shoulder. He seemed much more interested.

"What's that about?" James whispered pointing at the two of them. I glared at him as if to say 'you know exactly what that's about.' He nodded before popping a piece of beef in his mouth.

Jared took his attention away from Telly for a moment. "Are you seriously interested in any of the properties we saw?"

James and I looked at one another. I couldn't say for sure, but it seemed like the places I really liked, James really didn't and vice versa. We'd seen a variety of places and my guess was they were the best of the bunch. If we couldn't agree on one, who knew how long it would take to sift through apartments until we found one we both loved. I didn't want to compromise, but I didn't want James to compromise either.

"I think so," James said. "We'll let you know what we decide."

Jared accepted this with a shrug and turned back to Telly. "What about you? Did you like what you saw?"

"Yeah, I definitely liked what I saw," Telly said. I thought the two of them were going to start making out right then and there.

"Wanna get dinner later?" he asked her quietly. She nodded and bit her lip.

"You guys want to get dinner with us later?" Jared asked as he flipped through emails on his tablet. We considered it for a second before Telly shook her head at us. She stopped and smiled when Jared turned back to her.

"We've got to get going," James said, pulling cash from his wallet and placing it on the bar. "I'll call you later."

"Okay, man. See you later." Jared shook his hand.

I hopped off the stool, wishing goodbyes to both of them.

On the car ride to James' place, he seemed deep in thought, and I wished I could penetrate his mind. Was he having second thoughts about moving in together? Was he having second thoughts about us being together?

"You okay?" I asked.

"Yeah, I'm fine. You?"

"Uh-huh. You haven't said much about the tour today."

"Honestly, I'm a little disappointed. None of those places felt right. I was hoping we'd find something right away."

Whew. Was that all that was bothering him? What a relief.

"It's only the first tour. I'm sure there are others."

"What about you? Did you like any of them?"

"I really liked the last one. I could see us there," I said with a sheepish tone. I could tell he didn't like it, though I didn't know why. It was spacious, updated, and it had a garage. "You didn't like it?"

"It was nice, but the neighborhood didn't seem like the best for dog walking."

I couldn't disagree with that. The neighborhood was awkward that way, and when I hopped out of the car I realized how canine friendly his street was. As we walked into his building, James' dog Marvin, let out an alerting bark that boomed through the hallway.

Inside, the hundred and fifty pound Great Dane waited patiently near the door.

"There's bound to be a place out there for us," I said.

"There is. I'm sure we'll stumble on it soon," James wrapped his arms around me and kissed the top of my head. Marvin nudged between us.

"You feeling left out?" I scratched behind Marvin's ears.

"He probably needs to go out," James said and grabbed his leash.

The three of us walked the block, stopping every so often for him to do his business. Yeah, Marvin and I had come a long way since the early days. Somehow, he'd warmed up to me and we'd become buddies. I think I even loved the little horse dog, and perhaps he loved me too.

"Why don't you move in with me?" James asked. Uh. . .

"Don't you think your place is a little too small for the three of us?"

"Nah," he said and put his arm around my shoulder. "It's cozy."

"It's a loft." I cringed.

"So?" He sounded offended.

"And it's not very private."

"We're in love, baby. What do we need privacy for?" I suddenly remembered what happened when you combined your life with someone else. It was just the beginning. Do we move into your place or mine? Keep your couch or mine? Your shower curtain or mine? Your way or mine?

I looked at him, wanting him to let it go. For us to just get engaged, then married, then buy our own place instead of renting something that was temporary. I wanted roots and a foundation on which we'd build our life together. Was that so much to ask?

"You're right," he said finally. "We can move into your place."

"No pets allowed." Which was a shame. My place was bigger and closer to everything.

"What? You don't think we can hide Marvin at your place?"

I laughed. Marvin would be impossible to hide any place. There was no easy solution, but I tried not to be discouraged. Maybe it had just been a long day after a long night and a long week. That night I slept at my own apartment, alone.

7

The Other Book

"YOU OKAY, DR. JOHNS?" my patient Amy asked after sixty seconds of total silence.

"I'm fine," I said, taking off my reading glasses to rub my eyes. Yeah, I had to start wearing reading glasses, the kind you pull off the rack at the pharmacy, somewhere between aging gracefully and time's running out (your ass is old).

"You don't seem fine. Is something on your mind?" she asked as if she was imitating me.

"Amy, we're not here to talk about me. We're here to talk about you."

"Yeah, but I'm tired of talking about me," she said.

Frankly, I was tired of listening. I gave her the silent treatment.

"Is it about your husband?" Amy leaned forward slightly.

"I'm not married," I said sternly. Her expression changed with my tone. I didn't usually speak to patients that way, but she'd hit an open wound.

"Boyfriend then?"

I sighed, pushing my hair behind my ears. "Let's focus, shall we." I leaned forward as if to plead with her. "You were talking about the incident at work. It made you jealous, why?"

"I dunno," she answered.

"Are you usually a jealous person?"

"Eh, yeah, but it helps that I'm not dating anyone."

"I know what you mean."

"You do?" she asked, utterly surprised by my answer.

"Sure." I shrugged.

"Do you get jealous with your boyfriend a lot?" she asked.

"Again, we're not talking about me."

"Yeah." She lowered her head. "It's just that you're my therapist right?"

"Right."

"So, it's easy to assume that you probably have your shit together, right?"

"Right . . ."

"So how do you do it? How do you not beat yourself up every day over the things you have yet to accomplish? How do you not get nauseous over the prospect of dying alone?"

I took a moment to really think on her question. It scared me. I did beat myself up over the things I hadn't done, and the thought of dying alone terrified me. Maybe lately, I didn't have my shit together, at least not the way she thought I did. Amy had a colorful and lively personality. She had everything going for her and yet she struggled with numerous insecurities. I guess I did too. What was wrong with us?

She needed a good answer, one that would inspire hope, for both of us.

"It may sound cheesy, but I have faith."

"Faith?"

"Yeah, faith that in the end I'll do the things that really matter and have people to share it with. That can mean a lot of things, because happiness comes in many forms. Sometimes it's not as conventional as you expect, and sometimes unconventional can be even better."

She turned her head as if in thought. "Hmm . . . Faith, huh?"

"Yep."

She thanked me for the advice and scheduled her next appointment. It was a good reminder for me too. Things may not have panned out the way I imagined them, but with a little faith they just might.

After she left, I made a few notes and checked my voicemail—message from Ginger.

"Hey, Marin, it's Ginger. I was just finishing the final invite list for my wedding, and somehow your address didn't save in my phone. I don't have your cell, so it's a good thing I remembered where you work. It's so cool that you're a therapist. Anyway, give me a call as soon as you can." I dialed her on my cell as she rattled off her phone number. Just as I was hanging up from the voicemail, I heard her wish me an incredible day.

"Ginger, it's Marin," I said when she picked up the line.

"Hey, girl! It was so great to see you the other night. What are you up to?"

"I was just about to head to lunch."

"Where are you going? Can I meet you there?" she asked.

"Sure . . ." I said. I really liked Ginger and all, but I had the feeling she thought we were going to be besties.

Twenty minutes later, we met at the bistro around the corner from my office. Sick of the salads I had eaten all weekend, I ordered my usual panini with lots of mozzarella cheese. Ginger, on the other hand, ordered a vegan kale salad.

"So, did you two find a place?" she asked.

"Not yet, nothing seemed to fit. We're still looking," I said with an uncontrollable frown.

"I didn't want to say anything in front of the others," her voice lowered, "but I think I can help you with your problem."

"What problem?"

She shot me a patronizing look.

I had no clue what she was talking about.

"Getting James to marry you," she said.

"Who told you about that?"

"You did at the bar. Don't you remember?"

I shook my head earnestly. What did I say that night?

"You told me all about your birthday and expecting the ring. You said you didn't know how much longer you could wait. I know you were drunk, but you really don't remember any of the conversation?"

I continued to shake my head, horrified, but not surprised. It wasn't unusual to spill my guts after one too many drinks. I really shouldn't drink like that anymore. "Anyway, I was once in your shoes, you know, with Jon."

"You were?"

"Yeah, but then I found this," she said and handed me a purple book with a silhouette hand wearing a glistening diamond on the cover. The title read *How To Get a Ring on It: Get Him Down on One Knee in 90 Days or Less* by Charlotte McQueen. The paperback book had frayed edges and creases down the spine so deep the title was barely visible.

"What's this?" I asked.

"This is how I got Jon to propose in two and a half months after years of refusing to settle down."

My eyes widened. "Are you serious?"

"Completely," she said.

It was as if I'd been sitting miserably on the couch, flipping the channels until I found that one infomercial with the one solution I was looking for. I didn't know if the book was a cure-all, but I was definitely intrigued by the possibility.

"So what, this book has the secrets to a proposal?"

"Yeah, it talks about what men really want in a wife and how to portray those qualities. You get what you want and he gets what he wants."

"It sounds a little manipulative."

"That depends on your perspective. You could say couples therapy is manipulative."

"How so?" I furrowed my brow.

"You take these couples and get them to try all these things they don't want to do so that in the end they can see how much they love each other and it's really about growing as a selfless human being."

"I dunno, Ginger. I feel weird about playing games with James." Especially considering what happened the last time I found a book that I thought had all the answers. I burned all my copies of *Unspoken: The Secret Lives of Men* when James and I got back together.

"You want to get married, right?" She pursed her lips.

"Yes."

"You want to have children soon, right?"

"Uh-huh."

"You believe that James and you will be happy together as a family, right?"

"Right."

"Then this isn't a game. This is your life. Look, you can go down the road you're on and hope and pray for a proposal, meanwhile growing more and more resentful every day, or you can read this book and get it done." She pounded the table in unison with the last three syllables. "And, since I've already done this, I can help you. Make sure you don't make some of the same mistakes I did. I bet we can turn that frown upside down in six weeks." Ginger spoke with such conviction that I wanted to follow her lead.

"You really think so?" I stared at the book for a moment, wondering if its insights would lead me astray like *Unspoken: The Secret Lives of Men.*

"I know so. You just gotta have a little faith," she said, sitting up straight.

A little faith, huh? "I guess there's no harm in reading it."

"Yes! That's incredible!" She clapped like a giddy cheerleader then quickly quieted and leaned in. "One thing, don't let James see this book. That's very important. Got it?"

"Got it."

"Are you wearing Ballerina Shimmer?" she asked.

I puckered my lips and struck a pose. "I knew it would look great on you."

After lunch, I stuffed *How To Get a Ring on It* deep inside my oversized purse. When I got back to the office, I shut the book in my middle drawer. No one ever checked the middle drawer.

Just as I was preparing to leave for the day, I got a call from James.

"Some of the guys invited me to watch the game with them tonight, we didn't have anything planned did we?"

"No, but I was hoping we could watch a movie," I said, pouting.

"Can we watch a movie tomorrow night?" he asked.

"We can, but it's so cold today. Wouldn't you rather snuggle in bed with me with a hot drink or glass of wine? Mmm, sounds good doesn't it?"

He chuckled. "It does, but I already told the guys—"

James pretty much always picked me over a game or

night out with his friends. The least I could do was give him the night off. I wondered what Charlotte McQueen would have to say about that. "Okay . . . go have fun with your friends. I'll see you tomorrow."

Since I had the entire night free, I had Chinese food delivered to my office. While I waited, I opened the middle drawer and began the journey through *How to Get a Ring On It*. Before I could turn to the first page, my cheeks flushed and I winced. That's when I realized that I had become one of those women who read self-help books about love. Not that I was against self-help books about love, I was a couples therapist after all and recommended them all the time. But now I was one of them. It was a hard reality to swallow.

I tried to remind myself that at least I had found someone to love who loved me back. All I wanted now was to keep that love forever with a real commitment. With a ring and a promise. The feeling of ridiculousness didn't subside, so I had to force myself to read. Charlotte McQueen illustrated an almost identical situation with someone she called "Tanya," a girl that thought she had everything until she realized she had no ring. The author created a six-step process, which she dubbed the *McQueen Method*. All I had to do was play out the steps and wait. What was the six-step *McQueen Method?*

Step One: Happy Couples- You should only socialize with happily married or engaged couples.

Step Two: Family Matters- If his family is important to him, then you must become part of it and vice versa.

Step Three: Play House- Whether in a separate or together living situation, you must demonstrate yourself as the ideal spouse. Showing value by assuming wifely responsibilities is key.

Step Four: Mother Material- Men have a need to spread their seed and leave a legacy. You must allow him to see that your motherly nature and nurture are worthy of his children.

Step Five: Sexy Getaway- No one wants a stale sex life. You must perfectly plan and execute an exotic getaway, making him believe that spontaneity and spice still exist.

And lastly, Step Six: Break Up to Make up- He won't truly understand what he's got until it's gone. Take time away from the relationship and he'll surely come crawling back with an engagement ring.

Aside from the last step, of which I was very wary, the steps didn't seem so manipulative. They were actually very straightforward and generally good advice on being in a relationship. I made a few notes for some of my patients too. The trick was to overload him with these experiences in a short amount of time in order to inspire the proposal.

I knew that in order to pull it off, I'd need to bring in some help. So I called Ginger the next day.

"I read the book," I told her.

"Already? That was fast."

"I had a free night."

"So what'd you think? Did you love it? Did you hate it? Tell me everything!"

I would if she'd stop talking for two seconds.

"I think I want to try it, but I need your help."

"You got it, girl. You and James should have dinner with us on Friday night."

"Can't. We have plans with our friend Andy."

"Is Andy single?" she asked.

"Yeah," I said.

"Then cancel and don't make plans with him again until after the proposal, better yet, after the wedding."

"Is that really necessary?" I asked.

"Absolutely. If you want this, you have to take it seriously and follow all the steps to a tee."

"All right, I guess I can do that, except for that last step."

"Break up to make up?"

I scoffed. "Yeah, I'm not going to break up with James just so he thinks he might lose me for good."

"Marin, you have to. It's the most vital step of all."

"I'll do everything perfectly except that."

She sighed sounding disappointed. "Okay, then I can't guarantee success. But I'll help you," she said.

"Thanks, Ginger. I'll see you Friday."

After my lunch break, I found Andy behind my desk on some kind of hunt.

"Can I help you?" I asked with my hands on my hips. Andy looked up, surprised to see me.

"I think the question is, can I help you?" Andy held

up the book without blinking an eyelash.

I stomped over and tried to snatch the book from him, but he was too quick. "What are you doing snooping in my drawers? Don't you have any boundaries?"

He held the book high. "Do you really want to talk to me about boundaries right now?"

I reached for the book again, but he moved it from my grasp. With my fists clenched, I wanted to punch it away from him. Barely into my quest and already Andy had swooped in to shit on it. Well, surprise for him, I wasn't going to let him. I was getting my ring.

"I came in looking for a piece of gum, okay," he said.

"Is that why I'm always running out of my Dentyne Fire?"

"Probably." Andy was a lot of things, but somehow in the midst of our young friendship, I put gum thief and snoop past him.

"Okay then, if you're always taking my gum then you would know that I keep it in the top drawer. Why were you in the middle drawer?"

"There wasn't any in the top drawer. I thought you moved it somewhere else because you were on to me. But there's a bigger issue at hand."

"What?" I asked.

He gestured to the book again.

"So what?"

"Do you really think this book is going to help you. . . get a ring on it?" He gave a wry grin.

Could he be anymore condescending?

"Maybe, but it's none of your business."

"You're right. It's kinda ironic though, don't you think?"

"What's ironic?"

"Two years ago you used a book to prove all men were unfaithful, now you're using a book to prove that all men can commit?"

He was right, but these were different times and they called for different measures. I wasn't going to let Andy talk me out of it.

"Should I clear my schedule for you next week? I have a feeling you may need to revisit treatment."

I snatched the book from his slimy little hands. "This is not cool, Andy, which reminds me. We can't have drinks with you on Friday."

"Why? Because of the gum?"

"No, because you're single."

He pursed his mouth and narrowed his eyes. "Fine, I wouldn't be able to look James in the face right now anyway." He walked out of my office and when he was out of sight, I placed the book back in its rightful spot. Andy popped back in.

"What?" I grimaced.

"I get what you're trying to do, and I really like James, but if he doesn't scoop you up with a proposal, then it's his loss, not yours. That's all." He walked away again then turned toward me. "I'll buy you ten new packs of gum."

"Make it twenty!" I called after him. The man was a little much, but he seemed to know the right thing to say when it really mattered.

8

Happy Couples

STEP ONE: HAPPY COUPLES

James and I met Jon and Ginger at Bacco, one of our favorite Italian restaurants. The four of us got acquainted over a bottle of red and a couple delicious appetizers. We didn't know it before dinner, but Jon was actually Jon Cash, the sportscaster from the local news. This prompted loads of boring conversation about the world of sports, and eventually Ginger and I spawned our own conversation about wedding dresses and honeymoon destinations. Ginger and Jon had planned a trip to Maui. I'd been there once as a teenager with my parents and hoped to return again one day with my own family.

"So, tell me about how you got engaged," I said to Ginger. Her grin widened and she pulled on her fiancé's arm.

"Honey, Marin wants to know about how we got engaged."

Jon leaned back in his chair with a proud grin spread across his face. "It's a pretty romantic story. James, are you sure you want your girl to hear this?"

James looked at me and smiled. "I think she can handle it."

"Okay," he said as a warning.

"So, Jon and I had been on a little break. I was in Paris for a trade show." Ginger glared at me when she said the words "little break."

Subtle.

"When I got back to my hotel, the front desk clerk handed me this little white envelope. It was a note from Jon." It sounded like a movie already. "The note said to meet him on top of the Eiffel Tower at seven. Have either of you been to the top of the Eiffel Tower?"

"Only in Vegas," James said.

"Well, the Eiffel Tower in Paris is twice the height," Jon said.

Was Jon trying to engage in a secret competition with James? The Paris tower is taller, i.e. my dick is bigger. I sighed. What I wouldn't give for the boys to play the 'who could get married first' game.

"Yeah, so I was so scared going to the top. It's ridiculously high and it's outside. I felt like I was going to fall off even though it was all caged in. Anyway, when I got to the top and saw Jon, I forgot all about the height. He handed me a single rose and said, 'Ginger, I'm lost without you.'"

"Aw!" I said. "How sweet."

"Then he got down on one knee and asked me to

marry him!" She showed us her ring as if she were revealing it for the first time. "Isn't that incredible!"

Oh, yes it was! Ginger had told me that they had been dating for three years when she followed the steps in McQueen's book. And boom! Engaged, on top of the Eiffel Tower no less.

"That's a very romantic story," James said.

"Isn't it?" Ginger beamed. "I'm sure you're very romantic, too, James."

"I can be, but I think I'm more thoughtful than romantic." He looked at me and I kissed him.

"You're thoughtful and romantic, baby," I said.

The night had been perfect. Ginger and Jon were the perfect happy couple, and I could almost feel the commitment rubbing off on James. So much so that we spent the entire weekend together, mostly in bed. My next two weekends were booked with other happy couples including, my brother Michael, and his wife Jennifer.

So far things were moving along according to plan. The next morning I met Holly and Rachel for brunch. I warmed my hands on the hot coffee mug on that cold February morning, and longed to be snuggled up in my bed, preferably with James and good TV.

"I thought Telly was coming," Rachel said. "Where is she?"

"She texted me earlier and said she's tied up this morning," I told them.

They each shot me a look as if I had more to share on the subject.

"What?" I asked.

"Tied up literally or figuratively?" Rachel asked.

Good question. "I dunno. I guess I should ask her to clarify." I sent Telly a quick text.

"Did you and James decide on a place yet?" Holly asked.

"No, we're still looking."

"Well, I work with a teacher whose husband's an agent, and she told me that the market's flooded with houses for sale," Rachel said, sounding proud to contribute to the conversation in a meaningful way.

"Yeah, but we're not buying." I sighed.

"Oh, right." She took a moment to chew her omelet. "I'm sure it's the same for the rental market. Besides, what's the rush?" The rush? The rush is that I'm thirty-three, you twenty-eight year old married princess!

Still, something was up with Rachel. It was something I'd noticed about six months ago when she and David stopped therapy—against my recommendation, I might add. I could only describe it as emotional teetering. One day everything was great, the next was like *what's the rush*!

I didn't respond, instead, I watched Holly text for what seemed like the tenth time since we sat down.

"Whatcha got going on there, Holly?" Her eyes widened like she was trying to make something up on short notice. Rachel peeked over.

"Oh, she's just texting Noom again," Rachel said.

I raised my brows. "I thought you two broke it off forever ago."

"Yeah, we did." Holly finished her text then set her

phone on the table facedown.

"So . . ." I started. "What's going on with you two?"

"We're just catching up. It's nothing. We're friends." Holly fidgeted around the words.

"O . . . kay." I shrugged.

An awkward silence hung over our table. Maybe we all wanted to say something, but thought better of it. Me with my non-engagement, Holly with her non-boyfriend, and Rachel with her non-emotional stability.

Whenever we talked about Noom, Holly clenched up and changed the subject. She seemed uncomfortable with the topic, probably because the two had been passionately on again and off again too many times. I never understood his appeal or why she let him get under her skin. Based on the facts, I was in no way in favor of the very long distance relationship, separated by eight thousand miles, language, and two inches in stature. Maybe it was just as inexplicable to her, and perhaps she wanted to fight it as much as I thought she should.

"You're both still coming over for dinner on Friday, right?"

"Yep," I said, hoping Rachel and David would behave as the picture perfect couple, as they usually did during social events.

"What's the occasion again?" Holly asked, taking a bite of her soy chorizo breakfast burrito.

"Nothing special. David and I just got back from St. Bart's a couple weeks ago, so we can show you all the cool photos. Plus, we got this underwater video camera. You have to see some of the videos we took."

"Videos, huh?" I bounced my eyebrows.

"Marin!" Holly snapped. "See what happens when you hang out with Telly all week."

"I haven't seen her since the showings last week. I think she's banging my realtor."

"Is that who has her tied up?" Rachel asked.

I checked my phone for a response from my missing friend.

Ha! I wish I were. Call you later.

"Nope, she's just busy," I said.

"Well, on that note, I've got to get to the gym. I'll see you girls later." Rachel dropped her napkin on her half-empty plate and gave each of us a goodbye kiss on the cheek.

When she was out of the restaurant, I leaned in. "Is she okay?"

Holly scrunched her face as if she was trying to solve a difficult crossword puzzle.

"I dunno," she said.

"Something seems off. Has she said anything to you, about David maybe? Her job? Is she pregnant?"

"I know what you mean, but she hasn't mentioned anything."

"Do you think she'd talk to me?" I asked.

Holly shrugged. "You were her therapist, so I don't see why not."

"That's exactly why not. She probably sees me as her doctor and not her friend." I probably never should've been their therapist in the first place, but under the circumstances, it was the best of few options.

"Let's see what happens at dinner on Friday."

James and I showed up twenty minutes late for Rachel's dinner party that Friday. She wasn't keen on tardiness, so we brought a nice bottle of pinot noir and cannolis from an Italian bakery as a peace offering. She greeted us with hugs and inspected the dessert, seeming to salivate.

"Sorry we're late," I said.

"No problem. Dinner's not going to be ready for another thirty minutes." Damn, I was hungry. "We're in the living room watching videos from St. Bart's."

James and I joined Holly who was swapping her attention between the video and her phone. David, almost asleep in his chair with a splash of scotch left in his glass, shot awake when he saw James.

"What's up, man," David said, slurring his words some. "It's good to see you."

"Yeah, you too."

David walked over to the wet bar and poured himself another. "You look pretty, Marin."

I thanked him, though he stared at me a moment too long. He'd probably indulged in a little too much scotch.

"James com'ere," he said, almost in a whisper.

"Where are you guys going?" Rachel asked.

"The garage, we'll be right back," David said.

Rachel shot him a pissy look.

"You okay?" I asked.

Her frown quickly turned up with a smile that could light a dark room.

"I'm great!" she said and sat on the couch. "Oh, oh.

Check this out. David and I went fly boarding." I watched David as water from a jetpack looking device propelled him into the air.

"That looks really fun, Rach. Did you do it too?" Holly said.

"Yeah." She grinned and fast-forwarded the video to her fly boarding experience. Rachel was not as sturdy in the air as David had been. The three of us watched a few more videos from their St. Bart's excursions and she streamed a ten-minute slide show. The sound of a timer beeped from the kitchen. Rachel excused herself. Holly's attention was diverted to her phone once again.

"Who are you texting?" I asked.

"No one. I'm responding to work emails," she said, keeping her eyes on her phone. Though I lacked proper ninja skills, I managed to snatch the phone from her and saw that she had, in fact, been texting Noom. Again. I tossed the phone back and shot her a look.

"It's nothing," she said.

"If it's nothing, then why are you trying to hide it?"

"Because it's private," she snapped.

"Well, can you put the phone away? We're about to have dinner."

Holly tucked the phone in her back pocket. "Yes, mom." I gave her a playful shove and she smirked.

"Come on, you guys, dinner's ready!" Rachel called from the dining room.

The table was filled with warm food that created a little bubble of heat. The smell of wine seeped from the open bottles and I filled my glass for the second time.

The five of us took our seats at the table, passing around dishes and keeping the conversation light. Rachel began telling stories from St. Bart's and every so often she'd say 'isn't that right, honey,' or 'didn't you think so, honey,' to which David replied a simple 'Mmhmm.' Eventually, the table fell uncomfortably silent. In fact, the entire night had been a little off, something about the energy amongst us. I shared a look with Holly. Maybe she should've saged the place.

"Telly wants to have lunch tomorrow," I said, breaking the silence. "You girls wanna join."

"Sure," Holly said.

"I can't," Rachel said and I pouted my lip.

"Oh, don't be sad, Marin," David said. "She's got Bobby tomorrow."

"Who's Bobby?" James asked.

"He's my fitness trainer." Rachel's eyes didn't leave her plate. "How's the meatloaf?"

We all responded positively, half of us with our mouths full of the delicious beef.

"And, how's the lentil-loaf, Holly?" Rachel asked her vegetarian sister.

"Really good. Thanks for making it."

"Holly, I'll never understand why you would choose to go without this delicious meat," David said holding up a tender piece of beef with his fork.

"You don't have to," she replied, almost under her breath.

"But I want to. This meatloaf is so good. Exactly why won't you eat it?" David was in one of his pricky moods. I never saw them much, but Rachel confided about them in one-on-one sessions. He took another bite and moaned with pleasure as he chewed. The last time I'd been that uncomfortable in their house was when we found out about David's affair.

"David, can you please not patronize my sister right now?" Rachel asked through a tight, phony smile.

"It's okay," Holly said, leaving her napkin on the table. "I'm gonna go."

"No," Rachel begged.

"C'mon, Holly. I was just messing around," David said.

Holly left a kiss on both mine and Rachel's cheeks and a severe glare at David before heading out. "I'll see you tomorrow," she told me.

And then there were four.

James and I ate quickly and excused ourselves too. The night had been a huge bust. So much for the David-and-Rachel-happy-couple-show. Considering the influence David had with James, I didn't know how bad the damage from the evening would be, but his silence on the drive home wasn't a good sign.

James' right hand rested on the gearshift, so I took it.

"You okay?" I asked.

"Uh-huh," he said, giving me the impression that he was definitely not okay.

"That was pretty weird tonight, huh?"

James sighed. "Yeah, it was."

"What's up with David? Have you ever seen him act like that?"

"He can get a little belligerent when he's drunk."

"Drunk or not, I've never seen him that bad before. What were you guys doing in the garage?"

"Nothing. Just talking."

"Did he say anything?" I asked. His hand stiffened under mine.

"About what?" James acted distant and uncomfortable. I didn't know what was going on and James wasn't willing to share.

"Never mind," I said and took my hand back in order to cross my arms. "Something's going on with him and Rachel, something bad."

"I think we just caught them on a bad day."

"Maybe," I said, my words drifting toward the passenger side window. "Do you think they're happy?"

James shrugged as if he couldn't care less. "I think only David and Rachel are the ones with the answer to that."

Maybe James was right and we caught them on a bad day. Maybe the weird stuff with Rachel was in my head . . . and Holly's. If there's anything I've learned in my profession it's that things are not always what they seem.

James pulled up to my apartment. When he kissed me instead of shutting off the car, I knew the night was over.

"Aren't you coming in?"

"I've got the hospital in the morning," he said.

"Okay." I looked at him for reassurance, but his eyes seemed empty. I was smart enough to know that if I pestered him, it would just piss him off and start an argument. But that little insecure voice in my head told me to hold on for dear life. I was losing him!

"I'll call you tomorrow," he said.

I climbed out of the car and turned to shut the door.

"Hey," he said.

Our eyes met.

"I love you." He smiled.

My lungs seemed to re-inflate with fresh, hopeful air.

"I love you."

9

Family Matters

THE NEXT DAY AT LUNCH, I could barely get a piece of romaine in my mouth when Telly blurted, "I can't go on any more of your apartment viewings."

"Why?" I sighed, already knowing the answer.

"It's Jared."

Yep, there it was. She'd slept with him. My fork clinked against my plate as I dropped it in frustration. "What happened?"

"Well, we went out a couple of times this week, which was great until last night."

"What happened last night?" Holly asked.

"We slept together." Telly lowered her head. Was she ashamed? I'd never seen her less proud of her sexual conquests.

"Congratulations," Holly said. "You waited two whole weeks. That must be some kinda record."

Telly perked up, the shamed look transformed into

93

pride. "Thanks. It's a new thing I'm trying."

"What thing? Sleep with guys you *kinda* know?" I asked.

Telly glared at me. "No, I really like Jared."

"So, what's the problem?" Holly asked.

Telly grimaced. "The sex was really bad."

"How bad?" Even though there was no substantial evidence to suggest otherwise, he didn't look like he was bad in bed. In fact, with his confidence, I imagined Jared was pretty good.

"Bad, like Carrie and Berger first time bad."

Yeah, that's pretty bad.

"Carrie and Berger?" Holly asked.

"*Sex and the City*," Telly and I said.

"Ah." Holly went back to her veggie wrap.

"And it's weird because we had such a great week." Telly seemed genuinely disappointed.

"First times can be awkward. Maybe you should try it again?" I never thought I'd be encouraging her to start seeing my realtor, but anyone was better than Will, who I hadn't heard about in a while, which usually meant he was due for a visit.

"Marin, I wrote the book on first-times, and this one was far and away the absolute worst of my life. There's no coming back from that. So I can't see him again, which means no more tagging along on your house huntings unless you get a new realtor."

"Oh, I know a good one," Holly said. I gave her a grateful smile, then shrugged at Telly. I couldn't take that damn girl anywhere.

"You okay after last night, Holly?" I asked.

"What happened last night?" Telly leaned toward Holly.

"Yeah, I'm fine. David can be an ass sometimes. I think they're just going through a tough time again."

"I think so too. James was acting really weird after dinner. I think he knows something."

"Oh, God, I hope there's nothing to know." Holly fidgeted as if she was shaking off the thought. "Can we talk about something else? What's going on with the apartment search?"

"I never realized how picky James was before. It's like he's looking for *the one*, and he won't settle for anything less than perfect."

"Do you think that's why he hasn't proposed?" Telly asked. Holly and I glared at her.

"How could you say that?" Holly demanded.

Telly turned to me. "Marin, you know I care about you, which is why I think you should consider all the possibilities. I've said it before, but it bears repeating. I don't sugarcoat shit. Life's too fucking short."

"Well, I appreciate your candor as always, but that's not it. I am the one and I'm going to prove it."

"Prove it?" Holly's tone was low and flat, a sign that she wasn't impressed.

"Yeah, I have a plan," I said.

"Here we go again." Telly dropped her fork and rolled her eyes.

"What do you mean you have a plan?" Holly asked.

"I mean James and I are destined for one another.

How else would you describe our meeting? It's like out of a romantic comedy film or a cheesy chick lit novel. You see how we are together. We have that thing. That thing people search their whole lives for. We're . . . meant to be. So it'll happen. I just need to give him a little push."

"I don't know what you're planning, but don't do anything stupid like last time."

"Don't worry. This time it's all aboveboard. I promise."

After lunch, I went to James' house to walk Marvin and used that time to reflect on my next move. I was concerned that last night's dinner did more harm than good, but I was determined to move forward.

Step Two: Family Matters

Admittedly, I hadn't been great with my family, but I think it was because they made it so difficult. James' family was the total opposite, warm and loving, utterly supportive. I had only just met Mr. and Mrs. Young on my trip to Montana, but we had talked on the phone many times before that. Sometimes we'd even get into deeper discussions about things like having a career and a family or lack thereof. Mrs. Young was on her way to getting her degree, but gave up school when she had the girls. By the time James was all grown up, she no longer had the courage or much desire to return to school. All of her children were incredible people, so I think her decision to raise them full time was a good one. She'd made three great contributions to society.

When we returned from the walk, I conjured up a reason to get her on the phone.

"Hi, Gloria, it's Marin," I said.

"Hi, honey, how are you?" she replied. The two of us went on and on with small talk about the weather, the family—particularly Grandma. Everything was good.

"So is something going on, or are you just callin' to shoot the breeze?" she finally asked.

"A little bit of both. James is doing a long shift at the hospital today, so I wanted to make him something special for dinner tonight. I thought I could make one of his favorite childhood recipes. You know, bring a little bit of home to the city."

"Well, aren't you so sweet."

I blushed, hoping it would turn out sweet. Cooking was not my strong suit. I mostly used my kitchen to house the coffee. But Charlotte McQueen agreed with the old adage that the way to a man's heart was through his stomach. I thought it best to start honing my culinary skills.

"James loves my homemade tomato soup and grilled cheese sandwiches," she said. Soup and sandwich didn't sound too difficult. I grabbed a pen and paper to jot down the recipe, which she gladly shared. "You know, that was my favorite food growing up too. My mom made it for us when we were kids. Who knows, maybe one day you and James will have a little one to make soup and sandwiches for."

I smiled at this notion and that James' mom was suggesting it. "I hope so, Gloria."

"I told him to scoop you up before someone else does."

"You did?"

"Yep."

"What did James say?" I asked.

"Oh, he just told me to relax, said the two of you were happy." That sounded like him. "But, I told him that a girl like you won't wait around forever."

"I appreciate that, but it's not like I've got other proposals coming in." And I wondered if it would make a difference if someone else did propose. Did I want James or a ring? I wanted both.

"Well, if there's any girl he'd want to marry, it'd be you."

I smiled, hoping that soon he'd want to marry me. "Thanks for everything. I gotta get to the store before it's too late."

"Okay, Marin. Nice talking to you. Let me know how it goes."

"I will!"

I took the scribbled recipe straight to the store. I bought fresh, ripe tomatoes, garlic, heavy cream, and three types of cheese: cheddar, swiss, and white American, among other items. I even picked up a new rawhide bone for Marvin, which weighed down my canvas shopping bag.

When I got back to James' house, I organized all the ingredients on the table and began reviewing the recipe. Marvin sat busy on the floor with his new chew. With the ingredients laid out in front of me, I second-guessed my recipe notes. What was I thinking trying to recreate his favorite childhood meal? The only soup I'd ever made was the kind that came in cans or easy mixes. My nerves seemed to jumble over the task, so I called Mrs. Young back for clarification. Twice. She didn't seem to mind me pestering her. I think she may have found my effort endearing.

I didn't have much time, so I hurried to smash cloves of garlic and whip tomatoes in the food processor. I set the pot to boil and soon the kitchen was filled with the smell of warm vegetables. The griddle was hot. I placed the buttered bread and cheese and watched the cheddar mix melt between the slices. James would be home any minute and the soup was ready. I put on a new sandwich and let the other cool while I served the soup. I grabbed the hot metal handle and slammed it back on the stove, spilling red liquid all over the floor.

"Ouch! That's hot!" I yelled. Marvin rushed over and began lapping up the scalding soup. "No," I scolded the dog and pushed him aside. I grabbed a kitchen towel and had soaked most of the soup up when I smelled something burning. "Shit!" My grilled cheese was smoking and turning black. I moved it off the heat, the smoke alarm blared, and Marvin moved away, shaking with his tail between his legs.

"Dammit!" I waved a towel under the alarm trying to quiet it. Then, James walked in.

"Hey, what's going on?" he asked, looking puzzled.

"I was trying to make you dinner, but I just made a mess," I whined, still trying to hush the alarm.

He cringed and glanced around the kitchen. "What were you trying to do?"

Finally, the smoke alarm shut up.

"I was trying to make you tomato soup and grilled cheese like your mom made you when you were a kid."

"How did you know about that?" he asked.

"I talked to your mom earlier and she shared her recipe. I wanted to do something nice, something that felt like home."

"Aw, Marin, you are my home." He pulled me in and I rested my hands on his firm chest.

"I am?" I asked.

"Yeah."

I gave a half smile, and his eyes met mine. It was strange, no matter how much time had passed, gazing into his eyes was like coming home.

He kissed my forehead. "Okay, you've got one good sandwich and some soup left, why don't we split it?"

I agreed, then cut the one good grilled cheese in half and he grabbed the bowls to serve the soup.

"Careful, that handle's hot," I said.

"Thanks." He covered the handle with a towel and poured what was left in the bowls. "Hey, what's Marvin got?" he asked.

"I got him a new rawhide at the store."

"That's sweet. Thanks." He kissed the top of my head.

We sat at the table, and I watched James slurp the soup.

"Mmm, it's good." His words said good, but his face

said bad. I took a bite. Yuck! Bland and tart, I couldn't have made it worse if I wasn't trying at all.

"James, this is terrible," I said.

"It's not terrible."

Liar.

I dropped my spoon. "You wanna get take out?"

He hesitated. I could tell he was trying to be polite, but then he lowered his spoon. "Yeah, I'll drive."

We ordered from our favorite Chinese place and had a good laugh about my attempt to cook. He told me over and over how much he appreciated the thought, then regaled me with stories from his childhood about coming home from playing sports and sitting down to a hot bowl of soup and a warm sandwich.

I was worried that my attempt to play wife was a big fat failure, but there was no harm done. That night he couldn't keep his hands off of me, and I could feel him wanting me more as the hours passed. I was no longer concerned about the incident at Rachel and David's house. We were way past that.

In fact, the next day provided the ideal recovery. Michael and Jennifer were in the city visiting a specialty furniture store and we joined them for dinner afterward. Somehow, everything I went through with James in the beginning set me on a path to get closer to my estranged brother. Before James, I'd go six months before seeing Michael, who only lived forty minutes away. Now, we didn't go six weeks without a visit. The best part was getting to see my niece and nephew more often. Oh, how I loved those little angels.

We were on our third glass of vino, well, Jennifer and I were each on our third glass. "You look like someone hit you in the mouth." Jennifer giggled, her lips the color of red Napa grapes.

"And you look like you blew a wine bottle." She stopped laughing for a moment and the table was silent. A second later, we were all barreled over cackling. I may have been drunk, but I was fully aware of my mission that night.

"No seriously," I said. "You guys seem so happy. How long has it been now?"

Michael and Jennifer caught their breath from the laughing spelled.

"Ten years in a couple of weeks," Michael said with a smile.

"What's your secret?" I asked.

Jennifer cupped her hands around her mouth. "He's really good at oral sex," she whispered, sotto voce.

"Jenn!" Michael blurted, while we chuckled wildly.

"Oh, my God," I said. "I'm not sure how I feel about that answer."

"It must run in the family," James lifted his glass to toast Jennifer. I swatted James on the shoulder and tried to contain my flushing cheeks. Luckily, Michael didn't seem too disturbed by his remark.

"But seriously, we take time out for ourselves. Go on short getaways a few times a year, have an adventure. You have to. Otherwise . . ." Jennifer simulated an erection going flaccid with her finger and made a sad little noise implying its death. Michael pulled her hand down and seemed to hold it hostage in his. Sometimes, drunk girls can't be trusted.

"Which reminds us," Michael said. "We have a favor to ask you guys." It sounded serious and allowed us to sober up for a moment. "We're leaving for a long weekend at the end of the month for our anniversary, and we were hoping you two could watch the kids. Mom and Dad will be in Phoenix, otherwise, we'd just have them do it.
What do you think?"

"Yeah, that's no problem," I said.

"It'd be easier if you could stay in Berkeley for the weekend," Jennifer said.

Good, my apartment was too small for two young kids to run around in.

"That sounds like fun," James said before sipping his red wine. "Mind if we bring Marvin?"

"I don't see why not," Michael agreed. "But no boozing."

I gave my brother a thumbs up and winked. It was perfect! *Step Four: Mother Material*, here I come.

10

Surprise From Thailand

THEY SAY THAT YOUTH IS WASTED ON the young. While I believed that was true, I also thought nap time was wasted on the young. For some reason, every weekday between two-thirty and three o'clock my nap alarm went off. Today was no different.

The smell of fresh coffee beans permeated down the hall. Andy was already there, pouring sugar in his freshly made cup.

"Bless you, you're an angel," I said, taking a cup from the cabinet and basking in the warm scent of caffeine goodness that he just brewed.

"Thanks. No one's ever called me that before."

No surprise there. I snickered.

"Let me ask you something." He had my attention. "It seems like ever since that fucking *Fifty Shadows of My Repressed Sexual Abuse* book came out, all my clients are into sadomasochism."

"You're terrible with titles," I said, sipping caramel-colored liquid.

"Are your clients into it too?"

"Maybe a small percentage. I'm sure you're just lucky. I figured you'd be titillated by that kind of talk."

"I would be if all my patients were Victoria's Secret models."

Typical Andy.

"So how's project ring-way?" he asked.

I shot him a wry expression. "I can't tell if that's a clever pun or another one of your terrible titles."

"Let's go with clever pun."

"It's going well," I said cautiously. He already knew too much.

"Good, does that mean we can all get a drink tonight?"

Aw, did Andy miss us? It was cute, but no go.

"After the engagement. You're welcome to help. You know, encourage James to go ring shopping or book a romantic getaway to Paris."

"No way. You're on your own, kid."

"Fine. I'll see you later then."

Andy gestured a farewell with his coffee mug. The exchange reminded me about asking Katie for a double date. Katie was the founder and third partner in our practice. We didn't get together socially very often, but she and her husband were the ideal couple. He was the supportive spouse, and she was the thoughtful wife.

Her door was open. "Come in," she said, when she saw me hovering outside her office.

"Hey, do you have plans this weekend?" I asked.

"I'm not sure, why?"

"I thought you and Ray could join us out for dinner."

She didn't answer. Instead, she stared at me as if she might be trying to come up with a believable excuse. "Can you shut the door?" she asked finally. She only ever asked for the door to be shut if she had something really, really private to say. I had the feeling she was about to reprimand me for something, and I quickly tried to pinpoint what I could've done.

"Ray and I are separated," she said.

What? I covered my mouth, leaving only my raised eyebrows and wide eyes.

"No," I whispered.

"I'm not public about it, so if you can keep it to yourself, I'd really appreciate it."

I lowered my body into the closest chair without breaking my shocked gaze on her. "What happened?"

"We just grew apart." Katie shrugged.

"Grew apart?" I couldn't believe it. Of all the couples I knew, I would've never expected those two to grow apart and separate. It was madness!

"Yeah, it happens."

"I know it happens, but not to you and Ray."

Katie cracked a half smile. "You really are a romantic, Marin. It's one of your strengths in this profession, but it's also one of your weaknesses."

"What do you mean?" I asked.

"Sometimes you can't wrap everything up in a neat bow. Sometimes you're just disappointed."

When I left her office, I was just that—disappointed. I thought about all the events and conversations I'd had since my birthday. It was as if the universe purposefully put obstacles in my way, hoping that I would give up. Maybe it was my residual karma after the way I treated James in the beginning. Would I ever live that down or would it haunt me forever? Then again, there was still the possibility that I was cursed.

I needed reassurance. Ginger would definitely tell me that it would be fine and I was so close. Telly would tell me that I should forget it, dump James, and go out with her tonight. And Holly . . . well, she'd tell me something thoughtful, something real.

It had been days since I last talked to her, and it seemed as if her voicemail was the only thing answering her phone. When I still hadn't heard back from her, I got worried and moved my last appointment so I could pay her a visit at work.

EcoWorld, whose green logo featured the planet Earth in place of the first 'o,' and who was known for their worldwide green and ecofriendly initiatives, took up the entire building. Theirs was one of those hip offices with glass walls and long high-top tables instead of cubicles. Not to mention that it was bustling with energy, as if everyone inside was trying to save the world against a ticking time bomb.

As I made my way over to Holly's desk, I ran into Corrine. She didn't seem as preoccupied and hurried as the others.

"Hey, Marin. What are you doing here?" she asked.

"I was looking for Holly. Do you know where I can find her?" I asked.

"At home would be my guess."

"Home? She left already?"

"No, she's been out for a few days. She's taking some time off. Didn't she tell you?" Corrine sounded surprised.

"No, I hope she's okay." Now I was really worried.

"Oh, I think she's fine."

I was about to thank her and catch another cab to Holly's when Corrine asked me about James.

"Things are really good. We're in the process of finding a new place," I told her.

"Yeah, I remember. I was thinking about you the other day."

"What about?"

"I was thinking about all the happily unmarried couples like Goldie and Kurt and even Oprah and Stedman. It's unconventional, but it works."

"Those are celebrities, though," I said.

Had I given up on marriage with James, I might have indulged her parallel, but it hadn't come to that, and I believed it never would.

"So?"

"So, the rules are different for them. Their lives are totally different. I appreciate the thought, but my proposal's still coming."

"That's good. Keep the faith, girl!"

"You too, and thanks for the info."

"Tell Holly I said 'hi.'"

I agreed and maneuvered my way out of the madness that was EcoWorld.

Twenty minutes later, I knocked on Holly's door. No answer. I tried again. Still no answer, but this time, I heard muffled sounds from inside and knew she was home. I used the spare key she'd given me to let myself in. No sign of her. I walked toward the bedroom. As I got closer, I heard her whimpering cry.

Oh no, what had happened?

I pushed the bedroom door open and the next thing I knew I was watching my naked friend grinding on top of a tanned, small-framed man whose moans sounded like Holly's.

"Oh, my God!" I yelled and covered my eyes.

"Marin?" Holly called out, confused.

"Sorry," I said. "I didn't know you were busy. I'll call you later." With my hands obstructing my sight, I turned to leave and felt the door hit my nose. "Shit!"

"Are you okay?" Holly asked between the sounds of them rustling around to get dressed.

"Don't worry about me. Carry on." It wasn't the first time I'd walked in on Holly having sex, but since we were no longer roommates, I thought those days were behind me. I rushed to let myself out and scrub my brain of the memory, but Holly was after me.

"Wait," she called.

I turned to see that she had managed to put on a small T-shirt that she stretched down to cover her lady parts.

"What are you doing here?" she asked.

"I came to talk to you about this whole James thing. I had no idea that you were seeing someone. Who is that?"

Holly hesitated, and the guy tiptoed out into the living room wearing only a pair of pants. His bare chest was narrow. He didn't look a day over nineteen.

"Hi, I am Noom," he said in a thick Thai accent and approached with his hand extended.

Wow, he looked really young for his age. Good genes, I guess.

I gave him a crooked smile. "You didn't wash your hands just now, did you?"

Noom cocked his head and Holly pushed his arm down.

"Noom came to the states to be with me."

I glanced at her, then at him, and back and forth a few times, trying to figure out how the two of them were a physical, mental, and emotional match. Everything about the last few minutes took me by surprise, and I didn't know what to say or how to say it.

"Okay, then. Nice to meet you, Noom. Holly, I'll catch up with you later."

11

Miss Independent

MY HEART WAS STILL POUNDING when I got outside and my hands shook slightly, making it difficult to dial Telly.

"I need to meet you for a drink," I said as soon as she picked up the phone.

"Now?" she asked.

"Yes, this is an emergency. I'll meet you at Fly in fifteen minutes."

By the time Telly arrived, ten minutes late by the way, I'd already had two shots.

"Okay, I'm here. What's the emergency?" Telly rambled, strapping her purse to the back of the bar seat.

"Have you talked to Holly lately?" I asked.

"No, why?"

"Well, I hadn't either. So I went over to her apartment just now to check on her and when I walked in I saw something."

Telly's expression transitioned from irritated to intrigued. "What?"

"She was having sex." I cringed.

"Uh-huh . . ."

"With Noom!"

Telly gasped. "No way! Are you sure it was him."

"Yes, it was traumatizing."

"It's about time Holly got laid," Telly told me before ordering the bartender to pour her a whiskey neat, whatever that meant.

"You're missing the point," I urged on.

"Which is?"

"Noom is here in the states. That was the whole reason they could never make it work to begin with. What if he's here to stay? What if they're back together for real? What if he takes her back to Thailand for good?"

"Okay, what if?"

"He's so wrong for her. They don't make any sense. Literally, he barely speaks English. They don't make verbal sense to each other."

"They don't make any sense? Or they don't make any sense to you?"

"Both!" I took a gulp from my cosmopolitan.

"What happened to love-conquers-all-romantic-Marin, huh?"

"Holly should be with someone who's handsome and tall, understands her work is everything to her, and preferably lives in the Bay area."

"But if she loves this guy, God forbid, then she needs your support. Geez, I sound like you now."

"Hey!" I said, and she rolled her eyes. "Does she

have your support?"

"Never," Telly hissed with sarcasm. I laughed.

Telly took another swig from her short glass and cleared her throat. "Okay, I want to talk to you about something too," she started. My nerves jumbled again. I couldn't take any more life changing news this week. "So, I'm thinking about doing something big. Like really, really big. Something I never thought was possible until now."

Oh, my God. If she was getting married, then I might just kill myself. Tonight. Yes, I'd be known as the girl no one would marry.

"What is it?" I held her gaze for a moment, looking for the answer telepathically.

"You know how I've been getting consistent referrals from Man Test the last nine months or so?"

I nodded.

Telly was so intrigued by the Man Test Company after Rachel and I had used them that she contacted the owner about creating a strategic alliance. Telly was a divorce attorney, after all. At the time, Man Test already had a referral attorney, so they turned down her offer. Telly didn't take it lying down. She began to use all of her connections to link up with the owner, Serena. Shortly after, the two had become friends and Telly had become their go-to lawyer.

"Anyway," Telly said. "I've been bringing in so much business that I thought I'd be a shoo-in for senior partner. Nope. So I thought to myself, fuck 'em. I'll take my Man Test clients and start my own practice where I'm the boss."

A smile grew across my face and my stomach flipped. Was Telly really taking the leap of entrepreneurship? What an incredible declaration!

"Are you saying what I think you're saying?"

Telly beamed and nodded her confirmation. A scream left my lips and echoed throughout the bar. I grabbed Telly and we jumped around in excitement.

"Oh, my God. We have to celebrate." I turned to the bartender. "We need another round."

"It's crazy right. I mean, can I really do this?" Telly asked and gulped more of her whiskey.

"It's not crazy. It makes total sense. So what's the plan?"

"Well, I already spoke to a junior associate at another firm that interned with me a few years ago. She wants to come on with me. I'm scheduled to look at office spaces this week. All I need to do is hire an assistant and I'm good."

"What does Serena think?" I asked, knowing this was her biggest referral source.

"She's totally on board and wants to coordinate our branding."

Impressive. I wondered if they could use a couples therapist? Everything seemed to be coming together for Telly. I had just one more question. "Are you ready to work your ass off?"

She raised her glass to mine. "I was born ready, baby." We toasted to her new venture.

Telly and I left the bar an hour later, fully celebrated and inebriated. I missed three calls from Holly, a little out of spite and a little because I didn't want to take the spotlight off of Telly. There was no answer when I tried to call her back. Two could play that game. Oh well, we'd have to talk about it eventually.

If Holly was, in fact, in love and Telly was really starting her own firm, then I was happy for them. The three of us had grown a little stagnant in our day-to-day lives. It was time for something new, for our lives to evolve. My relationship with James was definitely due for an evolution. Yes, we were apartment hunting. Yes, I was on a quest to make it official. But, nothing substantial had happened yet. I'd have to be patient, as usual.

James hadn't called me that evening as promised and I grew worried. He answered the phone just before it went to voicemail. What was he doing?

"Hey, stranger. Everything okay?" I asked.

"Mmhmm," he mumbled. "I was asleep."

"Asleep? It's not even seven o'clock. Do you want me to come over and wake you up?" I asked, hopeful since alcohol stimulated my libido.

"If you want, but I'm not feeling too well."

Oh, no!

"Really, what's the matter, baby?" I asked in a sweet, maternal tone.

"I have no energy and my body's achy. I probably need a good night of sleep."

"Yeah. I'll let you sleep and check on you in the morning, okay," I said.

"Okay." He made a kissy noise.

First thing the next morning I called my tired boyfriend back.

"Feeling better?" I asked.

"No, I think I have a cold. I'm not going to work today." His voice cracked and I bit my lower lip. A cold? James was healthy as a horse. I couldn't ever recall him getting sick. There'd been a few times when he thought he was coming down with something, but then the next day, he was good as new. Interesting that a bug finally got him.

"Aw, baby. I'll be over as soon as I can."

"No, you don't have to. Just go to work, and I'll call you later."

"Forget it, James. You're sick. I'll be there as soon as I can. Go back to bed."

I hated that he wasn't well, but I had to embrace the fact that this cold had given me a good opportunity to demonstrate my value as a caretaker.

12

Play House

LUCKILY, I HAD A LIGHT DAY on the schedule at work, so I called Katie to move my patients back. Then I immediately headed over to the grocery store for supplies. As I walked the aisles of the store carrying my basket of get-well goodies, I was happy. Not happy that James was sick, but that the day had given me a purpose, to help him in his time of need. With no pets, children, or husband, I rarely had the opportunity to exercise my nurturing instincts.

James was tough, the kinda guy who didn't need help from anybody for anything. Taking care of himself for a decade probably had a lot to do with it. Then again, some other men weren't nearly as self-sufficient as James. David was a good example, and Rachel babied the shit out of him. Hopefully, James would let me baby him a little today. He'd never been too good at it before.

Armed with soup, cold meds, vapor rub, and vitamin

C, I was ready for the next step.

Step Three: Play House

James was upstairs in bed, watching something on his laptop.

"Hey, baby," I said.

"Hey, you." He cracked a smile that quickly turned into a cough. Poor thing. I slipped off my shoes and slipped into bed next to him.

"How are you feeling?" I placed the back of my hand against his forehead. He was really warm.

"Like shit." He frowned like a helpless little boy.

So cute.

My poor James. I pouted my lip and pushed his hair back. "Well, I'm here to take care of you."

"Marin, you don't have to do that. I'll be fine. You really should be at work." As he talked, I pulled a thermometer from my purse.

"Don't you worry about that, now open your mouth," I said holding the temperature gauge to his lips. He hesitated for a moment, but when I pursed my lips and raised my brows he relented. After almost a minute, the thermometer beeped.

"See," I said, holding the meter to his face. "A hundred and one point four."

"Well, that explains it. Man, this sucks," he pouted. "So I guess I'm stuck in here for a while."

"Afraid so. You're watching *Ace Ventura*?" I asked pointing to the movie on the screen.

"Yeah, I used to watch it on sick days as a kid," he said.

I relished the moments that I learned new things about James, like I was constantly discovering him, and he was ever fascinating. Even the silly facts about *Ace Ventura* on sick days enchanted me.

"I haven't seen this movie in almost fifteen years. Are you hungry?" I asked.

"No, I had some oatmeal."

"Okay, I'm gonna go get some stuff from downstairs. I'll be back in a minute, okay," I said.

He nodded and I went down stairs and returned with water, warm tea, honey drops, cold meds, and the other supplies from the store.

"What's all this?" he asked.

"Just some stuff to make you feel better."

He smiled and pulled me over. "You're the best, you know that?" he said.

I smiled and blew him a kiss. I wanted to kiss his sweet face, but I wasn't about to get sick too, because I was the biggest baby of all. James and I snuggled in his bed and watched the movie, and by the end, snot-filled tissues covered the bed.

Finally, he got the chills and his eyelids became heavy. I grabbed an extra blanket from his closet and tucked him under his covers as if swaddling a baby. He seemed to fall asleep quickly and he breathed heavily in and out of his mouth.

I headed downstairs to check in at work and start some lunch for James. No special recipes this time, but instead, a reliable premade carton of tomato soup. Minutes later the soup was hot. I heard rustling around upstairs, so I went up to check on James. He had thrown his covers completely off, but he seemed to be sleeping still.

"Hey, are you okay?" I asked and nudged him alert.

He looked up at me and grimaced. "Oh, my God. It's so hot."

"Here, drink," I said, handing him a glass of water. He sipped it while I ran a washcloth under cool water and faced the fan toward him.

"Better?" I asked, patting the washcloth on his forehead and neck.

"Yeah, thanks," he said and kissed my hand. I'd have to wash it in a second.

"Are you hungry? I made tomato soup," I sang in a way to tempt him. "Okay, I heated premade soup."

He rose sluggishly out of the bed and let out a chuckle.

"Wait, I'll bring it to you," I said, trying to push him back in bed.

"Don't take this the wrong way, especially since you're taking such great care of me, but you don't have the best track record with carrying soup."

"Good thinking," I said, helping him out of bed and downstairs.

The soup was much tastier, and I was relieved I didn't screw it up. Poor James was so stuffed up. He could barely keep his mouth closed to swallow.

"Did you clean the apartment?" James studied the

space from his seat.

"Yep, and I took Marvin for a walk."

"Man, I must've slept hard."

"Well, you're sick, sweetie," I said, playing with his soft hair. "Oh, I have some interesting news, actually a couple items of news."

He gestured for me to continue.

"Telly's going to start her own firm."

"Really? Good for her," he said. "I hope she's ready to work her ass off."

"That's what I said! Oh, my God, that's not the shocking news."

"What's the shocking news?"

"So yesterday I went to Holly's because I hadn't heard from her in a while, and . . . I walked in on her having sex. . . with Noom." I quickly covered my mouth with my hands like I'd let the words escape by mistake.

James looked confused.

"Who's Noom?"

"Noom! The guy Holly was seeing off and on from Thailand."

"Oh, is he visiting?"

"I certainly hope so, but I haven't talked to her since it happened. I knew they were communicating again, but she never said he was coming to California."

"Since when do you and Holly keep secrets from each other?" he asked. Probably since I started trying to prove James was a cheater a couple years ago.

"Since now, I guess." I ran my finger along his black kitchen table, catching a glimpse of myself in its shiny reflection. Why had Holly kept it a secret from me? Was there something more she wasn't telling me?

After lunch we started a movie, which turned into an afternoon nap. Well . . . at least for him it did. I let him sleep while I went downstairs to call Holly.

"Hey," she answered.

"Hey, so . . . yesterday was weird, right?" I asked with hesitation.

"Little bit."

"What happened? What's he doing here? Is he moving in? Are you two a couple? Why didn't you tell me he was coming?"

"Marin! Calm down," she told me, and I silenced. "I didn't know he was coming. He just showed up."

"He did?"

"Yes, it was completely unexpected and . . . totally romantic."

I grimaced. "How long is he staying?"

"He's here for good."

"I'm confused. I thought you two broke it off for good. Months ago."

"We did, but then he started calling and texting and emailing—'*Holly, I love youuuu,*'" she said, impersonating him and it wasn't sexy or romantic; it was whiny. "Then he showed up here a few days ago and said that it doesn't matter where we are as long as we're together, we're home."

"I don't know what to say," I said.

"Say, you're happy for me. Happy that I found someone who's willing to move halfway across the globe for me."

"Yeah, I'm happy if you're happy. I just don't understand why you're happy—with him I mean."

"I know, but you don't have to understand."

True, I didn't, but I wanted to.

"One day you will."

"I'm sorry about walking in on you guys. I had no idea."

"I know, it's okay. I'm sorry I didn't tell you sooner."

"So we're good?" I asked.

"Yep, we're good."

I went back upstairs and crawled into bed next to a snoozing James, making sure to keep my distance so I didn't catch his cold. He was so handsome, even with a hundred degree fever, chapped lips, and obnoxious, stuffy nose snoring. I spent the night with him, keeping an eye on his fever, and tending to his needs.

Just before I fell asleep, James opened his heavy eyelids. "Thanks for taking care of me today."

"You're welcome," I said. "Go back to sleep."

13

Fell Street

A FEW DAYS LATER, James was good as new and wanted to treat me to a cup of hot chocolate from my favorite chocolate shop. Marvin let out a loud bark when I unlocked the door to his place.

"Hey there, beautiful," James said. I rushed over and wrapped my arms around him, pressing my mouth against his in a heartfelt kiss. It was as if I hadn't seen him in years, and I didn't want to let him go, even though it had only been a day since he last held me.

"I missed you," I said.

"Yeah, me too," he replied. "It was nice having you here for a couple of days."

"Oh, yeah?"

"Yeah, making food, keeping the house clean, hangin' out with Marvin and takin' him for walks."

"So you wish I was your stay-at-home girlfriend?" I asked with a tinge of feminist attitude.

"No way! I'd never ask you to quit your job. All I'm saying is that it was nice having you here."

I pulled him in for another kiss. He was definitely my man.

The three of us headed to the shop across from the park. The sweet smell of sugar and cinnamon swirled around me when I walked in. I wanted so badly to eat some of the little chocolates, or better yet, a fudge brownie.

"What do you want?" he asked, waiting by the register.

"Everything," I said and he cracked a smile. "Just a large chocolate coconut." Mmm, coconut. Just saying it made me long for warm days on the beach, margaritas, and my bikini. Then I remembered that I'd have to plan a sexy getaway. I might be wearing that bikini sooner than expected. "Make that a small," I said.

I tightened my scarf as we left the shop. The cold wind prickled my face. Spring was supposedly around the corner, but for some reason it was taking forever. I lifted the cup to my nose and smelled the sweet aroma of chocolate and coconut. My mouth watered for it, but the steam shooting through the top warned me to wait.

Marvin led us across to the park, walking ahead briskly as the little horse had been cooped up in James' apartment all day.

"This is nice, huh?" James said, and put his arm around my shoulder. "You, me, Marvin, hot chocolate, a walk. It doesn't get any better than this."

I smiled for a moment. It was pretty great, but what if that was all he wanted? Maybe this was all he needed? Was it enough for him? Could it ever be enough for me?

They say doctors make the worst patients, and that was true for me. I always admonished my patients for being indirect with their communication, and yet here I was about to pull out the old passive aggressive questions.

"This is nice, but I think we can do better, don't you? Like, where do you see yourself in five years?" I asked.

"Hmm," he said and rubbed his chin. He squinted as if really contemplating the question. Like he wanted to give me the best answer. "In five years I'll be almost forty, wow. Hmm, I'd like us to have a house, not a big one, just big enough with a fireplace. A small backyard and a garage. In the city would be nice, but just outside in the suburbs would be cool too."

Okay, he wanted a house with a yard. Bigger houses meant family.

"I want to have my own practice by then, or maybe partner with someone." He'd always dreamed of working with professional athletes as a physical therapist in his own practice.

I nodded, assessing all of his words.

"Let's see . . . Maybe by then, you and I will have a kid. A boy. He'll play sports like me or a girl would be cool too. Maybe she'll play sports." There it was, the kid thing. We'd had this type of conversation before, and so I always thought that kids must've meant a marriage preceding it.

"Is that it?" I asked.

"Yeah, that sounds like the life," he said and went on to compare his work situation to Telly's, saying he should really start thinking about moving along with his plan, but that it never seemed like the right time. It got me thinking about time, and how timing really was everything.

I thought about how James and I met. Had Anderson and his girlfriend not walked into my office that day, I probably would have left the office early. My phone wouldn't have rung and so I would've made it safely out of the building and all the way home. We never would have had that moment when he rescued me in more ways than one.

Then again, James was best friends with David. It was likely that we would've crossed paths again in a different way. Maybe by that time I would have been past that whole 'men are all cheaters' thing and our relationship would've started off completely normal. Maybe that would have been better because then James wouldn't know how crazy I was, and he'd want to marry me because he'd see that we were two imperfect people who were perfect for each other.

I could play the *what if* game all day long, but it wouldn't change the reality of the situation. Then again, maybe James did want to marry me. Maybe the *McQueen Method* was working.

On the way back, we drove through Alamo Square, one of my favorite neighborhoods in the city. James knew that I loved passing by to look at the Edwardian style homes. I stared out of the window looking for my favorite ones. Most of the houses were over a hundred years old and had been rehabbed. But still, it was like going back in time to a place where things were simpler. James pulled the car over.

"What are you doing?" I asked.

"See that?" He pointed to a house on his side of the car. There was an agent setting up a sign. James got out of the car and approached her. I followed and looked up at the blue house with white trim on all three of the bay windows. A single car garage was tucked underneath and I must've counted over twenty steps to the doorway.

"Just listed it for sale," the agent told James.

"How much?" James asked.

My heart began to race. What was he thinking? We weren't in the market to buy a property, especially not one in this neighborhood.

The agent quoted him a price.

Wow, much lower than I had expected. "It's priced to sell. The couple's retired now, selling it to downsize. You interested?"

"What do you think?" he asked me. What I thought was there is no way we could get that house. It was like the housing version of James; a picture perfect idea that seemed so close but still out of reach.

"I literally just listed the house. The ink's barely dry. I'm sure you can see it now if you want," the agent suggested.

"Just a second," he told the agent and pulled me aside. "This house is a great deal. Let's check it out."

I gazed up at the property again, and felt myself become attached. "I don't think that's a good idea. We can't afford a place like this," I said.

"Sure we can," he said.

I pouted my lip.

"Marin, what's the problem? You love this neighborhood. How amazing would it be to buy this place? It could be ours."

Okay, James may not have been proposing marriage, but now he was proposing a home purchase. It was a big commitment. "Okay, let's take a look," I said.

We walked up the steps with the agent and rang the doorbell. Two columns framed the doorway and the entire area was trimmed with light blue and white molding. My heart raced as the door opened. An old gentleman, at least seventy-five, stood inside.

"Cindy," he said.

"Hi, Mr. Wallace. I was posting the *for sale* sign and this nice couple drove up. They're interested in the property. Since we're all here, do you mind if I show them around?"

Mr. Wallace peeked over the agent's shoulder and looked us over for a second. His suspicious expression turned into a welcoming one in a matter of moments, and we were invited inside. It was lovely, like having an out of body, real estate experience. The house was tastefully done with beautiful hardwood floors and crisp white moldings. There were fireplaces in both the living room and the bedroom, and I imagined sitting in front of them with James and a glass of pinot on a cool night like this. The bathrooms and kitchen needed a bit of updating, but overall it was . . . a dream. We walked out onto the back deck and down the stairs to the backyard. Like most of the homes in the area, the yard was long and narrow but big enough for a dog and maybe a swing set.

Elation from inside my chest made me feel as if it was already mine. I wanted it so badly, I could cry. Then at that very moment, James whispered, "Let's buy it."

I looked deep into his eyes, wanting it to be our home, feeling as if we were already home.

"But how?" I asked.

"Don't worry, I'll tell you later," he said.

Huh? What did that mean?

Mrs. Wallace, the lady of the house, followed us through each room. "How long have you lived here?" I asked.

"Oh, about forty-five years, I'd say. It's been a great home. We raised our two boys here. They're grown now and have families of their own."

"Why would you want to sell this place? It's a dream," I said.

She laughed a soft, warm laugh. "Yes, living here has been a dream, but dreams change. It's too big for just the two of us. We're moving to a condo in Juniper, Florida to be closer to one of our sons and grandchildren.

"That's nice," I said.

"Oh, yes. It was seventy-five degrees in Jupiter today." Mrs. Wallace grinned.

I looked into her sweet eyes. It seemed like she and Mr. Wallace were living the dream and now moving on to greener pastures and much warmer weather. I imagined us following a similar path, and the thought moved me to tears.

"Are you okay, dear?" she asked.

"Yes," I laughed the tear away. "I'm fine."

James and I waved goodbye to the Wallaces and to the house. Outside on the street, Cindy asked if we wanted to put an offer on the house.

"Let us sleep on it and let you know in the morning before you officially list it. We're very interested, but we need to talk it over first," James told her.

"I'll give you 'til ten tomorrow morning, then I've got to put it in the system."

"We can work with that," he said.

She handed James her business card and reminded us about her ten a.m. deadline before heading off.

"What street is this?" I asked. James walked a little way to the corner sign.

"Fell Street," he said and started laughing. "Oh, my God. That's too funny."

"Why is that funny?" I asked.

"Think about it, Fell Street? The first time we met, you. . ."

"Fell," I said.

James wasn't really the type to believe in signs. If the whole thing didn't already astonish me, then I was really surprised to hear him say, "I think it's meant to be. What are the odds?"

He was right, what were the odds of us meeting the way we did, of stumbling on this amazing property that would no doubt be gone within a day? It had to be meant for us. The only thing that would make this even more perfect would be if he got down on one knee and pulled a diamond ring from his pocket. But what were the odds of that?

That night we went back to his place and talked about nothing but the house. We flipped through the pictures we took on our phones and talked about the things that were perfect and things we could make perfect. It was the most exciting conversation we'd had in a long time.

"But James, what about the price?" I asked. "It's way above anything I could afford."

"Well, you're not buying it on your own. We'd buy it together."

"Even so, the mortgage would be a bit higher than our rent. I have some cash, but not enough for a decent down payment. What about you?"

"I've got enough," he said.

"You been holdin' out on me, Young?"

He laughed. "No, when my grandfather passed a few years ago, he left all of us a nice chunk of change. It's enough for a down payment on this house and to fix up the kitchen and bathrooms."

"Wow. I had no idea. Are you sure you want to use it for this?" I asked.

"Yep, I knew I'd put it into a house someday. I wanted to wait for the right house, the right girl, and the right time."

"And you feel like this is it?" I said, hopeful.

His eyes were fixed on mine and in that moment, I wanted to believe he was thinking the same thing that I was, that we were Mr. and Mrs. Right about to buy the perfect house on Fell Street.

"Yeah, I think so." He leaned in for a kiss. It had

been a crazy day and all the talk about buying a house and being committed to it together really turned me on. James may not have asked for my hand in marriage, but tonight I let it go to enjoy being in this right time with him.

The next morning, I awoke to the smell of french toast and bacon. The sounds of the newscast echoed from downstairs. As I blinked away the sleep in my eyes, I recalled the house on Fell Street. Our house. I could barely sleep the night before thinking about our life there.

"Morning, beautiful," he said and poured me a cup of coffee.

"You makin' my favorite breakfast?" I asked.

"You know it." He served me a plate of morning goodness. "I called Cindy this morning about the house." He paused and his silence made my stomach flip.

"And . . . ?" I asked.

"We got the house!" I threw my arms in the air, and he picked me up right out of my chair.

"Cindy's going to bring the offer by later to sign."

"Wait, what about the loan approval? Your grandfather didn't leave you that much in cash, did he?"

"I wish," he said with a smirk. "I got a pre-approval letter from a guy Jared hooked me up with a few weeks ago in case we wanted to discuss buying. I was curious what we could get."

"You were approved for the whole thing? Already?" Seriously?

He *uh-huhed* and laid one on me.

"Oh, my God, I can't believe this!" It was true. I couldn't believe it. Everything seemed to be falling into place. Everything except one thing and it was the only glitch in the plan. "Wait, are you sure this is a good idea, buying a house together? It's not like we're married."

"Lots of unmarried couples buy houses together," he said. Not the answer I wanted to hear.

"But what if something happens?"

"What's going to happen?" he asked before sipping his coffee.

"We could break up. One of us could die . . ."

He put down his mug and approached me. "We'll work out all those details." His hands slid up and down my arms to comfort me, but I lowered my head.

Was this a smart decision for me?

"Look," he said. "I'm not going into this lightly. I want to have a life with you, and I think this house is a great addition to that. Don't you think so?" He moved his head to make eye contact.

"You're sure this is what you want?" I asked, staring into his sweet blue eyes.

"Yes," he replied. I let myself believe that if I followed this path, it would eventually lead to the place I so desperately wanted to be.

James and I made house plans over breakfast. In the two months before closing, I'd have to pack, give notice to my landlord, forward my mail to the new address, and transfer the utilities. Not to mention we wanted to do some work on the house like update the kitchen and repaint the bedroom. My thoughts drifted to light shades of blue and soft hues of beige. Were we really buying a house together?

14

St. Patrick's Day

I WANTED TO TELL SOMEONE THE GOOD news and knew the one person who would truly appreciate it. So I met her at the dress shop where she was being fitted for alterations.

"Marin!" Ginger called from a small platform. A thin woman with a dark bun crouched by her feet, pinning the bottom of the dress. Even though Ginger's dress was unfinished and her hair was in a messy ponytail, she was stunning, like some kind of bridal dream. That boob job of hers didn't hurt either.

"You look . . ."

"Incredible, right!" She giggled and bounced with glee, and I joined her.

"I need you to stay still please," the lady with the pins said.

"Sorry." Ginger quieted and the pin lady cracked a little smile.

"You know," I said. "I still haven't received your

wedding invitation."

Ginger let out a sigh. "Ugh, I know. It's my fault. I keep changing my mind on the invite. I want everything to be perfect."

"I know what you mean." I thought back to my engagement with Chad, standing where she was with pins in my white gown. I had the same hopes, the same dreams, the same desire for perfection. But like Katie said, sometimes you can't tie everything in a neat little bow, but that didn't mean you couldn't try. Ginger and I weren't so different. We were optimists.

"So you said you had some news. Is it what I hope it is?" Ginger asked.

"Not exactly, but we're getting closer."

"Are you pregnant?" she whispered.

"No, I wish," I said. An "accidental" pregnancy would probably seal the deal, but I'd never do something like that. Call me a romantic, but I wanted James to marry me because I was the one he wanted, not for any other reason.

"Then what is it?" She hurried me to answer.

"We're buying a house! Together." My grin was from ear to ear. It was the first time I was able to share the news with anyone.

Just when I thought her grin couldn't get any wider, it did. "Are you serious?"

I nodded vigorously, unable to contain my cheer.

"That's incredible!" And she was right. It was pretty incredible. "So where are you with the steps?" she asked.

"I'm in the midst of Step Three, getting ready for

Step Four in a couple weeks. I really need to plan that getaway. Where did you go for yours?"

"We went to Miami."

"Miami?" That's not a place I would've picked.

"Oh yeah, Miami's very sexy."

"Have any other ideas?" I asked as I was out of places that didn't involve wine country.

"I could think of a few places, but it has to stimulate James. You know who you should talk to?"

"Who?"

"Rachel. According to her Facebook page, she's always going somewhere." Why hadn't I thought of that? I had to admit, Ginger was turning out to be a good friend. I needed some alone time with Rachel anyway.

Turns out, Rachel was difficult to get alone. She was too busy to meet for coffee so I had to meet her where she was, which was the craft store on Market Street.

I followed her around while she perused through sheets of scrapbook paper and paper cut outs of ocean waves and palm trees.

"I need your help with something," I said.

"Oh, yeah?" She didn't lift her eyes from the two pieces of paper she was comparing.

"I want to do something nice for James. I was thinking a weekend getaway. Like a sexy weekend getaway."

She turned to me for a moment. "I'm listening."

"You and David have been everywhere. Where can we go for a long weekend? Somewhere James would like."

"I have no idea. Do you think I have time to research vacation spots?" Her words were chilly, and I didn't know how to respond.

She must have caught a whiff of her tone, because after one look from me she changed it. "You can hire someone to figure that out for you. I'll text you the name of my travel agent. She's amazing and she'll take care of everything." Okay, that last part sounded much better. Not to mention, it was a relief.

"Thanks, Rach," I said.

"No biggie."

"So, how are things with David?" I asked as if it was a mundane inquiry, but really I was dying to know.

"They're good," she said like she meant it.

"Are you sure? Because you know you can tell me if they're not."

She gave me one of those perfect smiles that was too perfect to be believed. "No really, everything's good. Everyone has bad days, Marin. You should know that better than anyone." Was she talking about my bout with insanity or my profession?

"Okay, I had to ask. You're like a little sister to me."

Rachel headed down the next aisle, returning to casual conversation. "Speaking of sisters, did Holly tell you about Noom?"

I thought about telling her everything, but it wasn't something Holly would want me to share with Rachel. It was bad enough that I couldn't keep my mouth shut to Telly and as for James, well, I told him everything. Okay, mostly everything.

"Yeah, it's so weird, right?" I asked.

"Yeah, I want to be happy for her, but they're so mismatched. He's gotta go. And given his history, I'm sure he'll be out of here soon. We just have to be patient. That reminds me, we're taking them out drinking for St. Patrick's Day. You guys should come."

"Wait, I thought you wanted him gone?"

"I do, but I don't want Holly to know that. I have to support her regardless. She's family. Besides, maybe he's a bad drunk."

Yeah maybe, like David.

"Ooh, look at this!" She handed me a square sheet of pink glitter paper. It was strange the things that excited her. I shot her a wry glance. Some things never changed.

St. Patrick's Day fell on Friday that week, and it was quite a lucky day because it was the day our contract on the house was ratified, which meant it was official. Goodbye landlord, hello mound of debt. There was no one I'd rather have a mound of debt with than my love, James.

On the evening of St. Patrick's Day, James and I were getting ready to meet our friends and Noom as promised.

"What do you think?" James asked after he slipped on a green t-shirt with a St. Paddy's design that said 'I love beer' with a shamrock in the place of love and a beer drawing in place of the word.

"Cute."

"I know what you're trying to say, but you can't use the word cute. I'm a guy."

"Sorry, it's really clever."

"I'll take clever," he agreed. "You look pretty." He knew the right words to use. No novelty t-shirt for me. Instead, I went with a white sweater and bright green skinny jeans. Not getting pinched tonight. I hated that.

"You're missing something, though." James knelt down and reached into his overnight bag. My heart began to pound wildly. Did he plan a St. Patrick's Day proposal instead of a Valentine's Day one? Men really could be clueless sometimes. My eyes lost focus and I felt faint. "Here it is," he said.

This was it!

He pulled out a green headband with shamrocks attached to little springs and handed it to me. I let out a nervous laugh and slipped the festive fashion accessory on my head.

"How do I look?" I asked, striking a pose.

"You look hot, baby. How 'bout me?" he asked and adorned his face with a pair of green, shamrock shaped sunglasses.

"Very sexy," I said, winking at him.

The pub was packed. Everyone was sporting some kind of green, some with leprechaun hats and other getups. I didn't feel as silly in my Lucky O'headband. Rachel, David, Holly, and Noom sat at a tall bar table in the center. The way they were laughing, it looked like they'd already had a couple glasses of green beer.

"You guys made it!" Holly said, unusually elated. I hugged her and introduced Noom to James.

Then, "Ouch!" What the fuck? Noom had pinched me.

"Happy St. Paddy's Day!" he said, followed by a ridiculous laugh. I soothed my fresh sore.

"Noom, she's wearing green," Holly said. "You only pinch people if they're not wearing green."

Noom apologized, still laughing.

"Sorry, Mar. He's still learning about our crazy traditions."

"Mmhmm," I murmured.

James and I settled in and he poured me a glass of green beer. "We have some news," I said, pulling everyone's attention. "You tell 'em."

James smiled with pride. "We bought a house!" Everyone roared with cheer and raised their glasses to us in a toast.

"Where is it?" Rachel asked.

"Alamo Square," I told her. Everyone but Noom oohed at this.

"Let's get a round of shots," David announced. "On me."

"Thanks, man," James said.

"It's the least I can do. You're about to be broke!" He raised his glass and hooted a big laugh. James shot me a wink. They'd never know what a great deal we got. We sucked down the green-colored shots of flavored vodka and the party really began. Well, I should say it began for everyone else. No more drinks for me. I wanted to keep an objective eye on Noom, which wasn't difficult because he seemed to make a point of hanging out with me throughout the evening. The more he drank, the looser his lips became.

"Holly says you are romantic." Noom slurred his words.

"Do you mean a romantic?"

"Yes, yes. She says I am a romantic too." He showed his teeth, which looked ultra-white against his brown skin. His English was slightly better than I thought, especially after all those beers. "We are same."

"How so?" No way in hell that we were the same.

"You are romantic. I am romantic. You love Holly. I love Holly," he said. That might be all we have in common.

"You love Holly?" I asked.

"Yes, I love Holly since the moment I saw her."

Uh, oh. He was a romantic. I looked at Rachel, who was cringing just as I wanted to. Hopefully, she was right. Maybe he'd be gone sooner than later.

"That makes things difficult, I guess." I shrugged and sipped my Shirley Temple.

"Difficult?" He raised his eyebrow.

"Yeah, going back to Thailand and having to leave Holly."

Noom chuckled. "No, Holly and I are forever."

Forever? Noom wasn't just a romantic. He was a committed romantic. "Don't you want to go back?" I asked.

"I will go back. Holly will go back too." He delivered the words with confidence. Blood rushed to my cheeks and my heart pounded a little more.

Noom excused himself and Holly scooted in next to me. "Isn't he so cute?" It was rare to see her so giddy.

"He's adorable." I flashed a tight-lipped smile.

"That's why he's called Noom. It means cute, young. I'm so glad he's here. It sounds crazy, but I think he's the one."

Noom? The one? Was she high?

"Really? What makes you say that?"

"I can't explain it. It's a spiritual, chemical, emotional, and physical connection all rolled into one. All I know is I've never felt like this before." I took a moment to pray that she was only saying those things because she was drinking and getting laid on a regular basis.

"Okay, just be careful. You two are from different worlds." I patted her shoulder, looking into her eyes.

"Oh, Marin," she spoke in her soft, airy voice. "One day you'll see we're all from the same world, just different coordinates." Her eyes moved up as she toyed with the antennas on my headband. "What are you wearing this for?"

"James got it. He loves this goofy shit."

"Aw!" Holly curled into herself as if the feelings of love and happiness enveloped her. "You're buying a house and I'm in love. Isn't this great! I couldn't help but giggle at her lovable state. It had been a long time since I'd seen her so at ease. Over the past five years or so, she'd grown tenser over her work, saying there was so much to do and so little time. But it seemed that at least for the night, maybe the week, or maybe longer, she could let go.

15

Mother Material

HOLLY'S CARE OF MOTHER NATURE was admirable, but it was time to exemplify my own.

Step Four: Mother Material

The following Friday, James and I packed our bags for the weekend and headed to my brother's with Marvin in tow. The kids, Miles and Jillian, were still in school when we arrived. Jennifer gave me a quick rundown on all the need-to-knows, bed by ten and both had a shellfish allergy, so no iodine. Moments later, they couldn't get out of the house fast enough.

"So now what?" James asked. A few hours remained before the kids got home.

"I dunno. We have the house to ourselves. We can do whatever we want." Seconds later, James had me pinned against the counter, kissing me wildly. I pulled his shirt over his head and slid my fingers down to his belt. I didn't know if it was that we were alone, that it was my brother's house, or that it was definitely naughty, but it really turned me on.

James carried me up to the guestroom, where we were ordered to stay, and threw me on the bed. He felt amazing, the kissing, the sucking, the tickling, the grabbing, the moaning. After all this time, sex with him was still pretty. . .

I took a minute to collect myself after we'd finished, shaking my head and blinking. Trying to get the blood to flow back to my brain.

"Mmm," he moaned. "You really are so sexy, you know that?"

"I think maybe the house makes me sexier," I said.

He pulled me in. "I can't wait to see how sexy you are in our house."

Our house . . . I smiled. James got quiet, as he often did after sex. He usually fell asleep for about twenty minutes. I stayed still until his breathing became heavier then slipped out of the sheets.

"Where are you going?" he mumbled.

"I'm gonna run to the store. Stay here and sleep." I grabbed some of my clothes off the floor and headed back to the kitchen to find my t-shirt lying over the knife block. Would we remain the type of couple that gets a little rowdy in the kitchen?

I drove James' SUV to the store down the street. The rows were bustling with retirees and stay-at-home moms.

For the moment, as I pushed my cart up and down the grocery-filled aisles, I was one of them. After years of shopping for myself, it was good to shop for a family, my family. Granted, it was my boyfriend, niece, and nephew, but nonetheless, they were my family. I liked the idea of going back to the house and preparing snacks for the kids to eat while we helped them with their homework, then cooking a meal for all of us to share at the family table. So, I pretended as I pulled a tub of cookie dough off the chilly shelf.

"My kids love those," a woman browsing the same section said.

"Mine too." I smiled. "Have a good day." Yeah . . . I could totally be one of them.

Jennifer kept a nice home for having two children. Nothing was out of place. Not a speck of dust on the counters or buildup on the faucet. Did she have the kitchen detailed? I searched for cookie sheets and pre-heated the oven. There was something soothing about cutting chunks of dough and placing them in neatly ordered rows on a sheet of foil. It seemed like forever ago that I had "baked" anything.

James wandered downstairs, digging a Q-tip in his ear while his wet hair rained droplets on his shoulders.

"They've got a nice tub," he said. "Maybe we can take a bath later."

"While the kids are home?" I asked, not taking my eyes off my maternal task.

"We have to do something when they go to bed."

I smirked. He was still trying to get me naked. I

couldn't be mad at him for that, but I'd tease him anyway. "I thought that was our snuggle time." I pouted.

"We can snuggle in the tub." He grabbed my hips and planted a kiss on my cheek. "You makin' cookies?"

"Mmhmm."

"I kinda like suburban life."

I chuckled. "Well, that's too bad because we just bought a house in the city."

"Yeah, but the house is very suburban." The house on Fell Street may have had a homey, suburban feel, but it was nothing like Michael and Jennifer's house. Theirs was more like a Victorian estate with extra square footage for guest rooms, dens, home offices, and more bathrooms than I'd ever care to clean.

When the cookies were done, I organized them on an oversized ceramic plate. They looked and smelled irresistible so I couldn't resist and ate one. However, with one missing, my formation on the plate was unbalanced, so I ate another to even it out.

Marvin barked and ran to the front door. The kids were home. James had already made it into the entryway to get the dog, and Jillian and Miles stood with wide grins and colorful packs on their back.

"Aunt Marin!" they screamed and wrapped their adorable little arms around me. Marvin whined and pulled toward the kids as James held tight to his collar. Miles petted the dog, calming him enough to stand still though his tongue went wild. James and I laughed while the kids dodged Marvin's sloppy kisses.

Excitement was definitely high, and it took a while

before we had everyone peacefully settled in the kitchen.

"Are you staying here the whole weekend too, James?" seven-year-old Miles asked.

"Yep."

"And Marvin too?" Jillian, who was two years older, chimed in.

"That's right," James said.

You would've thought we told the kids we were taking them to Disneyland the way they reacted.

"Who wants cookies?" I asked.

Their hands shot in the air. "Me! Me!"

"Do you have any homework?" James asked them.

"I don't," Miles said.

"I do." Jillian frowned. They scooted onto the bench and I slid them each a plate of two cookies and glasses of almond milk from the fridge.

"Miles, are you sure you don't have homework?" I gave him an accusatory look. He squinted, so cute. I just wanted to kiss his cubby little cheeks the whole weekend.

"Oops, I do. I forgot." Miles covered his mouth after letting out a goofy chuckle. James sat with Jillian while she did her English and math assignments. Miles and I sat across from them while I helped him with his science worksheet. I could feel James staring at me from across the table, and I glanced up at him every so often. Watching him play the daddy role was hot. Yeah, my clock was definitely ticking. All I wanted to do was get in that nice bathtub with him and make our own baby.

"What's for dinner?" Miles asked.

"We're making pita pizzas," I said.

"What's that?"

"You'll see. We're gonna make our own pizzas."

"Yes!" Jillian hissed. "Everyone likes pepperoni on pizza, and I hate pepperoni."

Hate pepperoni? She hadn't gotten that trait from me.

"Well, you can dress it however you like. I'm gonna prep the ingredients, you guys wanna help?" They shouted *yes* and the three of us opened packages of cheese, pepperoni, olives, chopped onions, and peppers. Who knew that children could have so much fun sorting food? Each of us had designed a few pita pizzas, and Jillian and Miles waited patiently in front of the oven, watching the cheese bubble and melt over the vegetables.

"Can I have another cookie?" Miles asked.

"After dinner," I said.

We spent the evening at the kitchen table. First enjoying our pita pizzas, then playing *Operation* and finishing the leftover cookies. We played teams: James and Miles on one and Jillian and I on the other. We took turns winning since James and Jillian had the steadiest hands. Miles and I refused to let those two be on a team together. Eventually, it was bedtime.

"Okay, kids, it's time to change into your pajamas and brush your teeth," I told them.

"Aw, but we're having fun," Jillian whined.

"I know, but it's time for bed."

The kids began to move slowly from the table.

"Where are you gonna sleep?" Jillian asked.

"In the guest bedroom," I said and followed them

out of the kitchen.

"What about James?"

"He's sleeping in the guest room too."

"In the same bed?" Mile turned to me with widened eyes.

"Yes . . ." Did they not understand the nature of our relationship? Then again, I didn't know if I understood the nature of our relationship.

"But you're not married," he said.

Thanks, Miles. I'd almost forgotten.

I tried to usher the two of them up the stairs. "No, but we love each other very much." How was I supposed to explain it to a child?

"I thought only married mommies and daddies can sleep in the same bed."

If Miles wanted James and me to be a married mommy and daddy, I was right there with him. I looked around for James, hoping he could hear the conversation, but he was cleaning up the board game in the kitchen.

"Well, unmarried mommies and daddies can sleep in the same bed too," I said, then cringed. What was I saying?

"You're not a mommy though." Another slap in the face.

Finally, I got Miles to stop with the questions by getting him to brush his teeth with sparkly blue paste and a tiny brush. I helped Jillian brush her soft light hair that she got from Jennifer. "Can you read to us, Aunt Marin?" Jillian asked.

"Yeah, can you, please?" Miles begged. Did seven

and nine-year-old kids still want to be read to before bed?

"We've been reading *The Lion, The Witch, and The Wardrobe.*" Jillian showed the book to me.

"Sure." I shut off the bathroom light, then the three of us climbed into Jillian's full-size bed, with her pink and green floral bedspread. Was it normal for kids her age to have a full? When I was nine, I slept in a twin-size bed and so did all of my friends.

She handed me a paperback with a bookmark holding its place. The events of the day left me with little energy, but I managed to finish a chapter before sending Miles to his bed.

"Hey, Aunt Marin?" he asked before I turned off the light.

"Yes."

"When is James going to be my uncle?" he asked.

I sighed. Only James could answer that question. "I don't know, that's up to James. Now go to sleep, I'll see you in the morning."

I returned to the kitchen to a pile of dirty dishes. James had disappeared somewhere upstairs. As I rinsed off the plates and placed them into the dishwasher, I felt a mix of emotions. The kids were great, and being a mother was definitely a role I wanted to play. Not that being a mother meant my days would be like this one.

There was also a sense of uneasiness. The great thing about kids was the way they saw the world and their lack of verbal filters. If Miles was asking questions about my and James' future, then surely others were wondering. Even James' mom mentioned it. It's like everyone was on

156

board except for James. On second thought, I was still in the middle of the *McQueen Method* and had to have faith that it would all work out soon.

"You almost done?" James asked.

"I thought you were asleep upstairs."

"Nope, I have a surprise for you."

"Oh yeah?" I smiled. "Just a sec." I bent over to turn the dishwasher on, but none of the buttons I pressed seemed to do the trick. "How the hell do I use this thing?" James came over and we spent a few minutes deciphering symbols and pressing random buttons. Finally, it began to run. I just hoped it would clean the dishes too.

James led me to the bathroom where he had drawn a bubble bath, complete with candles, some kind of lavender scent—oil or maybe bath salts.

"Is this for me?" I asked.

"It's for us." He helped me remove my clothes and I helped him with his. We sunk in, letting the bubbles blanket us. I was too tired to get too excited, so I just let the warm water soak my tired muscles and breathed in the calming scent.

"You're right. We should get a tub like this," I said.

"Can you imagine ending our days this way?" he asked.

"Yeah, that'd be nice." I closed my eyes, imagining that we were in our own house and our own children were sleeping down the hall. "The kids really like you, ya know?"

"You think so?" he sounded unsure.

"Yeah."

"Actually, Miles asked me when I was going to be his uncle."

That didn't sound too uncertain.

"He did?" My eyes shot open. "What did you say?" This was going to be good.

"I told him I was his uncle. I already feel like I'm part of your family."

Hopefully he felt that way because he knew he was going to be part of my family. Soon.

"That's sweet. Thanks for your help today."

"You're welcome, but you did all the heavy lifting. You'll be a great mom someday."

"You think so?" I asked, sounding unsure even to myself.

James leaned back in the tub and closed his eyes. "Of course."

"Maybe we should have a baby," I said, my heart pounding as the words left my mouth.

"Let's get the house set up first," he said.

Nope, wrong answer. First comes love, then comes marriage, then comes the baby in the baby carriage. Duh!

"But that doesn't mean we can't start practicing now."

And that was the first time James and I made love in a bubble bath.

They say that when you have kids you can kiss sleep goodbye. I didn't think this applied to me given that the kids were old enough to sleep through the night in their own beds. But I supposed the old tradition of Saturday morning cartoons never went out of style, at least it was still in full force the next day. It wasn't even eight o'clock when there were more bodies in the bed than I was comfortable with.

"Wake up, it's time for breakfast. Can you make pancakes?" Wispy child breath tickled my ear. I shut my eyes tighter and covered my face with the blanket.

"It's too early, guys," I mumbled.

"Rise and shine, sleepy head," Jillian sang as she peeled the covers back. I opened my eyes for a moment and they stared back patiently.

"Okay, five more minutes," I said and took the covers back, but my respite was short lived. Moments later they had climbed on top of me and yanked the covers off. Must be nice for Uncle James, who was still snoozing on his side of the bed. Miles and Jillian didn't bother to torture him.

By the time I'd had some coffee and eaten a couple of pancakes, I was glad for the early morning. The sun streamed through the windows, lifting my sleepy spirit, and I had more time with the kids who adorably bounced around in the pajamas, singing theme songs from the morning shows and stuffing pancakes in their mouths.

"Aunt Marin, what are we doing today?" Jillian asked.

"That depends. What do you guys want to do?"

"Something fun," she said.

"Yeah!" Miles added.

"Do you guys wanna see the Redwoods in Muir Park?" I asked.

"Redwood trees?" Jillian asked.

I nodded.

"Those are the really big ones, right?" Miles raised his arm as high as it could go, jumping to give it more height.

"That's right," I said.

"Yeah! Let's go," Jillian hollered.

We arrived at the park just after lunchtime, which was perfect because we were all starving. The four of us sat at a dusty picnic table, chewing our turkey sandwiches, grapes, and granola. Jillian and Miles agreed that they were up for the hour and a half trail. Yes, they were balls of energy, but I was unsure about their stamina. I hadn't been to the park since last summer. Even though it was something I experienced regularly, the Redwoods still took my breath away. To me, trees were the ultimate symbol of life, staying grounded and having roots, while also reaching for the sky, pulling nutrients from the soil and the sun, and creating shelter and food for others.

Call it a hippie-Holly perspective, but the majesty of the Redwoods' height reminded me that nature was truly amazing. Jillian and Miles walked ahead, and James and I watched as their little eyes ran up the long trees to the sky, squinting and shielding their faces with their hands to improve their vision. To my surprise, neither Jillian nor Miles complained during the hike. In fact, the two were the most quiet they had been over the weekend. I imagined they were taking the magnificence of the forest to heart. They walked a little way ahead and James took my hand.

"Are you having a good time?" I asked, feeling a little

guilty that we had to spend the weekend on child duty and had to leave Marvin back at the house. No dogs allowed.

"I'm having a great time," James said with a smile.

"Really?"

"Yeah, I've always liked hanging out with them." He looked up, checking to make sure they were still in sight.

"I know, but we've never done it for this long."

"Why, are you tired already?"

"No way, I could do this all day, every day." Code for, I want a baby soon.

"I'll keep that in mind."

The kids were so tuckered out by the walk that they fell asleep on the ride home. Now that was the quietest they'd been all weekend. James and I were almost as quiet, and as much as I wanted to catch a nap when we returned home, I had to get dinner ready for the kids, which I did happily. But by the end of the night, I was spent. The five of us, Marvin included, cuddled up on the couch to watch one of the new animated movies I'd never heard of, but the kids couldn't wait to see.

"This is fun," Jillian said. "Can you come back next weekend?"

"Yeah and Uncle James too," Miles shot James a big grin and I laughed.

"Probably not next weekend but another time. Maybe you two can stay at our new house," I said. They shouted and hooted at this idea, even James.

I wasn't sure when it happened, but sometime during the movie I passed out and when I woke up, the TV was dark and the others were fast asleep, Marvin snoring on the floor. I whipped out my phone for a quick snapshot then nudged James awake.

"Hey, can you help me get the kids up to bed?" I whispered. He nodded in a sleepy daze. It was a good thing James was around because there was no way I could carry either one of those kids upstairs. Jillian maybe, but I didn't want to risk dropping her.

James lay them gently in their beds, and I tucked them in. I thanked James in a whisper, and he held me for a moment, probably to prop himself up. The poor thing barely opened his eyes.

The next morning was similar to the last. Only this time the kids had plain old cereal instead of fancy pancakes. Before we knew it, Michael and Jennifer were back and it was time for us to head home.

"How were they?" Jennifer asked.

"They were perfect." I smiled and she seemed relieved.

"Thanks for doing this. We really appreciate it." Michael shook James' hand and patted me on the shoulder. Not one for affection.

"Anytime," James said.

On the highway heading toward the city, James glanced at me. "I have to be honest, I was a little worried about watching them for two days, but they were great. You were great. Maybe we should think about having one of our own soon."

I couldn't help but grin from ear to ear. He obviously thought I was mother material. I had to hand it to Charlotte McQueen. James was making commitments with real estate and talking about a baby. He seemed to be more in love and enamored with me than ever. I couldn't be sure a proposal was coming, but I had the feeling that the sexy getaway would seal the deal and soon we'd be Mr. and Mrs. James Young.

16

South Of The Border

"CABO SAN LUCAS!" Brina, the travel agent, said, spirit fingers going. No wonder Rachel liked her. Both were enthusiastic cheerleaders.

"Isn't that where the college spring breakers go?" That's where I'd gone for spring break during my second semester in med school.

"Oh no, honey, I'm not talking about one of those cheap hotels that comes with condoms and hopefully Lysol. I'm talking about a honeymoon resort with beautiful pools, gorgeous beaches, five-star restaurants, helpful staff that speaks English. Comprende?" She was a little much, but I was still listening. Brina pulled up photos from a resort in my budget.

Impressive.

"Oh, look! If we book you now to go in two weeks you can get half off."

Two weeks? That could work. "Book it!"

She high-fived me. My first high-five in ages but totally appropriate. She arranged a suite, champagne, and all the activities that James would love.

I couldn't wait to tell him, so I didn't. That night I invited him out for Mexican food at Colibri, where we had our first dinner date almost two years earlier.

"We haven't been here in a while," James said, looking over the menu. We usually opted for the hole in the wall Mexican places that didn't skimp on the refried beans or the guacamole.

"I know, but I have a surprise for you."

James scrutinized me, most likely trying to guess the surprise before I could reveal it.

"You wanna guess?" I asked.

"I do, but I'll let you tell me. I know you like to surprise me."

He was right. I relished those few and far between moments when I could bring him some excitement and joy. "So, what's the surprise?"

"We're going to Mexico!" I said.

"We are?"

"Yep, pack your bags, baby. We leave in two weeks!"

He smiled and released a little chuckle. "Yeah, that's definitely a surprise."

"I got you, huh?"

"You did."

"I got this great deal on a resort in Cabo. It's just for a long weekend, but I thought it'd be nice to have a different kind of vacation. Something sexier than wine country."

"That's sweet, Marin. Thank you." He took my hand and leaned across the table. "But just so you know, there's nothing sexier than your purple lips after a few glasses of wine."

My cheeks flushed. I didn't know a single girl who wasn't embarrassed about purple wine lips, but if he thought it was sexy then I'd drink up.

"You know, they have wine in Mexico too."

"Mmm," he moaned. "I can't wait."

I bounced in my chair, clapping my hands. He chuckled, keeping hold of my hand and went back to surveying his menu.

"You know, this was the first place I took you to dinner," he said.

I peered over my menu at him for a moment, heart-a-flutter. How sweet. He'd remembered.

"Why do you think I brought you here?" I asked.

He raised his eyebrow as if he understood what it was all about, not just the restaurant or the Mexican getaway, but the whole thing.

From that night on, James and I spent every night together, his place or mine. It didn't matter. If we were together, we were home.

Telly met me over the weekend to purchase some provisions for the trip, meaning lingerie. I needed sexy, and Telly knew sexy.

"What about this?" She held up a skintight black dress that was slashed to show T and A.

"Um, I dunno. It's a little too . . ."

"What?" She didn't get it, because she was into everything and I was not.

"Slutty," I whispered.

"Grow up, Marin. Isn't this your sexy getaway? You've got to be a little slutty. You know what they say, lady in the streets, freak in the sheets."

True. The whole point of the trip was to show James that I was sexy, spontaneous, and adventurous.

"What about this one?" I held up a lacy red babydoll.

Telly tilted her head. A different angle, perhaps? If all went well, I'd be all over the place wearing it, or not wearing it. I mean really, lingerie stays on for what—ten minutes? I should just go naked.

"It's not bad, but I think we can do better. Like this." Telly pulled a sheer teddy that would cover my breasts in a V-shape, showing my navel, and a thong that was covered by a teeny-tiny skirt. Sexy, but not crazy. Just enough to drive him crazy. "You like?" she asked.

"Yeah," I said and nodded slowly. "I like it a lot." We perused the store a little more before finding another surprise.

"Rachel? Is that you?" Telly called from across the racks. Rachel jerked a little before turning around with a bright smile.

"Hi, Telly, what are you doing here?" she asked, fluttering her eyelashes.

"Shopping for Marin's getaway." That's when Rachel saw me, and seemed to clench her jaw. Weird.

"Marin. You're both here. Cool," she said.

"You trying to spice things up with David?" Telly

asked, pointing to the crotchless panties she clutched.

"Huh? Oh, yeah. Gotta keep the flames burning." Telly and I both looked at her strangely.

"Everything okay?" I asked.

"Yeah, everything's great!" Her voice rose to a higher pitch. "Oh, yeah. Oh, my God, Marin, I meant to call you yesterday."

"What's up?"

"Guess who was shopping at Gallery of Jewels?" She looked like she had the greatest answer in the world. Apparently I knew it too, because she started nodding.

"James!" I said.

"Yep!"

"Are you serious? Was he ring shopping? Did he buy something? How do you even know?" Please, please, tell me now!

"All I know is he called David and asked where he should buy jewelry."

"That's it. Did he say what he was looking for?"

"No, that's it."

"Are you sure he went? Maybe he was asking for someone else." I wanted so badly to believe that he was ring shopping for me, but I didn't want to get my hopes too high. It was a good sign though.

"He could've been, but David got the impression that it was for you."

"Can you text David and ask? This could be huge!"

Rachel's smile turned. "He's busy right now. I'll ask him later, I promise." She took her panties to the check out and bid us goodbye. "Oh, Marin," she called. "Don't tell David you saw me here. I want it to be a surprise."

"Okay," I said. Why would I tell him? After all, he was "busy." Were panties really a surprise? Hmm, maybe I should get some too.

"That girl is so weird sometimes," Telly said.

"She's probably just embarrassed to be lingerie shopping. I know I am."

"Seriously? How are we best friends?"

"We complement each other. I'm the angel, you're the devil." I smirked.

"I know that's right."

17

Sexy Getaway

J AMES AND I CAUGHT AN EARLY FLIGHT the
following Friday morning and arrived at the resort by
eleven a.m.

Step Five: Sexy Getaway

My lightweight suitcase dragged behind me, across
the black marble floors of the lobby. Sun lit the space
through the wall of windows and glass doors.

"Baby, this is really nice," James said.

"Right!" The pictures didn't do it justice and when
we got to the suite I knew it was worth every penny.
James and I had never been on a vacation like this, with a
suite, champagne on ice, and our own balcony with a Jacuzzi.

"What do you wanna do first?" I asked.

"What do you think?" I thought he was thinking
what I was thinking.

I pulled my sundress over my head and showed off a

170

new lacy panty and bra set from the lingerie store. Truth be told, I couldn't wait to strip. I was aroused the moment I got off the plane. James was ready to go too. He pulled me to him and moaned as he kissed my neck and slid his hands down my body, toying with my panties. I reached underneath his shirt and ran my nails lightly down his back. He popped my bra off and I pushed him toward the bed, pulling his shirt over his head. I didn't even care that the curtains were wide open. It was *muy caliente*.

Already the trip had been a success. James and I hadn't had sex like that in a while. Like kids in a candy store, we didn't know what to put in our mouths first. It started sensual and slow, him on top of me, me on top of him, then he passionately flipped me around and the sensation was amazing. He was amazing. Yeah, I could do it forever.

By the end, I was dizzy, tingling with exhilaration and exhaustion all rolled into one. After a relaxing hot shower, I searched my suitcase for my bikini. It was the least I'd ever packed for such a trip, nothing but lingerie, bathing suits, and sexy little dresses. James and I dressed and went downstairs to check out the resort and grab some lunch. Like new lovers, we couldn't keep our hands off each other, or rather, James couldn't keep his hands off my ass. I didn't mind one bit.

We were seated outside with a view of the pool and ocean.

"Gracias," James said, doing his best to speak Spanish. Luckily, most of the staff spoke English because I only knew a few key phrases. The waiter served us mango-flavored Mojitos and we sipped the sweetness quietly, beaming at one another.

"This is really awesome, Marin. Thank you," he said.

"You're welcome."

"I wish I'd thought of it first."

"Aw, you can plan the next one," I said, raising my glass to his.

"You got it, babe."

After the early flight, the crazy sex, the alcohol, and the gorgeous Cabo sun, we had little to say and spent the afternoon by the pool and napping in the room. By dinnertime we were well rested and starving. A table awaited us outside at the restaurant. Only this time the sun had set, twinkle lights and candles illuminated the restaurant enough to read our menus. I slid my foot out of my sandal and ran it up James' leg. He spent the entire dinner tickling my knees, kissing my hand, and kissing me from across the table between bites. It was like being in some kind of fantasyland, and I'd always remember it that way.

By the end of the meal, my lips were stained and my body was warm and relaxed, buzzing from the wine. James and I went upstairs and slipped into our bathing suits and into the balcony Jacuzzi. The only light glowed from the hot tub, but we figured out how to turn it off. As the light disappeared, so did my bikini.

We made love two more times that night, and I cherished every second of it. James may have been more in love with me after the last eight weeks, but I was definitely more in love than I'd ever been in my life. We spent the rest of the weekend by the pool or at the beach, late mornings, late naps, and delicious meals. Sunday afternoon would be our last at the resort, and Brina had arranged for us to go fishing.

James stood with his fishing rod over the boat, while I watched from the interior shade. The few days in the sun had given him a nice tan, and I stared at his shoulders, glimmering with sweat. Damn, my man was hot.

"You comin' out here?" he called.

"I'm okay here," I said.

"No," he whined. "Come sit next to me." I was sitting four feet away from him, but apparently that was too far. So I leaned over the rail next to him, he pulled me in and kissed my face before giving me a little pat on the butt.

"You're so sexy," he said and I blushed, but this time I believed him.

Later that night when we were packing for our trip home, James put on some mood music. He usually had a little music going in the background, but when he was in a good mood, he'd sing and even dance a bit. I recognized the classic love song before he reentered the room. One of my favorites. He sang the lyrics of the sultry Al Green song and did a little sway to the rhythm. He picked up my hairbrush from the dresser and used it as a microphone to serenade me. Surprisingly, he knew all the lyrics and even sang in key. He snapped his fingers and did a little twirl, like he was the King of Pop. I laughed. How cute was he?

"Dance with me," he said.

I began to move, singing with him. There in our Cabo suite, the two of us shook our hips around the bed. James was really into it, but I couldn't help but giggle every now and then. He took my hand and spun me around before pulling me in for a slow dance. In that moment, I wasn't thinking about the *McQueen Method*, my ovaries shriveling up, or anything else. It was just James and I and Mr. Green crooning through the speakers. Nothing else mattered. When the song ended, I tried to catch my breath, but kept laughing.

"You're . . ." I started, giving him that look. He gave it right back. I couldn't find the words.

"I know," he said. "I feel the same way about you." Then I really couldn't catch my breath, because he'd taken it away. "I have something for you." He pulled out a small gift bag from his suitcase. That's when I realized it had worked. This was it. This was definitely it. Rachel was right. He'd been jewelry shopping for me. My heart raced, and I wanted to cry. Finally, after all this time, he was ready to be with me, be my husband, and make me his wife. He took the box from the bag and handed it to me. My hands trembled as I tried to hold the box steady.

"Is this a watch?" I asked, because it wasn't a ring box.

"No," he said with a little laugh.

I lifted the top and there was a yellow gold . . . cuff bracelet? And a strange one at that. It had small pinholes throughout the entire cuff, almost looked like . . .

"It's a band-aid," he said.

Huh?

"You planned this thoughtful trip, and I wanted to do something thoughtful for you."

I stared at him, trying not to be upset, because in his mind, everything was perfect.

"It's engraved," he said. I flipped the cuff over.

If you should ever fall, I'll be there with a band-aid.

"It's lovely," I said, smiling but trying to hold a tear back.

"Oh, good. I wasn't sure, but when I saw this, I had to get it." He took the cuff and slipped it on my wrist. The cuff was a perfect fit and a perfect gift in his eyes, but to me it felt like a major failure. The *McQueen Method* seemed to be working perfectly. But the fact that James had gone to a jewelry store and had come back with a bracelet instead of a ring told me everything I needed to know. He was not going to put a ring on it.

I returned to my apartment alone the next day and retrieved my mail before heading inside. Bills, bills, credit card ad, furniture ads, *Psychology Today*, and a cream colored envelope with gold lettering. I dropped everything else and opened it.

Mr. and Mrs. Kyu Cho request the honor of your presence
at the marriage of their daughter
Ginger Kwan to Jonathan Joseph Cash
Saturday, the fifteenth of May at four o'clock in the afternoon
At The Westin St. Francis
San Francisco, Ca
Reception to follow

Just when I thought I couldn't feel any worse.

Office Space

"HEY, DID YOU GET MY WEDDING invitation yet?" Ginger asked on the other line.

"Yep, I'm sending in my RSVP today."

"Awesome. Oh, I saw your pics on Facebook this weekend. You two are the cutest! Do you have any news?"

"Well, I heard he was jewelry shopping and there was this one moment when I thought the proposal was coming, but he didn't buy a ring."

"Did he get you something?"

"A cuff," I said, disappointed to replay it.

"What?" she asked as if she didn't hear me.

"A cuff bracelet," I said into the phone.

"I heard you the first time. I'm just confused. Is it a nice bracelet?"

"Yeah, it's gold and designed like a bandage. Kind of an inside joke between us. It's engraved too."

"Aw, that's cute."

"It was really sweet, and I don't mean to sound ungrateful, but things have been going so well. I really thought . . ."

"I know, but you have to trust the system. It sounds like you've been getting great results, but you have to follow through on EVERY step." She was referring to *Step Six: Break Up to Make Up*, and I was no keener on it now than I had been when I read it the first time.

"Well, I am going away this week for a conference. I'm hoping the time away will help."

"That's great and all, but if you want a commitment you have to commit. You can't half ass any of the steps. Out of town for a conference is not the same as a break."

"Yeah, but I was thinking that I wouldn't talk to him as much, leave him wondering."

Ginger remained firm. "If you don't make a break, that's only going to piss him off. You can't be a shitty girlfriend."

"If I was going to do it, which I'm not, I wouldn't know what reason to give him anyway."

"You tell him that you want something more than you think he can give you, which is true isn't it?"

"Yeah."

"Just think about it and call me after your trip."

I did think about it, but the thought of a break up with James, even if I knew we were getting back together broke my heart. I'd have to take my chances without it.

The afternoon before my San Diego trip, I had one more patient to see before leaving for a few days. Felicia had been coming to me for about six months. What started as couples therapy soon became one-on-one sessions. Her marriage was built on a shaky foundation of convenience and so it crumbled.

She was well put together in her designer outfit, Prada shoes, and two hundred dollar haircut. Her ex was conveniently wealthy.

"I've been thinking a lot about Kevin," she said, looking off as if she were daydreaming.

"Who's Kevin?" I asked. It wasn't her husband.

"He's my ex from college."

"Oh, what made you think of him?" I adjusted my glasses and scribbled a note.

"You know when you're in the midst of a break up you start to examine your past relationships?" She looked thoughtful.

"I do." And I totally did. "What were you looking for?"

"A trend, I guess. Some sort of insight as to why I sabotage every relationship I'm in."

"What happened with Kevin?"

She shrugged and admired her manicure. "I didn't think his life was going anywhere so I dumped him like garbage."

"Was he garbage to you?" I asked.

Felicia folded her arms. "No, but I treated him like he was. I was young and didn't know what really mattered in life. I keep thinking that maybe he was the one I was supposed to be with."

"The one that got away," I said.

There's a tendency to romanticize past relationships because they feel so unfinished. Sometimes we want to believe there's more to the story. Maybe sometimes there is or maybe it would eventually lead to the same heartbreaking end. We never know, and that's what makes it romantic, the possibility of it all.

I'd had a college love too. Jack Ashbury from Stanford. For a long time, I believed he was the one that got away. That all changed after James.

"Have you thought about getting in touch with him?" I asked.

She scoffed. "And say what?"

"Tell him how you feel about what happened between you two. It could bring you both closure."

"Dr. Johns, some things are just better left in the past," she said. There are moments when I would have agreed with her, but this was therapy. Part of my job was sorting out and dealing with the past.

When Felicia left after her session, I decided to stop by Telly's new office suite. She'd been begging me to come by for a week, but things had been so hectic with moving preparations and the Mexico trip. I probably should have used the free time to research kitchen tiles, but I missed my friend.

After several glances at my text messages, I still wasn't sure if I had the right place. When I finally arrived at suite 204, there was no question about it. It was Telly's, from top to bottom. My footsteps echoed as I walked along the hardwood floors of the wide space. A loft style office, complete with large windows and exposed brick. Glass walls and doorways separated the space into six areas; reception, conference room, tiny kitchen, and three offices. Telly's was the largest with a view of the city through a bell-shaped window.

There didn't seem to be anyone around, and I was afraid I had missed Telly at a late lunch or a meeting. Then a whine resounded in her office. I slowed my steps as I made my way in, hoping it was a frustrated whine and not a sex whine. It wouldn't totally surprise me to walk in on her gettin' it on in her new office. Then again, it would've been nice if this year wasn't known as The Year I Walked In On My Best Friends Fucking. The closer I got the more I realized that the whine wasn't frustrated or sexual, it was a cry.

"Telly," I said, knocking on the glass door as I stepped inside. After a long sniff, she cleared her throat, then appeared from behind her desk. Was she sitting on the floor? She quickly swiped her fingers underneath her eyes, wiping away all traces of tears and runny mascara.

"I thought you weren't coming by until later," she said, and straightened her dress.

"I left a little early. Are you okay?" I approached her, but kept a fair distance. Telly wasn't the coddling type.

"I don't know," she said. "What if this is a huge mistake? I left a great job at one of the best firms in the city so I could what? Work longer hours and have more stress because it's all on me now?"

"No, you left because you weren't getting the respect

that you deserved and so you could have ownership over your work. I thought you couldn't wait to get out of there."

"I couldn't." She leaned on the edge of her desk and glanced around the office. "But now that I'm here, I feel like maybe I jumped the gun on this one."

I cracked a smile and sat in the chair in front of her. It was strange to see Telly in a position of fear. She was one of the bravest people I knew. Throughout her life, she had let down after let down and still she kept going despite it all. Her hair fell over her face as she looked down at me, hiding her leaky eyes.

"Don't you remember how excited you were when you told me the news at the bar? You had this immense enthusiasm and confidence. I know it's in there somewhere."

Telly brushed the back of her hand along her cheek and turned away, toward the wide window. She cleared her throat and her voice regained its firm tone. "That's my problem. I can never just be happy with where I am, with what I've accomplished. It's like I'm never enough. Like I'll always have something to prove."

"You're not alone, Tell," I said, feeling a tear surface. "I feel that way . . . all the time." I scoffed at myself and even at Telly. I think we'd proven ourselves enough. It was time to just take what we wanted and leave the rest.

"You do?" she asked.

"Yeah." I shook my head and bit my lower lip. "I never cut myself any slack." Telly nodded as if I was reading her mind. "Let me ask you somethin'. When you left to do this, did you feel like you were putting shackles on or taking shackles off?"

She looked up for a moment and took a deep breath. "I took them off and it's scary as hell," Telly said with a relieved smile. She wiped one last tear from her eye. "Jesus, I've been so emotional lately. I don't feel like myself."

"New birth control pill?" I asked.

"No, just been a big week."

"Come're," I said and draped my arm around her shoulder. Affectionate or not, she'd have to deal with it. "Show me the rest of the place and I'll buy you a coffee."

"Thanks, Mar," she said with an appreciative smile. I crinkled my nose and shrugged.

"Anytime," I said.

19

My Taste

AFTER THE OFFICE TOUR AND A LATTE, I met James at Pottery Barn. Every time I walked into that place, I felt a sense of calm that only beautiful interiors could inspire. However, I couldn't just look at everything, I had to touch it. The smooth gloss of a decorative bird statue, the plush softness of a cashmere throw, and the weight of a scented vanilla and lavender candle.

"C'mon, Marin, the beds are over here," James said as he pulled me away from the rows of elegant décor.

"But," I whimpered.

He took a decorative pillow from one of the bed set-ups. It was a creamy canvas material with a leafy green pattern. It distracted my attention, as that was surely his plan.

"This is nice," he said.

"What? The bedding or the bed?" I liked one, but

not the other. James and I hadn't been furniture shopping before. Though his apartment was well put together, it wasn't my taste. And our new house was going to reflect my taste, I mean, our taste. Who was I kidding? My taste.

"Both," he said.

I cringed. While I could appreciate the craftsmanship of the headboard, the bed looked like it belonged in the country more than the city. And our suburban-esc house was in the middle of the city.

"No?" he asked, timid.

I shook my head. We walked ahead and I spied a dark wood sleigh bed, which would look gorgeous in front of the fireplace in the bedroom.

"No," he said.

What?

"Why not?" I asked. The bed and its matching furniture was, well, a perfect match.

"I'm too tall for a footer on the bed," he said.

Woes of a six-foot man. I looked to see if the footer could be detached, but no such luck.

I sighed. "Okay."

As we moved along the bedding, we disagreed on poster beds and upholstered beds. Yes, he suggested using the posts as a stripper pole. Men. I was beginning to think that we weren't going to agree on anything and that one of us would have to compromise. Guess who that'd be?

"How about this one?" he asked and walked over to a traditional farmhouse style bed. The espresso finish gave it a contemporary feel, and the combination created a classic look. The side tables and dresser were nice too. A possible match.

"Yeah," I said. "How much is it?"

James turned the price tag over to show me. "It's in our price range," he said. "What do you think?"

I nodded with a slight smile. "Let's get it."

"Now wait," he said and held his hands up to halt the sale. "There's only one way to be sure if this is the right one." I shot him a questioning look and before I knew it, he'd lifted me from the ground.

"James, stop!" I giggled and he put me on the bed before hopping in next to me. "I don't think we're supposed to be laying in the bed," my voice was hushed and I was thankful that we went in on a slow Wednesday evening. I tried to slide off, but James pulled me back to lay with him.

"Why not? We're paying customers," he said. It was true, we were about to buy the bed. James rested his hands behind his head and stretched out his legs, one foot over the other. "Ahh, this is nice," he said. I turned on my side to look at him as he gazed up at the ceiling. I watched his lashes fall softly as his eyes closed. "I can see it now. You and me reading in this bed together with the fireplace going. Can you see it?"

"Mmhmm," I murmured. One of his eyes peaked open.

"You have to close your eyes too," he instructed.

I felt a little ridiculous already lying beside him in a display bed in the middle of Pottery Barn, so I hesitated.

"C'mon," he said.

I relented and closed my eyes.

"Can you feel the heat from the fire?" he asked.

"Mmhmm," I said.

"Yep, it's feelin' cozy." He was really getting into it. I let out a small chuckle. "What are you reading?"

"Hmm, *Pride and Prejudice*," I said and opened my eyes again. I didn't want to miss a moment of him lying there in Pottery Barn, imagining our future nights together. All inspired by a bed in the middle of the store.

"I'm reading *Game of Thrones*," he said, and I laughed.

"You're finally gonna get around to that?" I asked. He'd wanted to read the series for a long time, but the books remained untouched on his bookshelf.

He turned to me with the most gorgeous blue eyes. "You make me really happy."

I blushed, it was a sweet moment, a bubble in time. Like the life of a bubble it was over in an instant. I wanted to just take it as a compliment, smile, and tell him that he made me happy too, but all I wanted to say was, *then why won't you marry me?* There he was, blissfully creating our future in his mind like it was the most natural thing in the world, but somehow a ring and a wedding didn't fit. The bed that started out as a cozy little dream suddenly became a vast space and I was disconnected.

"Can I help you two?" a short man asked. He peered over the bed curiously as if he didn't understand why we were there.

"Yeah," James said, swinging his legs over the side to sit up right. "We'll take this bedroom set." The clerk's face changed from impatient to pleasant. I guess money talks.

That night, James and I sprawled out across my ivory nail button upholstered bed. A favorite place of mine. It was sad that in the coming weeks I'd have to give up my queen size Tempur-Pedic for a king-size-who-knows.

"I need to go to sleep," I told James as he lay behind me, stroking my shoulder.

"But you look so cute," he grabbed me and sucked me into his embrace, my limbs tangled up with his. I wanted it to be the kind of tangle that turned into a one of those impossible to get out knots, like a chain that lays in the bottom of a jewelry box and slowly, over time clusters into a little ball of gold. "Do you have to leave tomorrow?" He kissed the back of my neck, the warmth of his breath tickled my neck.

"Yes, I've been looking forward to it all year," I said.

"I know, you're right. I'm just gonna miss you," he said, loosening his grip. I turned to face him.

"I'll miss you too," I said, lying on my side as we looked at each other with one eye showing, the other buried in our pillows. "Now, go to sleep." I smiled and shut my eyes.

"Okay," he whispered. Moments later, he was out while I lay awake for a good hour, anxious about my morning flight.

20

Jack Is Back

SAN DIEGO WAS ONE OF MY FAVORITE cities and there were times that I wished I'd gone to grad school there versus bitter cold Boston. Palm trees and canyons grew larger as we landed on the tarmac. True, the conference didn't start until the afternoon, but I wanted to get in some pool time considering that it was almost ten degrees warmer and I was missing the southern heat of Mexico.

On my way to the Hilton, I watched the passing palms that lined Harbor Island Park and the blue water that bordered it. The scent of the ocean filled the shuttle as we drove along. The moment I checked in, I declared it bathing suit time. After slathering my skin with the sweet smelling Hawaiian Tropic, I took my teeny-weeny black bikini to the pool. As much as I enjoyed the solitude of lounging in the sun with nothing but my iPod and a magazine, I missed James. For a moment, I imagined that he was lounging next to me in a sexy pair of swim shorts and sunglasses. A fresh memory from the weekend.

He was probably with a patient, but I called him anyway. Yep, voicemail.

"Hey, you," I said. "I'm here, wish you were too. The weather is gorgeous. Maybe one day we can take highway one all the way here. Anyway, I'll call you tonight after the dinner reception. I love you, hope you're having a good day."

After a couple hours in the sun, I was ready for a bite to eat. As I walked back through the hotel sporting flip-flops and a floral jersey dress with water spots over my breasts and around my hips, I saw him. Even after ten years, I'd recognize that right dimple anywhere. It was Jack.

Jack Ashbury, my med school boyfriend, and I dated for only a year. At the time, I was convinced he was the love of my life. Medical school wasn't for me, so I ended up pursuing another field at a university on the opposite coast. He promised we could get through anything, including a long distance relationship, but he was wrong. A few months later, he admitted feelings for someone else. I was absolutely devastated. We hadn't spoken since.

For years, I'd fantasized about running into him somewhere. He'd be slightly overweight, strapped with a few kids and a ditzy, over tanned wife who didn't age as well as promised. I'd be fabulous looking of course, and he'd see me and regret the day he let me go. A day that he played over and over in his head and asked himself every day, what if?

My current scenario wasn't in the least reminiscent of my ideal. No, in this scenario, his suit fit his sexy physique. His dark hair had grown out and curled behind his ears like a Hollywood heartthrob. Jack smiled with his perfect bleached teeth. God, that dimple was cute. My heart raced as I wiped the beads of sweat off my nose and tried to remember if I'd put on deodorant before going to the pool. I wanted so badly to run a brush through my hair, but I resisted the urge to touch it. I didn't want to give him the satisfaction if he knew anything about body language.

"Oh, my God, Marin, is it really you?" he asked in his unique brogue. While he spent his early childhood in England, he'd lived in the states since the age of twelve and his elegant accent became slightly more American.

I grinned as he gawked at me. Was he just as surprised? "Yeah, Jack, Hi."

"It's been ages," he said, inviting me in for a hug.

"I just got back from the pool," I said, demonstrating my wet clothes.

"Who cares," he said, wrapping his arms around me. "You look amazing."

I surrendered to his hug and inhaled his scent. It all came back to me, every second that I spent totally, hopelessly, crazy in love with the man. When he released me, I shrugged it off like a bad nostalgia trip.

"What are you doing here?" he asked, grinning with apparent wonder.

"Um, I'm here for a conference," I said, and pushed loose hair behind my ear. Dammit, why couldn't I stop touching my hair?

"Me too! Which one?"

"It's a women's health educational conference."

"Oh, great. Is that why you were at the pool?" he asked, his hands on his hips. I shook my head and looked away shamefully. "I'm here for the Aesthetic Symposium."

"Are you a derm now?" I asked.

"A cosmetic surgeon, but I do work with cosmetic dermatologists." His chest welled with pride. Great, his chemically peeled skin hadn't aged a day, while I was using department store cream under my eyes. I didn't know why I used it, it didn't make a difference.

"Don't worry, I wore sunscreen," I said with a nervous laugh, he nodded politely. Holy shit, I needed to get out of there. As if Jack was the slightest bit worried about the amount of sun exposure I got. "Anyway, I should get going."

"Are you staying here?" he asked.

"Mmhmm," I said.

"We should have dinner later."

My mouth gapped for a moment too long. "Can't. I've got this dinner reception thing as part of the conference."

"How about a drink afterward? I haven't seen you since Stanford. I'd love to catch up. See what's going on in Marin's world." He flashed me a persuasive smile, one I couldn't remember turning down. Not much had changed.

"Sure, I'll meet you at the bar at say . . . eight?" Bad

idea, bad idea, bad idea. Did I mention it was a bad idea?

"Okay, love. See you then." He tapped my arm and walked away with a debonair stride. What were the fucking odds? In all the places in the world, why did his conference have to be here on this day? And he called me "love." Ugh. Did he not remember what happened? That he broke my heart into a million little pieces and that I spent YEARS getting over him. Now he wanted to swoop in and have a drink and call me "love" as if it never happened. Had he been wearing a wedding ring? Damn. I hadn't looked. That was probably a good sign. I only looked for rings when I was interested, which I hadn't been interested in anyone since James.

James. Would James care if I went for a drink with my ex-boyfriend? Would I care if James had a drink with his ex? Not if he brought me along. I'd have to tell him, and if he didn't want me to go, I'd cancel, no problem. Then again, maybe this would be a good opportunity for closure. I had a lot of unanswered questions with Jack, questions I eventually stopped asking. Did I really want to dredge up that part of my life when I somehow found a way out?

I couldn't help but be curious. Maybe he was single and miserable or divorced and miserable with a huge alimony payment. Maybe the alimony was so high that I had to pay for drinks. Yeah, who'd have the upper hand then? I could handle it. Just two mature adults having a catch up drink. In a couple days I'd be back in San Fran and he'd go back to wherever he'd come from and that would be it. I could dust my hands of him.

During the meeting later that afternoon, I could hardly focus on the speaker and my note page was desolate. Seeing Jack brought back a slew of memories. As I tried to focus on a subject I was anxious to hear about, I felt as though something had changed. It was like I was twenty-three again. While I longed for fewer lines around my eyes, twenty-three was not a place I wanted to return to. I didn't know myself very well then, which is why I'd ended up in medical school in the first place. I lacked clarity in many areas, but back then, Jack felt like a sure thing.

Everything made sense when he was around. Jack was the one who really encouraged me to leave because he knew it wasn't me. After I had left, he dumped me anyway. I believed that he took advantage of the situation and sent me packing. I used to imagine that he'd show up on my doorstep with flowers and a ring in the rain or snow and tell me he made a huge mistake, that I was the best thing that ever happened to him, and he was miserable without me. I was miserable without him. Eventually that passed, at least I thought it'd passed.

Later at the reception, I was in the middle of talking with a doctor from Phoenix when my ringing phone interrupted the conversation.

"Excuse me," I said and picked up the call.

"Hey, how's your conference?" James asked.

"So far so good. I'm at the reception now. How was work?"

"Good. You want to call me back after the reception?" he asked.

"No, it's okay, I can talk now. Actually, something kinda crazy happened." I stepped outside, dusk was falling and a cool breeze chilled my skin. "I ran into an old friend here. It was totally random."

"Yeah? Who was it?" he asked.

"Jack from Stanford," I said casually even though James knew the whole story. He knew everything about me.

"Jack, your ex-boyfriend?"

"Mmhmm," I said.

"Oh, what's he doing down there?" James' tone turned curious, the jealous kind. I had to say I didn't hate it.

"I don't know, some meeting. Crazy, huh?" I didn't want to fuel any suspicions in case he had any. He wasn't the jealous type, which I appreciated most of the time, but every now and then, I liked to see him get a little possessive. Show the world that I was his. "Anyway, we're meeting for a quick drink after this. Is that cool?" I asked.

"Sure, have fun," he said.

I couldn't tell if he was really okay with it or just acting like he was okay with it. Probably the former. James wasn't the passive aggressive type.

"Okay, I'll tell you all about it later."

"Sounds good, I'll call you tomorrow. I love you."

"I love you too," I said and hung up. Why was he so cool with it? If James was out of town and had a drink with his ex-girlfriend, I'd be bonkers. Then again, he really had nothing to worry about. I wished I could be as secure. I had nothing to worry about either.

Only fifteen minutes to eight, so I went upstairs to freshen up my makeup. I wasn't trying to lure Jack in by any stretch, but I wanted him to know that I was much more put together than a sweaty girl in a wet dress that smelled like chlorine. The decision to arrive early, on time, or late weighed on my mind while I puckered my lips for fresh gloss. Early would give the impression that I was anxious, on time said I had nothing better going on, and late would show him I really couldn't care less. I could only imagine what not showing up would say. Hmm, wasn't the worst idea.

No, that would be rude and cruel, and unlike him, I wasn't a mean person. I'd show up five minutes late, have one drink, and say goodbye forever. Besides, after tomorrow we wouldn't even be in the same city.

"There she is," Jack said as I arrived. He sat next to an empty seat and invited me to sit, but not before he planted a welcoming kiss on my cheek. I wiped my sweaty palm on my skirt and smiled, my lips trembling slightly. The bartender asked for my order and before I could answer Jack suggested, "Malibu Bay Breeze?" How did he remember my favorite cocktail? We hardly ever drank together, too busy studying for exams, and when we weren't studying, we were naked. Sex with Jack was always a stimulating experience. At least that's how I remembered it. But who knows, back then I was twenty-three and sexually inexperienced.

I smiled and ordered a glass of reisling.

"You're a wine drinker now, are you?" he asked.

"I suppose living near the best wineries in the country will do that to you."

"And where might that be?" He turned his seat toward mine and rested his hand on my chair, a little closer than I would have liked, but I tried to ignore it.

"San Francisco," I said.

"Really?" He seemed happily surprised. "I would have thought I lost you to the east coast for good."

"Nope, I'm a California girl at heart."

"So am I apparently. California boy at heart, that is."

"Have you been here since med school?" I asked and sipped my chilled white wine.

"Yep. I was in L.A. for a long time," he started.

"I can't picture you there," I said. Jack was charming, stylish, and pretentious at times, but he wasn't the vapid L.A. cosmetic doctor type at all. Not the Jack I knew anyway. Maybe that's what he'd become.

"Me either."

"Are you back in England now?" I asked, remembering that he always talked about going back. I used to imagine us there with a house in the suburbs and two little twin boys who would call me mum instead of mom, and I'd be the girl with the interesting accent.

"No, I live in San Francisco now, like you."

I choked on his news and my wine, which sent me into a coughing fit.

"Are you all right, love?" he asked as he rubbed my back. I tried to smile politely through my coughs, but there was no way to make it a poised moment. "Can we get some water please?" he asked, and the bartender filled the glass.

"Drink this," he advised. As I did, the coughing soothed, but my eyes had watered badly.

"Sorry." I coughed once more. "Wrong pipe." I took another long sip then composed myself. Finally. "Sorry, did you say you live in Frisco now?"

He nodded. "My partners and I are expanding the practice, so I moved there to get it going."

"So the move is temporary?" I asked.

"For now," he said. "But who knows. I think I might like living in San Francisco." His eyes twinkled and I was caught for a moment. I couldn't move, I couldn't think, I may have stopped breathing. It reminded me of the first moment I saw him wandering the campus just before school started. I was reading a book on a bench when he walked by and asked me if I knew where Green Library was. After I showed him the way, we were inseparable the rest of the year. "So, we've talked all about me. What about you? What brought you to San Francisco?"

"I did my internship there after grad school."

"For what?" he asked.

"Therapy. I'm in private practice with two other doctors."

"That's great! How's Holly? Have you seen her lately?"

"She's great. Works for an environmental organization in the city. I see her all the time."

"So are you married, divorced, boyfriend?" He sounded eager for me to answer and so I did slowly.

"Boyfriend," I boasted.

"I'm surprised. I would've thought you'd be married

by now."

You and me both, my friend.

"Is it serious?"

"Yeah, we just bought a house. We close escrow in a month."

"Congratulations," he said and lifted his glass to mine. I thanked him and asked about his relationship status in a way that was polite but not the least bit curious.

"Single. Just ended things with my girlfriend in Los Angeles."

"That's too bad. I would've thought it would be you who was married with two kids."

"Me? No, I don't want children. I work too much. That's probably why I'm still single."

Since when didn't he want to have children? Once upon a time, he and I had often talked about getting married and having kids. It was strange having a reunion drink with the man I once thought of as "the one." Life had a funny way of unfolding to prove you wrong.

We went on to talk about what we'd missed those ten years, classmates from Stanford, and best places to eat in San Francisco. There was this sense of familiarity, which never seemed to leave us. When I realized that it felt like we were back on our school campus, I decided it was time to leave. I took my last sip of wine and set my glass gently on the bar.

"Well, Jack. It was great running in to you. Maybe I'll see you around." I hopped off the bar stool and tucked my clutch under my arm.

"Where are you going? We've only just sat down."
He looked disappointed.

"I've got an early morning."

"Well, how about dinner tomorrow night?"

"I don't think that's a good idea."

"Why not? We're both here. We've got to eat . . . I
run into you after ten years in a random city, at a random
conference. Don't you think that's strange?"

"Yeah," I agreed nonchalantly. Of course it was
strange. It took everything that I had not to believe it was
some kind of great gesture from the universe. I wanted to
believe it meant nothing. That it was, like he said, random.

"If you change your mind, I'll be having dinner in
the hotel at seven."

"Okay," I said. "Thanks for the drink." I left before
he could say another word, trying to get out of there as
quickly as possible before his magnetic pull sucked me in
forever.

21

Sentimental Or Just Mental

THE MOMENT I GOT BACK TO MY ROOM I dialed James.

"Hey, I wasn't expecting to hear from you," James said immediately after answering my call.

"I just wanted to say 'hi.' I missed you today."

"I missed you too. How was your drink with Jack?" He sounded unconcerned.

I exhaled deeply before I could answer. "It was fine. I didn't stay long." And I didn't want to talk about it. I wanted to put it out of my mind and go home to James. "Did you hear anything about the home inspection?" I asked.

"Cindy said it's scheduled for Thursday at four. Think you'll be able to make it?"

"I'll probably be an hour late, but I'll be there."

"I can't wait to move in. It's going to be so great. Just you and me and Marvin." He must've been smiling. I imagined him talking with his eyes closed, envisioning our life there like he did on the bed in Pottery Barn. I tried to fill my mind with his words, our house, our family. It would be great.

"Well, baby, it's been a long day. I'm gonna get to bed. I'll call you tomorrow," I said.

"Okay, goodnight, babe." He blew a kiss into the phone.

"Goodnight."

Between the flight, the sun, and the run-in with Jack, the day had been exhausting. Even though I was spent, my mind still raced and constantly drifted back to Jack. The more I tried not to think about him, the more persistent the thoughts became until finally I surrendered. I mean the reappearance of my ex-boyfriend, once thought to be the love of my life, happened at the exact time I'd been defining my future with James. That couldn't just be a coincidence . . . right? I wanted to believe that it was totally arbitrary, but I had strong feelings to the contrary. Maybe, those were my repressed feelings for Jack. What if I'd never gotten over him the way I thought I had?

When you have a deep love and connection with someone and the relationship ends, the love doesn't disappear. The wounds of a broken heart can heal, but the love . . .where does it go? No, Jack had come back into my life for a reason, a reason I was determined to discover.

I spent the remainder of the women's health conference absentminded and looking over my shoulder for Jack. Knowing that he was in close proximity put me on edge. The hours seemed to drag on in anticipation for dinner. I had changed my mind and decided that I was going to surprise my old flame. Though, I didn't let him know in advance. There was a good chance I would chicken out and skip it.

The dinner was two hours away by the time the conference ended. My heart raced and I could feel cold beads of sweat along my neck. I sucked in one deep breath after another. Finally, my mind was clear enough to realize that it was going to take a lot more than deep breathing to calm me down. The hotel was just across the street from the beautiful Harbor Island Park. I slapped on my running shoes and grabbed my iPod before heading over.

The sun glimmered off the bay as I ran the trail along the water. I passed smiling people, walking their dogs on one side and a crowded harbor of boats on the other. My feet against the pavement provided a brief distraction. Within minutes, I was back to thinking about Jack. Only this time, I felt clearer on the situation as I often did while running. It was time to stop over thinking it.

That's when I heard it.

"Marin!" A familiar voice called from behind me. I turned around to see Jack in his running gear following close behind. Another chance meeting? We must be geographically linked. I slowed to let him catch up to me.

"Fancy meeting you here," he said and continued his jogger pace. I continued beside him.

"When did you start running?" I asked, remembering how I would beg him to jog with me around campus. Jack always refused, saying that he didn't enjoy cardio and could get his exercise during sex.

"A long time ago, I've done the L.A. Marathon for six years now."

I smirked. Jack running marathons, he'd definitely changed.

"What?" he asked.

"I'm just surprised is all," I said.

"Well, get used to it, because I'm full of surprises." He increased his pace, trying to pass me.

Did he want to race? Good. I'd show him.

I pushed through to gain on him and soon left him in my wake. Eventually, he hollered for me to slow down and so I did, with a smirk.

"I guess you're not the only one full of surprises, huh, pokey?" I said.

He panted, but maintained a steady pace. "I'm not surprised. You were always a step ahead of me." What did that mean? "Hey, look over there." Jack pointed in the direction of the park. A small wedding ceremony was taking place on the grass between two palm trees.

"Aw, that's sweet." I said. It was the kind of intimate wedding I'd want, just me, my groom, and our closest family and friends.

"Think you'll get married someday?" Jack asked as we stopped to catch the end of the ceremony.

"Yeah, probably."

"Probably? The Marin I knew couldn't wait to get hitched," he said.

"Hitched?" I looked at him strangely and he nodded. "Well, things change. If it's meant to be, it'll happen." I began walking back toward the hotel and he followed.

"Really?"

"It's the millennium, Jack. I'm a modern woman."

"Oh, yeah," he said. "Is that what it is?"

I didn't like his accusatory tone. So I answered with a short, "Yeah."

He glanced at his watch. "It's almost time for us to have dinner."

"Who said I'm having dinner with you?" I asked.

"No one." He shrugged. "But you are joining me, aren't you?"

"It's a surprise," I said with a sarcastic grin and dashed off. He let me go that time.

The park run-in with Jack took the edge off, but I still needed something stronger to calm my anxiety. When I was dressed and ready for dinner, I made an appearance at the hotel bar for a shot of whiskey, okay, make that two shots of whiskey. On an empty stomach no less.

I downed each shot quickly and thanked the bartender with a generous tip. As I walked over to the restaurant, I paced my steps by repeating in my mind, one, two, one, two, right, left, big, mistake.

Jack waited just outside the restaurant and smiled at my appearance.

"See, I knew you'd come." He reached out his arm in order to lead me inside. The sides of my mouth twitched as I smiled. My hands and head began to tingle from the whiskey that rushed through my bloodstream. I glanced at the tables around us for complimentary bread. I needed to get something in my stomach fast or I'd be giggling like a hyena.

Ten minutes later, while I was still trying to decide what to order, I busted out a huge laugh.

Jack grinned. "What's so funny?" He cocked his head to decipher my sudden outburst.

I snickered and tried to quiet myself. "I'm a little buzzed," I admitted.

"From what? We haven't even ordered our drinks yet." He looked confused.

I leaned in over my menu. "I had a couple shots at the bar," I whispered and started to laugh again but covered my mouth to hold it in.

"You really are a lightweight, aren't you?"

"I've barely had any food all day." It was true. My nerves had been buzzing for more than twenty-four hours and the thought of food made me uneasy. Now that the alcohol had kicked in, my anxiety vanished and my appetite reappeared in its place. "I'm starved, I'm going to have the filet mignon." I sat my menu down and sipped my water.

Not only were my nerves gone, but so was my filter. "Let me ask you something," I said, giving him a serious look. "Are you stalking me?"

He scoffed. "No, why would you think that?"

I shot him a wry glance. "Because you show up at the hotel I'm staying at in San Diego of all places. You magically ran into me again in the park. It seems a little too . . ."

"What?"

"Like a movie," I said. "I feel like this whole thing is

like out of a movie."

"Oh yeah? What kind of movie is it? A comedy, a drama, horror film, or romance?" He did that thing again when he trapped me in his gaze, like a moth flying into a spider's web, stuck and doomed.

"I dunno." I shook my head. "I'm just saying it feels scripted."

"You mean perfect?" He smiled. Man, his teeth were white.

"I mean, where's that waiter with our drinks?" I glanced around the restaurant for the young waiter with a tiny red wine stain near his top button, and also for an escape route in case things got out of hand.

"I know what you mean. This whole thing isn't a co-incidence. It's like it was meant to be. I can't help but think this is happening for a reason. Don't you?"

Why did he have to do that? Use phrases like *meant to be* and *for a reason*. For a romantic like me, those words were emotional kryptonite. Though, I had been thinking the same thing, I didn't want to indulge him or myself for that matter. There were too many reasons not to, the biggest one being my boyfriend, James.

"It's plausible." I shrugged. The waiter arrived with our drinks. It was about time. The conversation was getting dangerous. Jack sipped his glass of red wine, the same as mine.

"So, tell me more about your practice."

That's right, I was going to be the one in control of this conversation.

He rolled his eyes. "That's so boring."

"C'mon, I want to know. Do you do mostly boob jobs, facelifts, butt implants?" I raised my eyebrows twice.

"I specialize in this area," he said, circling his hand in front of his face. "You know, neck lifts, cheek lifts, rhinoplasty, blepharoplasty."

"Blepharoplasty?" I asked.

"Eyelid surgery." He winked.

I leaned forward and modeled my face for him. "What about me? What should I get done? Be honest."

He looked at me with a little spark in his eye. "I wouldn't change a thing."

I tried not to blush, but the alcohol made it impossible to control. "Is that your professional or personal opinion?"

Jack swirled his wine around in the stemmed glass and watched the tears slide back into the pool of burgundy then looked at me. "Both."

It turned out that I didn't need an escape route. That was the most he'd flirted with me through the whole dinner. I left an hour later on friendly terms, enough where I felt comfortable exchanging numbers in case we wanted to catch up in the city sometime.

22

Will Or Won't

THE NEXT MORNING, James waited outside of the gate when I arrived home.

"Hey, you," he said and took me in his arms. The moment I was back with James, I'd forgotten Jack completely. James was home to me.

"Hey," I said and cupped his face in my hands. "I missed your face." I said, gritting my teeth like I was talking to a cute puppy.

His eyes lit up. "Just my face?"

I gave him a light swat on his nose with my finger. "No."

"You want to get breakfast?" he asked and we walked hand in hand to the carousel.

"Yes, somewhere close. I'm starved."

James and I popped over to one of my favorite breakfast cafes. An overwhelming scent of coffee and cinnamon pancakes infused the air. My stomach growled angrily as I hadn't had anything but a cup of coffee on the plane.

"Is that Telly?" James asked. It was. Telly was having a cozy breakfast with none other than her on again, off again boyfriend, Will. It must be run-into-guys-you-never-wanted-to-see-again week. Ugh, I should've known she was sleeping with him again. The two of them were like magnets, somehow always coming back together. It was naïve to think that it was only the new practice keeping her from returning my calls. For a moment, I panicked. I didn't know if I should hide and pretend we didn't see them, or bump into them casually or confrontationally?

By the time I was close to a decision, it didn't matter. Telly had already spotted us, and the color drained from her face. She was caught. Naughty, naughty. James and I walked over.

"Hey, guys," James said.

"Hey, what are you two doing here?" Telly asked. I could tell she was trying to cover her shock with a pleasant smile, but it just came off as panic.

"I just got home from San Diego," I said.

"Yeah, how was it?" she asked.

"Good," I said, remembering that I still hadn't told James about last night's dinner. Now I was the one with the fake smile.

"Do you want to join us? We just put our orders in," Will offered.

"Yeah, thanks!" James said and removed his jacket to sit down. "This place has a twenty minute wait for a table." I followed suit sitting across from Telly and next to Will. Just the four of us having a friendly breakfast, another unwelcomed coincidence.

"So, what brings you two here today?" I asked.

"We've been coming every Saturday for a few weeks now," Will said, stirring more sugar into his coffee. "It's pretty much the only time I can see her since she opened the new office."

"That's right," James interjected while peering through the menu. "Marin told me about your new place. She said it was perfect for you,"

Telly smiled.

"I'm so proud of her. Aren't you proud of her, Marin?" Will asked.

I nodded politely then shot Telly a tough glance. Of course, I was proud of her, but at the moment, I was more disappointed that she'd been keeping him a secret from me. Will didn't seem to notice that I was completely unaware of his relationship with my best friend. The lie was irritating as was the surprise run-in. When the plates were clear, we paid our part of the bill and took our leave.

"I'll call you later," I said in a low voice to Telly.

"Can't wait," she replied.

Outside, James opened the passenger door for me. "That was fun, huh? Will's a pretty cool guy. I don't know why you give him such a hard time."

I rolled my eyes, of course he wouldn't understand. He was a guy. "It's a long story."

He hopped into the seat next to me and fastened his seat belt. As we drove toward my apartment, I stewed about Telly not telling me about Will. It was definitely something she should have mentioned instead of hiding it from me. But Telly wasn't the only one using omission. I also had something to confess.

I cleared my throat. "So, Jack and I had dinner after the conference," I said in an it's-no-big-deal kinda way and kept my eyes on the road.

He glanced at me. "Oh, yeah. How was that?" James may have been cool with the catch up drink, but by his tone he didn't seem as cool with dinner.

"It was good. We got to catch up. He's living here now. So maybe we'll run into him or we can all have a drink sometime," I said.

James nodded slowly. "Uh-huh." The car was silent and I found myself taking quiet shallow breaths, waiting for him to speak. "He knows about us, right?"

"Of course, baby. I told him all about you, and the house, and Marvin."

"Yeah, you know how guys are."

"Yes, I do," I said and ran my fingers through the hair on the back of his head while he kept his eyes on the street. "But it was totally cool. And . . . I'm really glad I ran into him. I feel like I got closure." Okay, perhaps closure wasn't an entirely accurate description, but I had no regrets about any of it.

"Well, good for you," he said as if he thought closure was bullshit.

"Aw, are you jealous?" I said in a sweet tone.

"No." He sounded defensive. "Maybe a little. But wouldn't you feel like that if I had dinner with my ex-wife and called it closure?"

"Yeah, probably, but if it helped you in some way,

I'd get over it. Wait. Did you ever get closure with her?"

"Fuck that bitch," he said as if he were spitting the words in her face.

My eyes shot wide. It was the most vulgar he'd ever sounded.

"Sorry." He sighed. "I just want to leave that in the past where it belongs."

James never talked about his ex-wife and if she ever was brought up, he instantly changed the subject. I used to be curious but then realized that if he didn't want to talk about her, then why should I? But as a therapist, I knew that not dealing with something didn't mean it stayed in the past. It could haunt like a ghost. He clearly had unresolved issues about the whole thing, and I wondered if that was a battle we would have to deal with later. Maybe we were dealing with it now.

He dropped me off at my place and left to run some errands. I quickly changed into a pair of comfy yoga pants and started my laundry. As I unloaded all the clothes from my suitcase, I recalled the moments with Jack in each one of them. My jersey dress, my running tank top, the skinny jeans I wore to dinner. There was something exciting about running into him the way I had. But, I needed to leave it in San Diego.

I thought about the past, both mine and James', and how we all had a funny way of remembering it. Even though we thought we'd kept the past in the past, it continued to linger on like a permanent mark on our soul.

When I was younger, I'd had this habit of journaling intermittently, usually when I was falling in love or getting my heartbroken, though I hadn't done it in years. I pulled a box out from the top shelf of my bedroom closet. Inside were a couple of journals and trinkets from my past relationships. Keeping those things in a box inside my closet felt a little silly, but I didn't have the heart to throw them out. They were part of my story. Whenever I opened the box, I could reminisce about being young and crazy in love, or maybe just crazy.

The pages of the journal were filled with memories, making the book feel heavier. I searched for passages from my break up with Jack, hoping to remember the details of our relationship. Things I had long forgotten. Seeing him made me feel nostalgic. I began to read one of the entries and quickly realized that I was indulging the idea of him and it needed to stop. So I made myself some tea, put on an episode of my favorite drama, and waited for my real love, James, to come home to me.

23

San Jose

B Y THE END OF THE WEEK, Jack seemed to be a distant memory. That was until Andy popped in my office just before lunch.

"Uh, there's a British guy in the waiting room asking to see you," he said as if the whole idea baffled him.

My heart began to race. Was it him? "Espresso-colored hair, dreamy eyes, like he could play a doctor on TV, but he's actually one in real life?"

Andy seemed to mull this over before responding. "I'd say dark hair, vacant eyes, and I wouldn't trust him to save my life."

"That's Jack," I said and marched past Andy.

Jack looked joyful as I approached, but the fact that he'd showed up at my office unannounced made me uneasy. "Hey, Jack. What are you doing here?" I kept a reasonable distance. Out of the corner of my eye, I could see the receptionist, Diana, watching us.

"I came by to invite you to lunch." He gave me an

216

innocent smile.

"Lunch?" I asked and raised an eyebrow.

"Yeah, I don't know that many people in the city and I thought we could be friends," he said.

"Friends?" Was it even possible?

"Yeah, liked we talked about in San Diego. Drinks with our significant others, the occasional lunch . . ."

I knew that we'd left on good and friendly terms, but maybe it was more than I remembered. I was pretty drunk. Was he expecting us to be best buds? I hoped not. James probably wouldn't like that too much.

"Did you eat yet?" he asked.

I shook my head.

"Then let's have lunch," he suggested. "As friends."

"Okay." But only this one time. "As friends."

Jack and I sat at the bistro around the corner from my office. The bustling sounds of chatter, a cash register drawer, and forks against plates surrounded us. Totally casual, nothing romantic or shameful about it.

"Is your office nearby?" I asked.

He took a bite of his sandwich and shook his head with a piece of lettuce dangling from his mouth. After a minute he said, "It's across town."

"So you came all this way on a whim during your lunch break?"

"Yeah." He shrugged.

"How did you even find me?" I didn't want to be impressed by his valiant effort toward our new and improved friendship, but I was. Even though I wasn't expecting it. At all.

"I Googled you, love. You're not that hard to find." Okay, maybe not so valiant.

"Are you doing anything for Easter Sunday?" he asked.

"We're going to see my parents," I said. My family was not at all religious, but we often spent Easter at my brother's house. An excuse to get together, I suppose. This year was different. Holly's parents invited my parents, James, and me to their house in San Jose. Rachel and Holly would be there too, of course.

"How are they?" he asked. "Is your dad still practicing?"

"They're good. He's still working, but he's slowed down a lot. They've been doing a lot more traveling over the past few years."

"That's good. I always liked your dad."

I smiled, knowing that Jack may have liked my dad, but Dad wasn't crazy about him. He said that Jack was an arrogant idiot. Then again, what aspiring doctor isn't, especially in the eyes of an established physician like my dad?

With every passing minute, I relaxed a little more. Talking with Jack over sandwiches felt like old times. Being with him was easy, just as I had remembered. Not that it wasn't easy to be with James. It was just a different kind of easy.

Ugh. I was comparing them. How could I do that? I cringed. It was enough to make me lose my appetite. It wasn't right and I needed to stop whatever we'd started. I shouldn't have been having lunch with my ex-boyfriend after we'd spent time together in San Diego. I shouldn't spend any time with him at all. Being friends just wasn't in the cards for us.

"You're not going to finish your lunch?" he asked while I gathered my things.

"Can't. I have a patient coming in soon."

He looked so . . . disappointed. Yeah, I definitely had to get out of there.

"Do you want me to walk you?"

"No, I'm good. Thanks for lunch." I didn't say much else before I left and didn't feel the need for a memorable goodbye. San Diego had been memorable enough. I had decided to leave Jack in the past where he belonged and move on with my life.

The following Saturday, James and I drove down to San Jose to stay with my parents, both of whom adored James. I think they were anxious for him to put a ring on it too, but not any more anxious than I was. We got there late enough to enjoy a brief dinner and settle in for the night.

Though my parents had changed houses since Michael and I moved out, it still felt like home just knowing that they were asleep in the next room. Having James with me made it even more apparent that I wanted him to join my family. While he mostly had, I wanted it to be official, for my parents to be his in-laws, and his parents to be my in-laws. The Youngs and the Johns' coming together over a wedding, grandchildren, and holidays. I reminded myself, once again, that moving in together was a huge step to becoming a family. But it still wasn't enough.

At least not for me.

Then, I had a thought. What if James was planning to ask me in front of my parents? He was old fashioned that way and would definitely ask their permission first. Maybe all wasn't lost. After all, it had been two months since I started the *McQueen Method*.

The next morning, I found James enjoying a cup of joe in the kitchen with my mother.

"There you are," my mother said, smiling widely.

James immediately stood to fix a cup for me too.

"We were wondering when you were going to get up," he said, pouring the steaming brew into a familiar mug. My parents may have changed houses, but most of the dishes remained the same.

"So lazy." My mom shook her head in disappointment. "I've tried to tell her that she's too old to sleep in."

"I'm not lazy. It's so peaceful up here. I didn't know it was so late," I said with a yawn.

"That's because this is the suburbs. No traffic on a cul-de-sac." James sat down next to me a slid the mug my way. Even the coffee smelled fresher at my mom's.

"Where's Dad?" I asked.

"He's in the garage riding his exercise bike," my mom said.

I nodded. It was great that Dad was being proactive with his cardio fitness. Years of high cholesterol foods had left his health less than stellar. In the last year he'd adopted a primarily plant based diet and moderate exercise routine. It seemed to be working well for him. Holly emailed him recipes on a regular basis. She was like their other daughter since the two of us spent so much time together as kids.

"What time is dinner at the Jensen's?" I asked.

"Two," James told me.

I slid off the kitchen stool and took my cup of coffee.

"I'm gonna go see Dad," I said.

James took a sip and nodded. As I walked out of the kitchen, my mom asked James about the remodeling of our new house. Their exchange warmed and excited me at the same time.

I walked into the tidy, sun-lit garage. A nice dewy breeze filled the room. The neighborhood street was so quiet; the only sound was the winding of his recumbent bike. Ear buds were tucked in his ears, but the music was loud enough for me to hear. He looked lost in thought as sweat beaded down his face.

"Morning, Dad," I said.

He seemed startled and pulled out one of the ear buds. "Morning."

"What are you listening to?"

"Journey," he said, slowing his pace. Journey's songs invoked memories of the eighties when my mom had wild, poofy hair and my dad sported a porn stache. And new memories of car rides and wine nights with Telly. One of those classic bands that would never go out of style.

"Am I interrupting?" I asked and sat down on one of those short stools that they use in boxing rings. I spun around on it one time, holding my cup up so as not to spill any of the delicious coffee.

"No, I'm just about done. Did you just wake up?"

"Yeah, sleeping on a dead end street is like a tranquilizer."

He chuckled, which was nice to see. When I was a child, he'd seemed so serious all the time and often too quiet. He still was, but the years had loosened him some. Less time at work had apparently helped with that.

"It's nice being down here. James and I should come more often."

"You're both welcome any time."

"Well, over the summer you'll have to stay with us at our new house," I told him. He got off the bike and wiped his face with a fluffy white towel.

"I'm looking forward to it. So," he said before taking a long sip of water. "Are you two thinking about getting married anytime soon?" My dad may have been serious and quiet, but he was very liberal, which is why his question caught me off guard. Did that mean James didn't ask him for my hand in marriage? Or that he did, and now my dad wanted to make sure saying yes was the right decision.

"I don't know. Are you worried about us living in sin?" I joked.

He chucked again. Two times in one conversation! "No. It just seems like the natural next step. Both your mother and I are wondering if we can expect any grandchildren from you."

I frowned. Always with the babies. They already had two amazing grandchildren. I didn't think I shelved the responsibility anymore. Though, I would've loved to give them more grandchildren.

"Don't worry, Dad. We'll get there," I said.

"I know. I'm not trying to put any pressure on you." He hugged me.

I lay my head on his damp chest and breathed in his familiar smell.

"We just want you to be happy."

"Thanks, Dad."

"But it would be neat to see a little Marin running around."

It would be *neat* to have a little Marin running around. Or maybe a little James. Or both!

For a moment, I imagined James having a similar exchange with our unborn daughter one day. My dad was a great provider and he was good to us, but James would be one of those warmhearted fathers. The kind that wouldn't let anything come between him and his kids, not even me.

"It would," I said. "Oh, that reminds me. Guess who I ran into recently?"

He shrugged.

"Jack Ashbury, my old boyfriend from Stanford."

"Oh, yeah." He gave me a curious look. "What's he up to?"

"He's a cosmetic surgeon."

My dad rolled his eyes.

"He asked about you." I smiled.

"Humph," he said.

"What's your problem with Jack?" I asked, hoping to finally get an answer. Their disapproval had always irked me.

"You're my little girl. No one was ever good enough for you."

"What about James?" I asked, hopeful.

My dad shook his head. "I like James a lot, more than any of your other boyfriends. Still, I don't think anyone will be quite good enough." He smiled and motioned for me to follow him back into the house. If my dad thought James was the best of the worst, I'd take it.

24

Just Say Yes

THE FOUR OF US ARRIVED AT THE Jensen's house with a bottle of white wine and a strawberry pie from the grocery store. My mother didn't bake either. Holly's parents still lived in her childhood home. Stepping through the front door was like traveling back in time. I inhaled the memorable aroma of lemon and something cool like spearmint, but slightly different. I spent so many days in that house, the living room where we watched *Saved by the Bell* after school, the dining table where we did our homework, the kitchen counters on which we sat when we made bean burritos.

I introduced Mr. and Mrs. Jensen to James and they led us to the backyard where they'd set up a beautiful Easter Sunday table with a light green table cloth, candles in mason jars and wild flowers in a skinny vase. It was nestled between two trees, the same place Holly and I'd set up a tent when we were kids so we could sleep outside. I never got any sleep in the tent and always snuck back to Holly's bed. She got mad every time.

James looked for David and I spied Holly on the wooden swing that hung by thick ropes from the biggest tree. Noom stood next to her, lightly pushing the swing forward. She giggled like she meant it. What could he have said that was so funny? I walked over to greet her, and it wasn't until I was standing right in front of her that either of them noticed me.

"Marin! You're here." She hopped off the swing and gave me a big squeeze. Noom bowed a hello that I returned.

"When did you guys get here?" I asked.

"We came a couple days ago, having some quality time with my parents," she said.

"It was nice of them to invite us all here."

"Since Noom's here they thought we could all spend the day together."

I turned to Noom. "Is this the first time you've met Holly's parents?"

He shook his head and told me that the Jensen's had visited San Francisco to meet him when he first arrived.

Wow! Holly hadn't wasted any time.

"Finally, you're here!" Rachel snuck up beside me with an ear-to-ear grin. I greeted my sweet, sweet Rachel with a hug.

"How are you?" I asked.

"Great! David and I are planning a trip to Italy this summer."

"Wow, Italy?"

Rachel gave a big nod and took my hand. "Come

with me to get some lemonade." I followed her into the kitchen, doubtful that Holly and Noom noticed we'd left.

She poured lemonade into two short glasses, then pulled a fold out stepstool from behind the fridge and reached for the high cabinet.

"You want some?" she asked, holding a bottle of Vodka. I shook my head and she shrugged as she filled the rest of her short glass with the clear liquid. I sipped from my glass of virgin lemonade and Rachel gulped from hers before letting out a refreshed sigh.

"You okay?" I asked.

"Never better." She beamed. We stood in the kitchen for fifteen minutes talking about my sex-mex getaway and the trip she planned to Europe before her mom came in to take the turkey from the oven. I took the welcomed interruption to head back outside to find James. He wasn't anywhere in sight until I checked around the corner of the house. There, he and David stood close together, talking. Their voices sounded somber, so I hid. Not sure why, but the conversation felt eerily private.

"You want some?" David asked.

"I'm good, man," James said.

Want some of what?

"So you're closing on the house soon. That's cool." One of them took a gulp of his drink.

"Yeah, we're excited," James said.

"So what do you think? You gonna make it official or what?"

Yeah, was he going to make it official?

"What are you talking about?" James said.

"Are you getting married?"

James was quiet for a moment or he said something so quietly I couldn't hear. Then his voice broke in. "It's possible," he said. Possible? What did that mean?

"You want my advice?" David asked.

"No, not really." James snickered.

"Don't do it."

"What's going on with you lately? Every time I see you at a get together like this you're hammered. I know you like to have a good time, but shit. You're starting to act like an alcoholic."

"It's fucking Rachel, man. She's being such a chilly bitch."

I stifled a gasp with my hand.

"C'mon, don't talk about your wife like that."

"Why not? She's my wife and it's true. I can't even remember the last time she gave me a blow job."

Blood pulsed through my veins. I didn't know if I was prepared to bear witness to this conversation, and I definitely didn't like the way David was talking about Rachel. I never would've imagined David saying things like that, especially after our therapy sessions. How naïve was I? What else were my patients hiding? Maybe that's what therapy should become, spying on your patients and analyzing their behavior. Yeah right, no one would go for that kind of treatment. I stood still, listening.

"What's going on with you two?" James asked.

"I don't know, I think I just really fucked up with that affair. Things haven't been the same. It got better for a while, and then it got worse. I don't know what to do, but I can tell you this. I can't take much more of it. All we do is travel, we do it to bond and get closer, but we always end the trip with a huge fight and it makes everything worse, plus . . ."

"Plus what?" James asked.

"I think she might be sleeping around to get back at me."

"Why do you think that?"

"Takes one to know one, I guess."

"So what, you're sleeping around again too."

"Not really," David said.

Not really? What did he mean—not a lot or not at all? Fucking men.

"You?"

"Nah, I got a good thing goin'," James said.

"Well, don't ruin it by getting married. Remember what happened with Vanessa?" The moment David mentioned James' ex-wife's name my stomach flipped and I held my breath.

"I spend my life trying to forget," James uttered.

That's when I realized, the residual pain from his divorce was worse than I thought. That explained why he was so reluctant to get married. Maybe it wasn't about me. After all, he had just signed documents tying us together with a fancy house and mortgage. It wasn't that he didn't want a life with me. Maybe he was afraid of having a life without me, like I was afraid of having a life without him.

I had heard enough. I stepped around the house so the guys could see me. "They're about to serve dinner.

You guys ready to eat?" I asked, smiling.

David cleared his throat and headed for the table. James and I watched him walk away.

"Is he okay?" I asked.

"Yeah, he's all right," James answered. I looked at him unconvinced, but he just smiled. "C'mon, I'm hungry."

James and I sat down at the long outdoor dining table over a delicious looking Easter feast. We passed around plates of greens, rolls, salads, starchy sides, and of course turkey. Aside from watching Holly and Noom feed each other green beans and David throw back drink after drink, it was nice that we could all come together during a holiday and enjoy a family meal. It felt so traditional and warm. I looked at James and he smiled at me while he chewed his salad.

What, if anything, was he hiding behind that smile? I knew he loved me and wanted to be with me, but it seemed like he didn't want the same things I wanted. Or at least, not the same way I wanted them.

After dinner, the ten of us spread out in the backyard while we stuffed our faces with strawberry pie and whipped cream. I was sneaking an extra bite from James' plate when Noom called for our attention. They stood by the wooden swing, his arms around Holly's waist.

"I want to thank Mr. and Mrs. Jensen for having us all over today for a real American Easter," Noom said. "It has been a great experience. I love California. I love Holly's family and her friends, but most of all I loooooove Holly." The girls awed at his sweet words. "There's something that I want to say to Holly." Noom turned to Holly and began speaking to her in a mesh of Thai-English. She seemed to hang on his every word, like she was trying too hard to remember every syllable. Or maybe she was just trying to understand him?

Rachel and David looked confused, while my parents and the Jensens smiled. I glanced up at James and he shrugged. Were we supposed to be watching them still? Finally, Noom took Holly's hand and kneeled.

I shook my head, clearing my vision. Was he about to propose? Oh, my God, he was. Holly yelled, "Yes!" and everyone applauded, it took me a moment to put my hands together. Holly and Noom engaged? How could it be?

Noom took Holly in his arms as tears fell from her eyes.

Did she really want to get married? She'd never said anything about it, and despite each of them telling me they were crazy for each other, I really didn't think their relationship was that serious. Yet, they were going to be husband and wife. They were going to be family.

"I can't believe it," I whispered to James. He leaned toward my ear.

"Believe it, baby. Go congratulate your friend."

I forced a smile before approaching Holly.

"Congrats, guys," I said and hugged Noom, then Holly. I looked into her tear filled eyes and could tell she was really, very happy. She was in love. I wanted to cry too, not because I was elated by the proposal, but because I was heartbroken by it. I wanted to be happy for her, I really did, but in that moment, I couldn't think about anything other than everyone else getting married. Everyone but me. Holly was going to be Noom's wife. How would it change our friendship? Would he take her back to Thailand?

I prayed that my true feelings didn't show, not that Holly would have noticed. This was her moment. "I'm so happy for you."

25

Friendly Advice

IT HAD BEEN AN EVENTFUL FEW WEEKS, and all I wanted was to take a step back from pretty much everyone. Holly must've called me at least twice a day, but I dodged every one of them. Not my greatest moment as a friend, I know, but I didn't want to risk saying the wrong thing because I was feeling, in my opinion, the wrong thing. The longer I waited, the more my rational senses returned, and eventually I was ready to take her call.

"Where've you been? I've been trying to get in touch with you since the weekend." Holly didn't sound upset, just concerned.

"Sorry, Hol, I've been tied up with house stuff." A little white lie that my honest friend would never tell.

"It's okay. Can we get together and talk?" she asked.

"Sure, what's on your mind?"

"Are you kidding? Everything. You're buying a house, I'm engaged. I just want to see you and catch up."

She sounded like she missed me, and I had missed her too. Things were just a little weird. I hoped they would return to normal again soon.

I agreed to meet her for coffee the next evening after I finished with my patients. My body stiffened and my smile turned phony when she walked into the café, an unusual and uncomfortable reaction. I hoped she couldn't tell. Little lies were easy on the phone, but I'd have to work really hard to lie to her face.

Her manner was awkward too, as she sat across from me with her steaming cup of tea in a ceramic mug. Holly insisted on using real drinkware. I looked at my paper cup and felt a little pang of guilt at the "waste" she'd say I was creating. Holly really was a much better person.

We made sixty seconds of polite small talk when she gave me sad puppy-dog eyes. "Are you mad at me?"

I sighed. "I'm not mad at you, I'm just . . ." I didn't want to sound like a big baby, but the truth was that I was, "—a little jealous."

"I had a feeling." Holly put her hand on mine. "I wasn't expecting a proposal at all. It just happened. I know the timing is weird for you. I'd probably be upset too." How many girlfriends would have reacted like Holly? Not many. Her friendship was my true fortune.

"I'm sorry. I really am, because I want you to be happy. And if this makes you happy, then I support it a hundred percent."

She smiled as if I'd said the magic words.

"Does this make you happy?" My face cringed slightly.

"Yes!" She beamed. "I've never been happier and I love him, Marin. He's my James."

Noom? Holly's James? That meant she'd do almost anything to be with him. Even move away.

Tears burst from my eyes and I covered my face. "Is he taking you back to Thailand?" I asked.

"What?" She snickered a little. "Is that what you're upset about? You think I'm moving to another country?"

I nodded and wiped my drippy nose with a rough brown napkin.

"Aw, Marin." Holly put her arms around me. "I'm not going anywhere. I'm sure we'll spend some time away, but we'll live here. My life and my work is here, and Noom wants to be here too."

I wanted to say something, articulate anything, but my words were smothered by my uncontrollable waterworks. What a fucking mess I was.

"Is that the only thing that's bothering you?" she asked and sat back in her chair.

"No," I said, finally managing to get a word out.

"What else is going on?"

"James doesn't want to get married." I sobbed harder.

"What do you mean?"

"It's his ex-wife. She ruined it for him and now . . ." I cried. "I'll never be his wife." I blew my nose hard into the coarse napkin.

Holly came to my aid, crouching next to my chair and rubbing my back. "Just give him more time. You'll see."

"I have and the more time I give him, the more he'll take. I don't know how much I'm willing to give up."

"What do you mean?"

"What if I'm wrong? What if he's not the guy for me? What if there's someone better, someone who can give me what he can't?" I couldn't believe I had admitted that to myself, let alone to someone else. The relief from releasing the words was short lived, quickly replaced with a queasy sense of guilt.

"Marin, James is the one for you. Maybe he's a little spooked about marriage now, but he'll come around. He's crazy about you. Why do you need a piece of paper and a title to believe it?"

Easy for her to say. She was the one wearing the engagement ring.

My crying slowed, and I took a deep breath. "I just do." Holly had no rebuttal. What could she say?

"There's something else," I said, regaining my normal tone.

"What?" Holly looked alarmed.

"I ran into Jack in San Diego."

Holly rose over me, frowning. "Jack? As in Jack-Ass-Face, Jack?" I nodded. "You ran into him? What happened?"

"It was a totally random run in. We met for drinks, then we had dinner, and he told me that he made a mistake, that he never should have let me go."

"That fucking guy," Holly said under her breath. She took her seat across from me, worry spread across her face. "Remember how heartbroken you were?"

"Yes, but things have changed. What if there's a reason he came back in my life? He even lives here now. I mean, what are the odds?"

"Wait, what?" She held up her hand and took a deep breath. "Listen to me, whatever ideas he's put in your head, you have to forget about them. This path you're on is a slippery slope, and as your best friend, I forbid you to see him again." Her tone was as severe as the time the Man Test came to Rachel and David's house.

I scoffed. "You forbid me?"

"Yep."

"Well, you can't forbid me. I'm a grown woman."

"Then start acting like it, Marin." She raised her voice. "No wonder James hasn't proposed. You're no more sure of him than he is of you."

I gasped.

Holly grabbed her bag. "James already gave you a second chance. You might not get a third. I'm saying this with love. Get your shit together before you blow it." Before I could defend myself, she stomped out of the coffee shop.

What had just happened?

I should've known Holly would react that way after everything that happened when I left med school. Maybe she was right and letting Jack back into my life would turn out to be a huge mistake. But what if it wasn't? I picked up my cup to take a sip then realized I was going to need something a little stronger to numb the pain of it all. That's when I called my therapist. Yes, alcohol and an objective pep talk from Andy were just what I needed.

We met at a desolate bar near his neighborhood. Burgundy and hunter green leather seats lined the old wooden bar top. The floor was sticky under my shoes and I noticed the tops of the tables were dirty as I walked over to meet him.

Next time, I'd pick the place.

"Hey there, Andy." The blonde bartender flashed her blue eyes at him. She couldn't have been older than twenty-nine, at least fourteen years his junior. "Haven't seen you in a while. We missed you around here."

"Yeah, you know how it is," he said and looked away shyly, which was odd because Andy didn't have a shy bone in his body.

"Is this your girlfriend?" She gave me a once over.

"No," I said abruptly. Andy looked at me as if to say 'okay, nutcase.'

"Liz, this is Marin. She's one of the doctors from my office."

The bartender perked up enough to match her silicone breasts. "Hey, what can I get you?"

"A glass of cab, please," I said.

"Your best cab," Andy confirmed. "She's having boyfriend trouble," he whispered.

I rolled my eyes.

"Don't worry. I've got the perfect wine for you." Liz winked and flashed a knowing smile. "What about you, Andy?"

"Usual, please."

"You got it!" Liz bounced away, and Andy's gaze followed her around the bar as she poured and mixed.

"Ahem," I let out, and it diverted his attention back to me. We sat quietly for a minute. A familiar song played faintly in the background. I listened for the lyrics, trying to identify the tune, while Andy stared at me. Taking mental notes as he usually did.

"So, what's goin' on?" he asked, playing with the paper bar napkin in front of him.

I let out a heavy sigh. "I don't even know where to start."

"Start at the beginning."

I hesitated for a moment, wanting to get the words right. Anything I said to Andy could and would be used against me in a later discussion. The guy never forgot a thing.

"James still hasn't asked me to marry him, and it turns out that he might never propose."

"What do you mean?" he asked.

"I overheard him talking to his best friend over the weekend."

"What did he say?"

"He said that marriage was possible, the same way people say a zombie apocalypse is possible. Then his ex-wife came up and . . . I could just hear it in his voice. She ruined holy matrimony for him. Maybe forever."

Andy gave me a sideways look, the kind that meant I was fucked.

"Here you are!" Liz sat the drinks in front of us.

I nodded a thank you.

"Thanks, Liz," Andy said with a wink before sipping his Jack and coke.

She leaned on the bar, boobs spilling out of her tight tee.

"You got it." She winked back.

"Andy," I said through gritted teeth, "this is serious. Can you please stop flirting with the bartender for two seconds? I need your help."

"I can do two things at once." He chuckled.

I sipped my cabernet and stared at Andy with disdain. "You're very arrogant, you know that?"

He smirked.

"What about you? You're divorced. Think you'd ever get married again?"

Andy grimaced. "Ooh, I doubt it."

"Why not? What happened with you two?"

He sat his drink down as if to prepare to engage in a long tale. Yes! I'd waited years to hear this story. I leaned forward slightly.

"You know how married people say marriage changes things?"

I nodded.

"A lot of couples who live together and share everything think it's a joke. That nothing's going to change. We'll have this big party, then a nice vacation, and come back to the same 'ole, same 'ole."

"Yeah, and?"

"It's not that simple. Marriage makes the relationship more complicated. For some couples it's a good complicated. The relationship deepens and becomes stronger, but for others, it's a bad complicated. You feel trapped, which is why I don't believe in long-term monogamy." I opened my mouth to speak, but he kept going. "The moral of the story is that getting married put unnecessary pressure on my relationship with my ex-wife and it destroyed us, what we had. And the divorce. Well, even the simplest divorces are excruciating."

"I guess I should talk to Telly about that," I said and watched Andy's cheeks turn pink. I smirked.

"How's your wine?" he asked.

Nice save.

"It's good," I said with a chuckle.

He gave me a strange look so I straightened up. "Well anyway, I don't think James had the same marital experience that you did."

Andy shrugged and stirred his cocktail. "Maybe not, but coming back from a failed marriage is easier on some than others."

"So you're saying what exactly?"

"If it ain't broke . . . what's the problem? He loves you. You two are buying a place together. Life's good, enjoy what you have. Why do you need a marriage certificate?" When did it become so wrong to want a marriage certificate?

"I just want someone to call my own, someone to grow old with, someone to raise a family with."

"Typical girl," he said. Then in a mock-girl voice, "When are we getting married? When are we gonna have a baby?"

I shoved him playfully to get him to stop, which he did and laughed. He had to know he was irritating me just a little.

"What's wrong with that?" I said.

"It's the millennium. You don't need a wedding to have a family or have a baby. You don't even need a man to have a baby anymore."

"I know," I said looking down and picking nervously at my nails. "But I want to be married. I don't think I should have to give that up."

"If it's that simple for you, then maybe you should just let him go. But if you love him like you say you do, then why would you give him up for a piece of paper that has no real value or use?"

I thought about it for a moment and sipped my dark wine. The smell of the cabernet reminded me of the visit to the vineyards last spring with James. By the end of the night we were so intoxicated we could barely get our clothes off. So we slept on top of the covers, fully clothed with wine stained lips. We made love that morning and I remember thinking that I could have lived in that moment forever.

My phone buzzed with a text from Telly.

I know this is a bad time, but I really need to talk to you. Are you free to meet?

"Telly needs to talk," I said while replying to her text. "I'm gonna tell her to meet us here."

"Us? No, I have to go." He took a big gulp, finishing his drink. "Liz." Andy raised his glass to get her attention. "I'll take the check whenever."

"Wha . . ." I started with my hands up in question. "Where are you going? I've got more stuff to unload."

"I told you I couldn't stay long." He'd never said

that. "Besides, you can get on my calendar."

"Yeah, but c'mon." I searched his face for the truth. It was Telly. Would she have agreed to come if she'd known Andy was here?

"What happened with Telly anyway?" I asked.

"I told you, nothing." He pulled a few bills from his wallet. "Keep the change," he told Liz.

"That's what she says, but I know it wasn't nothing. Just tell me, I can handle it."

"Fine, you want to know what happened?" He seemed serious, and I shook with anticipation. I'd been waiting to hear the story for over a year. Andy looked over his left shoulder, then his right, and leaned in. "Nothingggg," he whispered like a ghost.

"Ugh, just go," I said, shooing him away.

"I'm going." He stood up and put on his sports coat. "About James . . . just talk to him."

I gave him a half smile and he patted my shoulder before walking away.

"Hey, Andy," I called and raised my wine glass. "Thanks for the drink." He raised one hand to bid me farewell and I took a long sip.

"You doin' okay?" Liz asked.

"Yeah, thanks."

"He left you here all by yourself?" she asked, shaking her head with disapproval.

"It's okay, my girlfriend'll be here in a few." The bar was as empty as when I came in, so Liz hung around. "You like Andy?"

"Yeah, I like him." She shrugged.

"You're a beautiful young girl, aren't you more interested in guys your own age?" Sorry Andy, but I had to look out for the poor girl.

"Sometimes, it depends on the guy. But I like Andy. He's smart and he listens."

He listened? Her Andy and mine sounded like two different people.

26

Are You Positive?

"THERE YOU ARE," Telly called from behind me. "Jesus, why did you ask me to meet you here?" She looked around the bar with a disgusted expression.

I gave Liz an apologetic look, and she responded with a dismissive wave.

"Telly, this is Liz." Telly smiled indifferently and ordered a scotch.

"I heard about Holly's proposal. You okay?" Telly asked.

"Kind of. That's why I'm here. I was talking it over with Andy."

"Oh, where's Andy?" She looked around, seemingly panicked.

"He had to leave."

Telly let out a sigh as if relieved and quickly moved on to the topic at hand, which was still unknown. "Before I say anything," she started. "I want you to know that I realize I have the worst timing ever, but you're the only one I can talk to about this."

"Oh, my God. If you're engaged—" I started and her eyes began to water.

"It's worse."

"What is it? Is it your practice? Are you dying?" Telly shook her head at both of these. "Then what?"

"I think I might be pregnant."

Pregnant! My heart sank and, for a moment, I stopped breathing. "You think you're pregnant or you know you're pregnant?"

"I don't know, I've been so busy setting up the new office that I didn't realize my period was late."

"How late?"

"Four weeks."

"Four weeks!" I echoed.

She nodded and bit her lower lip like she couldn't argue her way out of a possible pregnancy. It was Telly. She couldn't be pregnant. It had to be something else.

"Did you take a test?" I asked and she shook her head. "You've been really stressed with the new practice. Sometimes that can affect your cycle." Liz brought the scotch and Telly picked it up from the bar, putting the glass to her lips.

"Telly!" I yelled.

"What?" She froze.

"Why did you order scotch if you might be pregnant?" I asked in an angry whisper.

She frowned and seemed to realize her mistake just in time. "See, look at me. I'm a mess. I can't be responsible for someone else's life." She lowered the glass, but didn't take her eyes off of it. I could almost see her salivating for the liquor. "Will you come with me to take the test?"

"Right now?" I asked.

She nodded and looked shaken.

"Okay."

I called Liz over to settle the tab. Then Telly and I scooted out of there and headed for the drug store.

In the aisle next to Telly's beloved condoms were several rows of pink and blue boxes of pee sticks that read, 'Results before your missed period' and 'Trusted by doctors.'

"What kind should I get?" she asked.

"I don't know. I haven't had a pregnancy scare since . . . since college." I thought back to the day when Jack came back from the store with the most expensive pregnancy test on the shelf. He wanted to be sure. I remember thinking that having his baby wouldn't have been the worst outcome. Wow, if I had been pregnant, I would have had a nine–year-old now. Hard to imagine.

"Let's just get one of each," she suggested.

I tried to calculate the very expensive pregnancy test bill, not to mention the amount of urine Telly would have to generate for all of them to be accurate. "How about the best three?"

Telly agreed and grabbed the three most expensive ones and we headed for the check out.

Back at Telly's place, she set all three tests haphazardly on the sink. The two of us sat on the floor just outside the bathroom, waiting for her timer to ding.

"Who's is it?" I asked.

"We don't know if there is an *it* yet."

"But if there is. Is it Will's?"

She kept her eyes to the floor and nodded slightly. That's all she needed, to be tied to that guy forever.

"This is the worst time, you know," she said. "I can't have a baby."

"Let's not get ahead of ourselves. Wait for the tests." I felt sick to my stomach not wanting to believe that she was pregnant, but knowing that in this circumstance, her chances were pretty good.

Ding!

Our eyes met with slight dread.

"Can you look for me?" she asked. Poor Telly. The girl who wasn't scared of anything couldn't even bring herself to check the results.

I walked to the sink. My heart dropped to the pit of my stomach as I glanced at the tests. Positive. Positive. Positive. I didn't even have to check the results key on the boxes. There was no doubt. Telly was pregnant.

"What is it?" she called from the hall. I couldn't say anything. How could I tell her that her life would never be the same?

She pushed me out of the way to get a look at the tests then said nothing as she stared blankly at the results.

"Telly, you okay?" I asked after a minute.

"Yeah," she uttered under her breath. "I think I need a minute."

"Of course, I'll be here."

"Can you shut the door behind you?" she asked, and I did.

I exhaled from the tense moment and went to sit on her couch. The silence was eerie, but moments later it was broken by her muffled sobs in the bathroom. She shouldn't be alone right now.

I sent James a quick text.

I'm at Telly's. It's a long story. I'll be there as soon as I can.

Are you okay? he replied.

I'm fine. Helping Telly with a personal crisis.

I couldn't help but feel the weight of everything changing. Holly was getting a husband. Telly was getting a baby. And I wasn't sure I'd ever have either. I sat on the couch, listening as Telly's grief spilled out. It was strange, listening to her pain. The crying in her office a couple weeks back was nothing compared to this. In the years I'd known her, I'd believed she was impervious to, well, everything. Was she going to keep it? Was she going to tell Will? Maybe I had it all wrong and she was crying tears of joy that she would be a mother.

More cries echoed down the hall. Nope, it didn't sound joyful at all. After twenty heart-wrenching minutes, I knocked on the bathroom door.

"Telly. Are you okay?"

"Yeah," she sniffled. "I'm okay, you can go."

"Are you sure? I can stay. I don't mind."

She was silent for a minute.

"Telly?" I called and she opened the door. Other than her pink eyes and nose, she looked totally normal. She cleared her throat.

"I'm fine. Seriously, it's all these fucking hormones," she said in a deep, serious tone.

Yeah, right.

She walked passed me and I followed her to the kitchen.

"Do you want to talk about it?" I asked.

"Actually, can we just pretend it didn't happen? At least until I figure this shit out." She leaned on the counter and turned her head toward the ceiling. "Ugh. I need a drink!"

"Sorry, but I'm not going to pretend enough to allow you to have a cocktail," I said.

She turned to me and let out a deep sigh. "Fair enough."

27

Three's A Crowd

WHEN I FELT COMFORTABLE ENOUGH to leave Telly alone, I headed to James' as originally planned. The day had turned into an overwhelming mess, and I felt this sudden sense of urgency to have a real, open conversation with James. When I entered his apartment, ready to spill my guts, David was sitting on the couch sipping on an amber-colored drink.

"Hey," James said and greeted me with a kiss. "Everything okay?"

"We can talk about it when he leaves." I glanced over to David who held up his glass.

James pulled me aside. "David's staying here tonight."

"Can we just get him a cab home? I really need to talk to you," I whispered.

"We can talk upstairs. He can't go home tonight,"

James said.

Oh, yes he could.

"What's going on?" I called to David.

"You should ask Rachel," he said.

I turned back to James, waiting for an explanation. But honestly, I'd had enough of other people's drama for one night.

"Tell you what. You guys have a boys night or whatever, and I'll go home."

"Cool!" David leaned back into the couch.

"Are you sure?" James asked.

"Yeah, it's late and it's been a long day. I should just go to bed."

"Okay, I'll call you a cab," he said.

I folded my arms in front of my chest. "That would be nice. Thank you."

I couldn't explain it, but I wanted to dash out of there. If I'd had my jogging shoes, I would've run the whole way home. Instead, James and I waited outside for the cab.

I sat on the cement stairs that led up to his building and he nestled in next to me. "What's going on with David?" I asked.

"Rachel asked him to leave. He's gonna stay with me for a couple of days while she cools off."

"Well, I can't say I'm surprised." I shrugged.

"Yeah, but I'm trying to be supportive." He rubbed his hand along my back.

"You're a good friend." I smiled.

"What happened with Telly? Is she okay?" he asked.

"Yes and no. She's pregnant."

"What? No way!" He pulled his body away, his eyes and mouth wide in awe. I nodded slowly in my own disbelief. "Does she know whose it is?"

"James!" I shoved him. "Of course she does!" Okay, it wasn't a totally unreasonable question, but I had to act like it was. What were friends for anyway?

"I bet it's Will's baby," he said in a singsong voice.

"Yep." I tried to imagine what Telly's new life would be like with Will's baby. Assuming she decided to have it.

"I knew it!" He snapped his fingers. "Those two are meant to be. I'm sure of it now."

"What are you talking about? They're sooo not meant to be." I shook my head with conviction. "And neither are Holly and Noom, for that matter. Why are all the mismatched couples committing and the perfect ones aren't?" I raised my voice slightly.

"What?" James asked with a slight chuckle, but there was nothing funny about it.

"Never mind. Are we still going shopping tomorrow?" I asked.

"Yeah, but David's going to tag along. Is that okay?" he asked, knowing that I probably wasn't okay with it. If he wanted to support his friend then I needed to support him. At least, that's what Charlotte McQueen would say.

"Sure, why not."

"Thanks, Marin. I'm sure he's not your favorite person right now," James said.

"He's not, but you are." I gave James a half smile and he kissed me.

He looked concerned. "Are you okay?"

"There's some stuff I want to talk to you about." The cab pulled up and I stood to leave, glad to leave our needed talk for another night.

"What stuff? Is it bad?" he asked.

"No, it's fine." I assured him with another kiss. "We'll talk later when David's not around."

"Okay," he said and I hopped into the cab and waved goodbye.

Then I was alone, which was a relief in some ways and unsettling in others. I took a long hot shower, trying to scrub it all away, Holly's engagement, Telly's pregnancy, the likelihood of Rachel's separation, and the "possibility" of getting married. It was too much for one week.

Sleep didn't come as easy as I thought. After tossing and turning for an hour I got up and opened a bottle of white and a container of hummus, not even bothering with a glass. I'd need the whole thing to knock me out.

With a TV drama playing in the background, pita chip crumbs littering my shirt, I swigged from a half-empty bottle of wine. My strong buzz imbued me with a false sense of inspiration. For whatever reason, I had the bright idea to drunk-dial Jack.

"Marin?" he answered.

"Jack," I said.

"What's going on? It's late."

"I dunno. I just felt like calling you, so I did, and here we are. Crazy running into each other, huh?" I slurred my words.

He snickered. "Are you drunk?"

"Yes. I'm drinking out of the bottle. Alone! And almost finished a tub of hummus. I'm a hot mess. Do you know what that is?" There was no way to stop it, and I'd definitely regret the hell out of it in the morning.

"I do know what a hot mess is, and I doubt you are one. Are you all right? Do you want me to come over?" he asked.

Drunk or not, the answer was a firm, "No."

"Why?" he asked.

"You know why," I told him seriously.

"What? You think something might happen?" He chuckled.

"Pff! Nothing's going to happen, okay. I am faith—ful!" I had my hand on my hip, pointing my finger with attitude.

"Is that why you called me and not your boyfriend?"

I thought about it for a moment, as much as I could in my state. Why had I called Jack?

"No, I called you because some crazy shit went down today and my boyfriend, who I love but won't marry me, is preoccupied at the moment with probably even more crazy shit."

"What happened?" he asked.

"Everything's a mess. My best friend got engaged to a guy she should not marry, my other best friend is pregnant and she should not be having a baby. Meanwhile, I'm with a great guy, I'm ready for marriage, for a baby, and I get nothing! What's wrong with me?"

"Nothing's wrong with you, love. You're perfect."

I scoffed. "Yeah, right. If I'm so perfect, then why

did you convince me that we could do a long distance relationship and dump me anyway?"

"Because I'm an ass. It was a mistake," he said and for a second, I stopped breathing. Did he just say letting me go was a mistake? My cheeks began to flush. "I never should have ended things when you went to Boston. I was young and stupid."

"Jack, you don't have to do this," I said, when what I meant was *don't do this*. For years, I wanted to hear him say those words. Maybe even up until he actually said them, I still wanted to hear them. Now that he was confessing the regrets of his soul, I couldn't bear it.

"No, I should've told you years ago," he said with a soft, regretful voice.

I glanced at the mantel of a photo of James and me in Napa, and felt a twinge of guilt and nausea. I couldn't have this conversation, especially not when I was drunk in the late hours of the night. Especially after the day I'd had.

"Jack, I gotta go. Sorry I called so late." I hung up before he could say anything and shook it off like a bad dream. The rest of the wine went down the sink drain, and I forced myself to go to bed. No more phone calls until I sobered up.

It wasn't even six on that Saturday morning when my head began to spin around yesterday's events, so much so that my stomach coiled. What a nightmare. I longed for the days before my birthday, when Holly was just a planeteer, Telly was, well, Telly. When Jack was only a memory, and James and I were just happy to have each other. So much was changing and it would never be the same.

My unsettled gut churned more and I rushed to the toilet. Gross. Drinking almost an entire bottle of wine by myself was out of the question from now on. I pulled the lever and watched the remnants of the night's indulgence flush into oblivion. If only the rest of the night could go with it.

I sat against the wall in the bathroom and took in a deep breath. Somehow my life had spun out of control. I had been so consumed with my shit that I got lost in it. I was acting like a spoiled child. In front of the bathroom mirror, I splashed cold water on my face and took a good hard look at myself. "It's time to grow up, Marin," I told my reflection. "You're no spring chicken."

I got dressed and tried to stomach some shred of breakfast. James showed up around eleven with a fresh coffee and tag-a-long David. I was happy to see one, but not the other.

I needed to be mature. Take the high road.

"You ready, baby?" James asked, handing over the warm paper cup. My face lit with a fake smile. Fake it until you make it, right? I followed the guys to James' car.

James and I had been planning a trip to the home improvement store to pick out paint and some new appliances. It was supposed to be a romantic outing, but I'd have to settle for a third wheel. I hadn't talked to Rachel to see what he'd done, so I didn't know if I should be pissed at him or not. Wives didn't kick their husbands out for nothing.

I sighed. For the sake of ignorance and maturity, I needed to remain indifferent.

"What do you think about this?" I asked James and opened the doors of the stainless steel double-door fridge with an ice dispenser. I'd always wanted one of those. I never had ice in my freezer because I always forgot to make it.

"It's nice." He pulled a piece of paper from his pocket then compared the measurements on it to the numbers on the tag. "Oh, yeah. It'll fit."

I grinned and tried to imagine the appliance in the new space along with all my other ideas about the kitchen update.

"I think you can go bigger," David added, pulling me out of my daydream state. "Like this one." He walked over to a towering hunk of metal, the kind of fridge that only a professional athlete would need.

"It's just the two of us. We don't need that much storage," James said.

"It won't always be just the two of us," I said smiling.

"Yeah, because I'll be moving in with you guys, and we'll need more room to stash the beer." David stood back and admired the oversized refrigerator.

"What's he talking about?" I whispered to James.

He shrugged.

It was like that the entire time we were in appliances. Eventually I asked James if we could come back another day, but he insisted that we finish the shopping trip.

As we walked the aisles, I realized that we were in a

fully stocked warehouse of home improvement items. Any issue with a house could be fixed with the objects that lined the shelves.

Wouldn't it be amazing if every city contained relationship improvement stores? Have a broken heart? You can paint it a new color and start fresh. Your husband's a pain in the ass? There's a part to fix that. Sure, relationship improvement stores would make my occupation obsolete, but I could always find another trade, like owning a winery or writing books about life's crazy shenanigans.

Oh, well. A girl could dream.

On the way to the paint department, I asked David if he wouldn't mind getting brushes, tape, rollers, and other supplies.

"I want to help you guys pick out paint. Rachel never lets me help with stuff like this," David said.

"There's probably a good reason for that," I said under my breath.

James shot me a disapproving look.

We browsed the array of swatches filed neatly in sections by brand. I didn't care about brands, just colors. After nearly four years in my apartment, I was sick of white walls. It was always my intention to put some color on them, but knowing that I'd have to change it back when I moved out had left me with little motivation to brighten my space.

I'd already been browsing Pinterest for ideas and I was set on no-nonsense neutrals. I went straight for the beige, grays, and a few fair blues for the bedroom, testing the swatches under different lighting.

"Do you like this Khaki?" I asked James.

"Yeah," he said.

"Or what about this Sandpiper?" I handed him another swatch.

"Honestly, baby, I'm sure whatever you pick out is fine. I don't care that much about paint."

Carte blanche with the paint? Hell yes!

"This color's pretty cool." David stood in another section holding a single swatch.

Even from ten feet away, I could tell it was a bad choice.

"Yeah, I like that too. Marin?" James handed me the wine-colored sample. I didn't like wine stains on my mouth, and I definitely didn't like them on my walls.

I scowled.

"Are you sure? It's called Bordeaux," James said.

"Cool name. Bad color." I turned back to my approved stack of shades.

"I wish I had this color in my bedroom. It's kinda sexy," David added.

Yuck. I rolled my eyes and looked at James. "I thought you didn't care about colors."

"I do and I don't. David's just trying to help," he said.

"Oh, you're gonna like this one." David handed over a hideous, dark hunter green card.

My face grew hot. Was he fucking with me?

"Why don't you two get some supplies or go look at power tools or something?"

"Babe," James said, "c'mon."

This was his fault for bringing his pain-in-the-ass friend.

"Please," I begged. "Give me twenty minutes alone and I'll be done."

"Yeah, man, let's go," David waved for James to follow him.

Thank God.

Half an hour later, James and David returned and the paint was almost done mixing. I'd only picked out enough for a few rooms, but the colors were perfect.

"What are these for?" James asked picking up the three sample sized tins of paint in green, blue, and purple.

I shrugged. "They're nursery ideas. I really like the colors."

"Are you pregnant?" David snapped.

"No."

"This is exactly what I'm talking about." David glared at James. "She's already got your whole life planned for you, colors and everything. Don't you think you're getting a little ahead of yourself? You haven't even closed on the house yet."

"C'mon, man," James said in an apparent attempt to get him to shut up.

"What? I'm just telling you what I wish someone had told me."

James inched closer to David. "This isn't the time or the place."

Was there ever a time and place for him to act like such an asshole?

James turned toward me. "Let's just pay for everything and go home."

I glowered then pushed the cart toward the check-out, the guys trailing behind.

"I bet you're buying all this shit too," David muttered to James just loud enough for me to hear. I squeezed the handle on the cart and it took everything I had not to say something back that would only make it worse. Instead, I ignored him.

The three of us were silent in the car on the way home. I sat with my arms crossed and my body turned toward the door. I wanted to call Rachel and tell her to come and get her husband. He was being a dick. We got back to James' and unloaded our purchases. Boxes piled high along James' walls and his shelves were almost bare in preparation for the move. Marvin nudged me with his nose, and I patted his head.

"Be right back," James said and ran up the stairs to the bathroom. I knelt down and scratched Marvin behind his soft ears. David whistled for the canine and he obeyed.

"Have you talked to Rachel?" I asked.

"Nope," he said, not taking his eyes off the dog.

"What happened? I thought things were getting better in counseling."

"Me too. I guess you're not as good of a therapist as you thought."

"What's with the shitty attitude? Even your wife can't stand being around you."

He shot me a dirty glance, and I folded my arms over my chest. "She can't get over what happened. That's why

I had to leave."

"What are you talking about? She forgave you."

"She may have forgiven me, but she'll never trust me again. People don't forget when you've hurt them. It's funny. The same day she found out I slept with someone is the same day James found out about all your lies. You think he forgot about that whole thing?"

I choked on impending tears and my muscles tightened.

He scoffed. "Yeah, I guess we're not so different, are we?"

The bathroom door creaked open.

I fought back the urge to cry.

"You guys wanna get some lunch?" James asked with a smile as he walked down the steps. It quickly faded when he entered the room.

"Can you take me home?" I asked James. He looked at me, then at David, then back at me.

"Sure."

I waited in the car while he loaded empty boxes in the back.

"Are you okay?" he asked, pulling the car out onto the street.

"Do I look okay?" I snapped.

"What happened?" He sounded alarmed.

"Like you don't know. David's been antagonizing me all day. You should've heard what he said to me when you were in the other room."

"What did he say?"

I never wanted to bring up that time in our life again,

as I was lucky enough to get out of it the first time.

"Never mind, you don't care anyway," I mumbled and coiled into myself.

"Yes, I do," he said.

"Then why didn't you stick up for me before?"

"I'm trying to go easy on him. He's having a rough time."

"He's having a rough time? What about me? I'm having a rough time."

"With what?" he raised his voice.

"You really don't get it, do you?" I stared out the window, anxious to see the buildings on my street.

"Marin, what are you talking about?"

"My friends are moving on with their lives. Holly's getting married. Telly's having a baby, and for all we know, Rachel's getting a divorce."

"And?"

"And, we've been together for almost two years. I'm ready to move on to the next step."

He let out an annoyed sigh. "We are moving to the next step. We close in two weeks."

"I'm not talking about the house. I'm talking about getting married."

"Can we please just move in first? We've known each other for two years, but we've only truly been together a year and a half." His words were a slap in the face after what David had said.

"I don't want to talk about this anymore," I said.

"Fine."

Neither of us spoke the rest of the way to my apartment. When we got there, he unloaded the empty boxes and said we would talk later. We were supposed to have the entire weekend to get ready for our move. Thanks to David, the whole day had been a bust. I had no motivation to pack up my stuff to move. Why would I want to live with someone who didn't want anything more and wouldn't even stick up for me in front of his friends? I wanted to scream and cry and throw a fit.

After everything I had done with the *McQueen Method*, I was no closer to getting a proposal than before my birthday. Maybe David was right. Maybe he and I would always be the ones who broke their hearts that day. It was a permanent strike against us. I thought I had earned my way out of that mess. Why couldn't James see what I could see so clearly? What if he never proposed? Was that the kind of life I'd want? A marriageless existence? Could I live with it? Was it enough?

An Affair To Forget

ONLY MINUTES AFTER JAMES LEFT, someone knocked on my door.

It had to be James, back to apologize and make things right with us. As he should.

I opened the door. "Rachel, what are you doing here?"

"I need to talk to you." She pushed past me and headed straight to my kitchen. "I don't know what I'm doing anymore." She retrieved a chilled bottle of vodka from the freezer and attempted to make herself a drink.

"What are you talking about?" I stole the bottle from her grip and she began to sob. "What happened?"

"I've been having an affair." Rachel covered her face. The two-carat diamond ring sparkled on her ring finger.

"Are you serious?" I asked with wide eyes.

Rachel nodded. "I don't know what to do." She leaned into me and began sobbing. I stroked her long dark hair, trying to calm her. After a minute, I peeled her off.

"Rachel, look at me. What happened?"

Her tears slowed, and she stumbled to the couch where she curled in a ball like a little girl sobbing. I handed her a tissue.

"I couldn't forget, Marin. I tried. Sometimes I could pretend and sometimes I even believed I was over it, but I wasn't. So I thought if I was with someone else behind his back we would be even and I could move on with my life."

"Was it only one time?"

"No, it was more than one time. It's been going on for a while."

"With who?"

"Bobby, my trainer." Always the fitness trainer. It all made sense as to why she'd been so off the last few months.

"Does David know?" I asked.

She shook her head. "No, I told him I didn't think it was going to work between us and that we should separate. I mean, how could it? He lied to me, I lied to him."

"Is that all? You said it's been going on for a while. Do you have feelings for the other guy?"

"I dunno. I dunno what I feel or think anymore. I just know I'm not proud of it. I want it to stop. I want something to change."

I could commiserate with her. I wanted something to change too.

"You need to tell David what you just told me."

She cried harder. "I know I should, but I don't want to hurt him like he hurt me."

"But isn't that why you did it in the first place?"

She lowered her head and said nothing. I thought back to her bachelorette party in Vegas, how she told me about her reservations outside the hotel. Maybe she should have listened to herself instead of listening to me.

"I'm sorry," I said.

"It's okay, you're right."

"No, I'm sorry about all of this. I feel like it's my fault."

"It's not."

"I should have listened to you when you confided your fears about marrying David. None of this would have happened if I hadn't gone all crazy after Chad. And I couldn't fix it, which forced you into a position of breaking your vows."

"It's not yours to fix. We made mistakes of our own free will."

We sat together for a while until finally I convinced her to find David and tell him the truth so they could move on. I didn't know what that meant for their future, but what was done was done and only time would tell.

"Just do me a favor," she said before leaving.

"What's that?"

"Whenever you do get married, make sure that it's the right thing for you. If you have even a shred of doubt, don't do it." Her words hit me hard.

I looked around my emptying apartment. Was I making a doubtful commitment by buying a house with James and not knowing where it would lead? Was I doing the right thing? Her words settled over me like an uncertain cloud. I couldn't just sit there anymore. I needed a run.

Sun warmed my cheeks against the cool breeze as I jogged swiftly near the lake. Physically, I could run out the negative energy but mentally, it lingered. I tried not to think about it all. Maybe I needed some time away to clear my head or at least quiet my thoughts.

"Marin," a voice called from behind. I slowed and turned back.

"Jack?" I said and stopped long enough for him to catch up with me.

"Hey, what are you doing here?" He smiled from ear to ear.

"Me? This is my park." Okay, now it was getting weird.

"What? You own it or something?" he joked, but I wasn't amused.

"Are you stalking me for real?" I kept my distance.

"Don't be so full of yourself, Marin. I don't even know where you live."

"So you say." I rolled my eyes.

"I'm glad I ran into you though. I've been worried about you," he said.

"You have, why?"

"Last night when you called, you sounded upset."

Life changes and alcohol could do that to a girl.

"Thanks for your concern, but I never should've called you," I said.

"No, I'm glad you did. You can call me anytime."

He gave me that look. The kind that said I could trust him, but if I was smart, I'd run far, far away and avoid him like the plague. But he was being kind and concerned. Was he the type of man now who would stick up for me in front of David?

"I think I need more fuel. Have you eaten yet?" he asked.

"No, I've got to get back to my apartment to pack," I lied.

"Let me take you to lunch, then I'll help you pack." He began running backward so he could face me.

"I appreciate it, but no thanks." I tried not to look at him, but kept my eyes on the run.

"Come on, I know you're hungry. That's probably why you're so cranky."

"I'm not cranky," I snapped.

He came to a stop. "Marin, please, I promise I'll be on my best behavior." I don't know exactly why I did it. Maybe it was because I was mad at James. Maybe it was because of what David said. All I know is an hour later the two of us were sitting together outside of a café. I was on my second cocktail, munching fries, and he had just scarfed down a burger. We had finished laughing at an old anecdote when we found ourselves sitting quietly for a moment. I took a swig from my Cosmopolitan.

"You know what I think?" he asked, as he looked around at the other restaurant patrons.

"What?"

"You're the prettiest girl here." He smiled and sipped his water.

"Pff!" I said and gave him a dismissive wave. "What are you talking about? I'm in jogging clothes. My hair's in a messy ponytail and I'm pretty sure my deodorant's wearing off."

"I didn't say you were the sweetest smelling girl here," he said.

I chucked a fry at him.

It was fun, the kind of fun that was exciting and familiar all at the same time. Aside from a few compliments, he kept his hands and his heart to himself. Was there a purpose to his reappearance? If I believed that all of my movie moments with James were a sign from the universe, then surely all my accidental run-ins with Jack had to be the same, right?

When the server brought the check, I should have said goodbye and left him forever. After all, I had pretty much dodged him every chance I could since he'd popped back into my life. Maybe that's why he kept showing up. Maybe there really was unfinished business.

"Do you need help packing?" he asked.

"Sure."

"Great! I can meet your boyfriend then." He closed the bill leaving a generous tip.

"He's not coming."

"Oh, are you sure it's okay?" he asked.

"It's fine. We're just friends, right?"

Right?

"Of course." He smiled.

We walked the rest of the five blocks to my place. With every step, I grew more unsure about having him at my place alone, but I stuck to my guns. Besides, no matter how mad I was at James, I wasn't Rachel, and nothing was going to happen.

"Here it is!" I opened the door, and he stepped inside, glancing around the room.

"This is a great place. Why are you moving?" he asked. Obviously, he hadn't seen the house on Fell Street.

"The new house blows this place out of the water."

"Really?"

I showed him around, careful not to invite him inside any other rooms. In fact, I had to keep him confined to the living room just in case he wanted to try something funny. I showed him the items in the living room that had to go first and handed him a small pile of newspaper. He inquired or commented about each piece he wrapped up, like he was trying to get to know me better. Then he got to the framed picture of James and me.

"So this is him, huh?" he asked, examining the photo.

"Yep." I gave a polite smile from across the room.

"He's a good looking guy. I just hope he knows how lucky he is."

"Lucky that he's good looking?" I asked.

Jack chuckled. "No, lucky to have you."

I looked away. Did James know how lucky he was to have me? He certainly hadn't acted like it today.

"It's so quiet. Can we put on some music? Where're your CDs?" He began opening my cabinets for the missing music.

"CDs?" I scoffed.

"We're old friends. We should listen to music the old way."

"Second cabinet on the right." I motioned to my stash, and watched him out of the corner of my eye as he sorted through the few CDs I'd kept after converting everything to digital.

"You kept this one?" he asked, pulling out one of my favorites from an infamous pop princess.

"It's a classic, Jack. You just wait," I joked.

"Oh, my God. You still have this?" He pulled a white case with a picture of the singer and his guitar.

"Of course. I love Mayer," I said.

"You used to have this on all the time. I still think of you any time I hear these songs." He opened the case and placed the CD carefully in my DVD player. The only place left in my apartment to play the discs. Just the scratchy sound of a guitar and it was as if we had been transported back to my dorm room, me in a t-shirt and panties, lying on my stomach, reading my anatomy text, Jack in his underwear studying at my desk.

"Good times, huh?" he said.

"Yeah." I smiled. After that, we packed in silence. Not an empty, awkward silence, but a comfortable peace. Track after track, we filled boxes with my belongings. Then, as our old song filled the room, his gaze caught mine and I knew he was thinking the same thing I was. How had we gotten here?

He opened his mouth as if to speak, but instead turned back to his task. My heart pounded, wishing he would say something. Do something, something that would give me some answers or at least a sign about what to do.

A moment later, almost as if he had heard my thoughts, he put down my white pillar candle and began moving toward the bar where I was wrapping my glassware. With each step he took, I grew tense and weak.

"Don't do this," he said with a frustrated look.

"Do what?" My heart began to race.

"This." He waved his finger around the moving boxes. "Move in with me instead."

"Are you serious?"

And crazy?

"Yes. Every time I wrap something in paper, I think to myself 'that would look nice in my place, or she would look nice in my place.' I think the reason we keep running into each other is because we're supposed to be together."

"Why would we want to be together?" I said. "We're not the same people we once were. Besides, I'm with someone and you don't even want kids." I walked to the other side of the bar, keeping my distance.

He followed behind. "I do. You make me want a family."

Was he saying that he changed for me? If I could change Jack's mind, couldn't I change James'?

"Seeing you again brought up all those old feelings. I don't think I ever stopped loving you."

I searched his eyes for the old Jack, the Jack I loved. Somewhere buried deep inside, did I still love him too? Could I love him again?

Next thing I knew Jack knelt before me, holding my hand tightly in his. My heart pounded and my stomach fluttered.

"I know it sounds crazy, but I think we should do this. You and me. If you want marriage, then we'll get married. We'll have a baby. We'll be a family like we always talked about when we were together."

"Jack . . . I can't."

"Why not?" He looked desperate.

"You know why not." I felt dizzy. Was this really happening? "Look, I'm sorry if I gave you the wrong impression, but I love my boyfriend."

"What if that's all he'll ever be, huh? Your boyfriend. I'm offering you a whole life. Everything you've ever wanted."

"There's nothing between us." I pulled my hand away and walked toward the door.

"That's a lie and you know it."

"Fine. Maybe there is still something, but it's not enough," I said.

"It could be more, just give us a chance," he begged.

"I can't, Jack. You have to go." I turned the doorknob and he took my face in his hands. I looked into his sad, sweet eyes for a second before looking away.

He tried to bring my gaze up. "Please, Marin, don't let this second chance slip away. Please."

He leaned in and I watched his mouth inch closer to mine. I wanted to stop him, but the pull between us was too strong. Jack's lips touched mine and I let them. The sensation was different than it had been when we were together years earlier, different in an unfamiliar sort of way.

"Stop," I said. "I can't do this. You have to go. Now!" I pushed him out the door while he tried to argue his way back. I slammed it, locked the deadbolt, and fastened the chain. My face felt hot and my stomach twisted in pangs of remorse.

I slid down my door and curled into myself. What had just happened? A moment later, tears burst from my eyes, and I cried on the floor for a while. Eventually, I took a deep breath and found my cell. My hands shook as I sent Telly an urgent text to come over as soon as possible.

29

The Commitment Test

A N HOUR LATER, Telly was at my door and I invited her inside.

"Are you okay?" she asked, sounding worried.

"I need to tell you something, and I hope you won't judge me for it," I said as she slipped off her heels.

"Please, I'm the unmarried, knocked-up one. What's up?"

"I kissed my ex-boyfriend today. Well, he kissed me." I covered my mouth with my hands.

"Are you talking about Chad?"

"Fuck no!" I snapped. "I'm talking about Jack, my college boyfriend."

"Oh, yeah, you told me about him before. What happened? I thought you hadn't seen him since you left medical school."

I let out a long sigh. "We ran into each other a few weeks ago when I was in San Diego." I bit my lip.

"Really?" She rested her chin on her hand, waiting for me to tell the whole story. "Is he hot?"

"He's gorgeous. He's a cosmetic surgeon for God sakes."

"So what happened?"

"James and I had a fight, then Rachel came over to confess her affair."

Telly gasped. "Rachel cheated on David? No way!"

I nodded. My shocked expression mirroring Telly's.

"Wow, I have a lot more respect for little miss goodie-two-shoes. That's how I would have handled it."

I rolled my eyes. "Anyway, I was really upset, so I went for a run and ran into Jack. Again."

"Again?"

"Yeah, he's popped up a few times."

"That's weird."

"Right?"

"So we ended up having a drink, then I invited him here to help me pack, and the next thing I know, he's down on one knee proposing marriage!"

She raised her eyebrows. "Marin, you have to stay away from this guy. He sounds crazy."

"He's not crazy. He's just . . . passionate."

"Does James know?" Telly asked.

"Know what? That another guy wants me worse than he does?"

"No, I mean, does he know you've seen him?"

"He only knows about the couple of times in San Diego."

Telly smirked. "Well, well, well. Look at you being all sneaky."

My cheeks flushed with shame. "I'm so confused. On one hand I love James, but I don't think he ever wants to remarry. And I feel like I shouldn't have to give up on marriage. Meanwhile, Jack's willing to give me everything I want."

"I hope you're not thinking of taking him up on his offer?" She pursed her lips with attitude.

"No. I dunno. Maybe I should. Like you said, it's weird how he keeps popping up. Like the universe is purposefully pushing him toward me. I can't ignore that. But I love James and I want him. Now I'm thinking that maybe he's not the one for me. Maybe we shouldn't be buying a house together. Maybe there's someone else out there for me."

"Like Jack?"

"Maybe." I covered my face in my hands. "I can't even believe I'm saying these things. What do you think?"

"I think you should bang this Jack guy and whoever's better is probably the one."

I lightly shoved her shoulder. "I'm serious. I need help."

"I can see that." Telly made a face. "You should talk to James. Tell him what you're afraid of."

"I know I should, but I'm afraid that I'm right, and I'm afraid that I'll have to walk away."

"Then you walk away. This is your life. You need to do what's best for you, because ultimately you're the one who has to live with your decisions."

I gnawed on my lip. "Have you made a decision?" I gestured at her belly, which was still flat as a board.

"Yeah." Her eyes met mine and her silence said it all. She wasn't going to keep the baby.

"Are you sure?" I asked.

"Yeah, I'm sure. I have an appointment tomorrow."

"Do you need me to take you?" Though, I knew Telly felt it was the right thing for her. I hated the idea that she had to go through with it. How awful.

"No, I've made other arrangements." Telly dropped her head and played with her nails.

"Will?"

"Yeah," she said, still not looking up.

"How's he taking all of this?" I scooted closer to her.

"He wants me to keep it, but I told him my body, my decision."

"Good argument. That's why you're such a great lawyer." I smiled and nudged her with my shoulder.

"And that's why I'll get to stay one."

The next afternoon, James was at my door, looking serious, almost angry.

"We need to talk," he said, taking a seat on my couch.

My heart thumped against my chest and I swallowed a hard lump in my throat. I sat next to him, keeping my distance so I could see his face.

"I know," I uttered.

"You've been weird since Easter, maybe even a little before then."

"I know. I'm sorry." I lowered my head.

"What's going on? Is it the house? Do you feel like we made the commitment to buy too soon?"

"You're kidding, right? My problem isn't commitment. My problem is lack of commitment." I stood up, ready to hash it out.

"What do you mean?" He looked so clueless, I almost felt bad for him.

"Do you remember our last night in Mexico, when you gave me the band-aid cuff?" He nodded. "I thought you were going to propose that night. I've been waiting for you to propose since Christmas and I'm afraid I'll always be waiting."

James said nothing.

Where was his band-aid now? "I don't want to be one of those people who gets their heart broken slowly over time. If it's not gonna happen you should be honest. Tell me right now that you don't want to marry me." A tear rolled down my cheek.

"It's not that I don't want to marry you."

"Right, you just don't want to marry anyone. Why?"

"I don't trust it. Look what happened to me, what happened to you, what's happening to Rachel and David, it's a curse."

"It's not a curse if it's the right person." I cried and he looked into my eyes in a way that made my heart plummet into my stomach. I shook my head and looked away. "You don't know if I'm the right person. If you did, we wouldn't be having this conversation."

"Marin, listen to me," he grabbed my shoulders like he wanted me to really hear him. "I don't know what the future holds, but I know that I love you and I want to be with you for as long as it lasts. For whatever it brings. Can't that be enough?"

"I thought it could, but I don't know anymore." My eyes were flooded with fresh tears. How had it come to this? This wasn't what I'd planned.

"What are you saying?" His expression looked panic-stricken.

"I don't know what I want. Maybe I need more than you're willing to give. I definitely know that I need some time to figure things out."

"How much time?"

"I don't know."

"What about the house?"

"You don't need me to buy that house." My tears slowed and I felt the end was coming. I'd have to say goodbye to any future I had with James.

"But I do need you." He squeezed my arms tighter.

"I don't think you do," I said, and released myself from his grip. I couldn't look at him.

"Are you sure about this?" he asked.

I nodded, keeping my eyes on the floor, but I saw him maneuvering around the boxes as he walked slowly toward the door. As much as I didn't want him to walk out, I had to let him.

"I think this is a mistake, but I'll give you the time you think you need. I love you, Marin." With that, he closed the door and was gone.

"I love you too," I blubbered to myself and broke down onto a pile of moving boxes. How had I gotten to this place? I thought about that day in Katie's office when she told me about her divorce. Maybe she was right. Sometimes you're just disappointed.

30

Breakups And Makeups

I SHOWED UP TO TELLY'S with ice cream and a bottle of wine. I figured that between her loss and mine, we could sulk together. She opened the door and looked surprised to see me.

"I'm still pregnant," she said, but I barely registered the words.

"James and I broke up." I held up the coping mechanisms I brought with me.

"You win." She let me inside and reached for the ice cream.

"I guess this is just for me, then." I walked to the kitchen, placed the wine on the counter, and rummaged in a drawer for the bottle opener.

"But I can eat some of this." Telly examined the nutritional facts on the carton. "I'm gonna get fat anyway. Might as well enjoy myself for once."

I poured myself a glass as quickly as I could fill it and downed it even quicker.

"What happened? Did you tell him about Jack?" she asked.

"No, I told him I needed some time."

"I'm so sorry," she said and rubbed my shoulder as I began to cry for what felt like the millionth time since it had happened.

"Me too. I just wish I was enough to change his mind."

"You mean change him?" she asked, and I nodded, covering my face. "That's the lie we like to believe. Women think they can change men, and men think their woman will never change."

I sobbed some more, sipping intermittently.

"Marin, you did the right thing."

"Then why don't I feel good about it?"

"Because you love him. And it just happened. Give it some time. You'll work it out."

"So you didn't go through with the abortion?" I wiped my tears away.

She shook her head and flashed a small smile.

"What changed your mind?"

"I don't know. I don't know if I'll change it again before it's too late. But I've done this before. In college. Even though I know it was the right thing to do, it still haunts me. I didn't think it would matter, but it did. Now that I'm older and can actually provide for a child, I think it would haunt me more. I just couldn't do it."

"What does Will think?"

"Oh, my God, he's ecstatic, and if I'm being honest. I'm kinda excited too." She rubbed her hand on her belly and I put my hand on top of hers.

"Telly, you're having a baby!" I smiled and turned on the waterworks again.

"I'm having a baby. It sounds so weird."

I took her hand and squeezed it. "It's gonna be great. I know it. I'm gonna help you with anything you need."

"Thanks. I appreciate that." Telly pulled a couple bowls from a cabinet and began scooping ice cream while I made myself comfortable at the table. "When was the last time you talked to Holly?" she asked.

"The night we found out you were pregnant. Why?"

"She called. She's worried about you. You really should talk to her about all this."

I sighed and frowned. "I know."

"Why don't you ask her to come over and join us?" Telly suggested.

I pulled out my phone, but hesitated to dial. "You think?"

Telly stuck a spoonful of ice cream in her mouth. "Mmhmm, call her," she said. So I called Holly to come over and we waited for her.

"I really appreciate your support with this pregnancy," she said.

"Of course, you're my best friend." I smiled.

"So is Holly, and I think you need to show her the same support with her engagement. That's what friends do," Telly said in a stern manner.

I shot her an astonished look. "You know, you're gonna be good at this mom thing."

"I know, right? I'm gonna be the coolest mom ever."

Telly did a little sexy dance and I smirked.

When Holly showed up she walked in hesitantly and kept a fair distance. Telly gave her some ice cream and a glass of wine and told her about the pregnancy. Holly was shocked, but overjoyed for her. Then they turned to me.

"Marin, is there something you want to say to Holly?" Telly asked.

I gave Holly an apologetic look. "I'm sorry about the way I've been acting. I haven't been fair, but I want you to know that I love you and I want you to be happy. If that means you and Noom get married then I totally support it, and I'm going to make a real effort to get to know him."

"Thank you," Holly said softly. "That means a lot to me." She gently squeezed my hand.

"There's something else," I said, dropping my head.

"What?"

"James and I broke up." Just saying the words made my heart break again. I tried to hold back more tears. "Well, we're technically on a break, but I think it's a permanent one."

"Oh, no," Holly put her arm around me. "What happened?"

"We want different things, and I told him I needed some time to figure things out," I cried.

"I don't understand. You love him and want to be with him and he loves you and wants to be with you too. That's why he's getting a thirty-year mortgage with you. How is that different?"

"Yeah, but I want to get married and he doesn't," I

said.

Telly watched our exchange while scarfing down another bowl of ice cream.

"I know this doesn't sound like much coming from someone who's getting married, but marriage isn't everything. Look at David and Rachel, they're married and miserable right now."

I let her words sink in as if I was hearing the message for the first time.

"All you need is love, and that's what you have with James. Isn't that what you told me? Movie night in, morning breath, grow old together love."

Sniffling, I nodded. "Yeah, I think so."

Later that night, I dreamt of James from the moment I fell asleep until I woke up. I dreamed he'd come back to me, with a ring, and that somehow we'd put it all behind us. Waking to the harsh reality that I'd only been dreaming left me feeling paralyzed. Physically and emotionally. I tried to remind myself that it was my decision and that I could make it all go away if I only accepted the life that James was willing to give.

A life of love but a marriageless life.

Was there really anything so wrong with it in the first place? Hopefully, time away would give me complete clarity to make the right decision for myself, for James, and for both of us.

I checked my phone again and again between appointments to make sure I hadn't missed a call, text, or email from James. So far, he had been silent, which I guess was good. It's what I'd asked him to do. My patients kept me busy throughout the day and helped take my mind off of things.

That afternoon as I left work, I opened my middle drawer and pulled out *How To Get a Ring on It: Get Him Down on One Knee in 90 Days or Less* by Charlotte McQueen. I headed to Neiman Marcus to return the book to Ginger. I found myself at the makeup counter, browsing the array of perfect color pallets and fifty-dollar tubes of mascara.

"Nice lipstick," the young woman behind the counter said.

"Thank you." That Ginger really could pick 'em.

"Can I help you find something?"

"I'm actually looking for Ginger Cho. I think she works in buying."

"Yeah, she's upstairs. I'll call her down for you."

Moments later, Ginger appeared, dressed like a Neiman Marcus princess with stiletto booties and chunky accessories.

"Hey, girl, what are you doing here?" Ginger asked as she pulled me in for a hug. Her chest was noticeably firmer than mine.

"I wanted to return this," I said and handed her the book. She took it and her smile quickly frowned.

"What happened?"

"The *McQueen Method* didn't work. James and I broke up," I said, looking at the floor.

"Are you serious? What happened? Is it permanent?"

"I don't know, but he told me he doesn't want to get married."

"And you told him you needed time?"

I nodded, trying desperately not to cry. As if I had any tears left.

"Marin, you totally pulled off *Step Six: Break Up to Make Up*." She smiled.

"No, that's not why I did it."

"It doesn't matter if it was real or fake. You completed the *McQueen Method*. Now all you have to do is wait. He'll be proposing soon. You watch." She winked at me.

"Trust me. He was very clear. It's not gonna happen."

"Mind if I test out some colors?" she asked, holding a pallet of eye shadow.

I shrugged.

Ginger sat me down in front of the bright counter and began removing what was left of my makeup from the day. She could do whatever she wanted to my face. No amount of makeup could cover my heartbreak.

"When did you two break up?"

"Two days ago," I said.

"Close your eyes." She brushed shadow across my closed lids and it helped me relax. "I have total faith that it's gonna work out for you two. I can feel it."

"I hope you're right," I said and maybe she was. Maybe it was time to have a little faith. After all, if it was meant to be . . .

"Are you still coming to my wedding this weekend?" she asked, sweeping my cheeks with blush.

"Yeah, but it'll just be me."

"That's okay. Holly and her fiancé are coming. You can hang with them. That's so crazy that she's engaged, right?" You're telling me. "It just goes to show, you never know where your life will lead. Here, look." Ginger handed me a mirror so I could view her work. My face looked bright with an even tone, as if I hadn't been crying the last two days. Maybe makeup could cover my heartbreak.

"Thanks, Ginger." I handed it back with a smile.

"See, there's the hope I was looking for."

31

Mr. And Mrs. Cash

THAT SATURDAY, I SLIPPED INTO ONE of my favorite dresses, the sleeveless navy with the hidden pockets. One of James' favorites too. He could pull the zipper and the dress suddenly disappeared. I still hadn't spoken to him, and though it hadn't even been a week, I missed him like crazy.

The sun had set by the time I got to the hotel and found the gift pile. I was just in time for the ceremony. Holly and Noom were nowhere to be found among the sea of guests that filled the room. I snagged a seat in the back. Floral garlands and candlelight set the tone in the room. It was classy, romantic.

Ginger waltzed down the aisle in her gorgeous princess wedding gown that cascaded down, leaving tufts of rose-shaped fabric along the way. That's exactly what she looked like, a princess with a tiara and all. There were moments when I wanted to flee the painful reality of watching someone else get something that I'd wanted for so long, but I stayed to support my friend. I paid close attention to my emotions and reactions to everything, hoping to gain some insight into my situation.

As the bride and groom exchanged vows, I felt a strong pull. I definitely wanted that. To stand in front of my loved ones and make a promise to the man I loved. Since Jack had already proposed marriage, I tried to imagine us exchanging vows, just to see how it would feel. Could I be Mrs. Ashbury? There was a time, years ago, when I wanted that so badly. I began to tear up, but I wasn't sure if it was because of the beautiful ceremony, the fact that I missed James, or the idea that I'd never have my own wedding?

Later, at the reception, I found Holly and Noom at my assigned table. They both greeted me warmly, but sympathetically too.

"You okay?" Holly asked. I nodded, wiping a single tear. "If not, I'll take you home. Just say the word."

"I appreciate that, but really, I'm fine." I took a deep breath and there were no more tears.

Holly and Noom introduced the three of us to the other guests at our table, none of whom we knew. Most were family members of Jon's. I didn't speak much, but used my fork to pick at my food and shielded myself with a glass of red. The more we drank and ate, the friendlier we became with our tablemates. One particular couple at the table caught my interest—Roni and Vinny, who looked to be in their late fifties. It was very apparent that Jon's Uncle Vinny was madly in love with Roni and that she was, quite possibly, the love of his life.

I sipped my second glass of wine and listened as the two lovebirds regaled us with stories from their travels, giggling and flirting in between. Common phrases seemed to translate into sexual innuendos for them. Between the way they acted and their bare ring fingers, it seemed as though their relationship was fairly new.

Good for them, finding someone to be crazy about in later life. My lovebird friends, Holly and Noom, had had enough chitchat and headed for the dance floor, leaving me alone with my almost empty second glass of wine.

I leaned over to Vinny. "Where did you two meet?" The location might make a good suggestion to my pre-retiree divorcee patients.

"At a wedding," Vinny said.

"Recently?" I asked.

They got quite the chuckle out of my question. "No, Roni and I used to work the wedding circuit. She's a photographer. I was a videographer. What year was that?" Vinny appeared to be doing calculations in his mind. "Eighty-seven?"

"It was the end of eighty-six. At that holiday wedding, remember?" She pulled playfully on Vinny's tie.

"Yes, I remember," he said, leaning in and touching his nose to hers.

"That's so sweet. How long have you been married?" I asked.

She scoffed and gave me a dismissive wave. "Oh, we're not married."

"Why do you think we've lasted so long?" Vinny said with a big laugh. Roni joined him and he took her hand.

"Really?" I asked. "Do you have children?"

"We both have children from our first marriages. My son's over there," he said pointing to a man on the dance floor. "We decided years ago that we had a full family."

"Wow, so you've been together almost thirty years and never got married?" I'd never known any couples like Roni and Vinny, though I may have seen one or two like them in therapy. They were a rare breed.

"You know, that doesn't shock people now as much as it used to. You must be one of those old-fashioned types. What about you? Got a boyfriend? Girlfriend? Husband? Wife?"

I laughed. These days you really could have it all. Well, if you were lucky you could have it all.

"Boyfriend," I said.

"He let you come to this wedding all by yourself?" Roni frowned.

Normally, I would have made up a polite excuse, but there was something about them that made me feel comfortable with the truth. Also I was a little buzzed. I shook my head. "We're having some issues right now, about marriage actually."

"Let me guess. You want to get married and he's not ready, right?" Roni asked.

"Is it that obvious?" I asked.

"Not obvious, but not unusual. A lot of women feel insecure without a ring."

"Well, yeah. Don't you?"

"No way! Vinny and I know what we mean to each other." Roni winked at him, making him blush.

He turned to me. "Tell you the truth, Roni and I have both felt a little insecure at times, but that would've happened with or without wedding vows. That's just being in a relationship."

"That's true. I'm just so torn between something I want and someone I want, because it doesn't seem like I can have both."

"Listen, honey." Roni leaned over and put her hand on mine. "The only way to find real happiness is to be true to yourself by following your heart. My love story with Vinny had a complicated beginning, but it didn't stop us from getting what we wanted, when all we wanted was each other."

What they had was so incredible, and it reminded me of what Holly had said—all you need is love.

"You're totally right. I need to be true to myself." I nodded.

"I'm sure everything will work out great," she said.

I gave her a half smile. "Thanks. I appreciate that."

A moment later, Vinny stood up and offered to dance with the girl he was still crazy about.

Now, that's what I wanted. No wedding, or romantic proposal could compare to the love that was shared between those two happily unmarried people. It had been a fortunate stroke of luck to be seated next to them at Ginger's wedding. Roni had said the wise words I needed to hear.

32

The Decision

AFTER THE WEDDING, I felt empowered with a fresh outlook on everything. I decided I wasn't going to be a victim. Instead, I was going to take responsibility for my future and my happiness.

The next morning, I got a text from James.

The final walk through is on Thursday at four. I need to know if you'll be there.

Part of me wanted to run to him and tell him that I loved him and that I was sorry about taking a break. But I needed more time to know if that was the right thing to do.

I'm not sure. I'll let you know.

My best strategy when dealing with major issues had always been running. Nothing sorted my thoughts better than my feet against the pavement. The steady breathing cleared my mind of unwanted junk. So I ran that afternoon and again that evening and again and again the following days. I thought about everything that I had been through with James, about Jack's reappearance, and what it all meant. I searched my soul for the things that truly mattered to me, and let go of the things that didn't. The longer I was away from James and the more I ran, the clearer things had become. After three days of intense mental, emotional, and spiritual deliberation, my decision was made. I wouldn't apologize for it, not to James, not to my friends, and definitely not to myself.

After my run that Wednesday evening, I called Jack to come over. My stomach was full of butterflies as I awaited his arrival, and I thought my heart was going to leap from my chest when he knocked on the door.

"I didn't think you'd want to see me again," he said.

I led him inside. "Well, if there's one thing I've learned, it's that life is full of surprises."

"You can say that again." We settled in awkwardly with the usual niceties, and I served him a glass of iced tea. Neither of us mentioned the kiss or anything that had happened that day.

"You haven't finished packing," he said, seeming confused. My apartment remained somewhere between staying and going, just as I had been that last week. Staying. Going. "Have you changed your mind?"

"That's why I wanted to talk to you. About what you said. Did you mean it?"

"Every word." He put down his glass and took my hand.

I could barely look at him. "There was a time when I wished you had said all those things. And I believe you. I think you could give me that life. The life I've always dreamed of. Maybe we could be happy together. We once were . . . but that was a long time ago. And despite your intentions or mine, I just don't know if there's enough between us, enough to keep us together."

"Then why don't we give it a chance to see what's there?" He squeezed my hand and I looked into his eyes.

"Because it's not fair to you or to me. No matter what, the truth is, I'm in love with someone else, and I can't change that. You may be the better choice for all kinds of reasons. And there may come a day that I regret not taking a chance with you, but I think I'll regret it more if I don't finish what I started with James. I want you to understand that. I want you to find happiness for yourself."

He let out a sigh. "What can I do to change your mind?"

"It's not my mind that needs changing," I said.

"Right. Well, I guess that's it then."

I nodded and he let go of my hand. I could feel that he was letting me go too. We stood and I motioned him to follow me to the door. "I'm really glad we ran into each other all those times," I said.

"You are?"

"Yes." I smiled. He took me in his arms and pressed himself against me. It would be the last time he'd ever get to hold me like that and so I let him. "You'll always be special to me, Marin."

"You'll always be special to me too." I pulled away.

"Maybe I'll see you around."

"Maybe."

I stood outside my door and watched him walk away. Even though I knew I'd hurt him, that I might even miss him a little, I had no desire to call him back. As the distance grew between us, it became all the more clear that I had made the right decision for both of us.

33

Coming Home

MY PATIENTS, ABBY AND DYLAN, sat on the sofa, near one another. I'd been seeing them for over two years. It all started when Abby had felt hopeless about their less than stellar sex life. I'd never forget the two of them screaming at each other in my office. No matter what Abby thought in the beginning, plenty of passion existed between those two.

"Dr. Johns," Dylan said. "We believe we're ready."

"Ready for what?" I asked, glancing back and forth between the two of them.

"Ready to graduate therapy," he said.

I smiled and could see the accomplished looks on their faces.

Abby leaned forward. "You've been so good to us, helping us through the separation, then coming back together. Our sex life made a one-eighty, which I never thought was possible."

"I totally agree," I said. "You two put in a lot of

work and I can see it's really paid off. I'm so proud of you both."

Abby and Dylan shared a sweet glance, then he turned to me. "Thank you, Dr. Johns, for saving our marriage."

I shook my head. "No, I didn't save your marriage. You two did." I was always encouraged when a couple graduated therapy. Each time it reaffirmed my belief in love. Real love.

Abby and Dylan left me with hugs and praise, and I watched them head off on to their new life together. It was almost three-thirty, and I also would be heading off on to my new life.

Shortly after, I left the office and took a cab to Alamo Square. I pulled out my phone to call James, but he was already calling in.

"Hey," I said, my voice a little shaken and my heart pounding so hard I thought I might have a heart attack. It was the first time we'd talked since the break.

"Hey, I didn't think you would answer." He sounded quiet and cautious.

"How are you?" I asked.

"I've been better. How about you?"

"I'm good." I tapped my hand on my knee, looking out the window, then tried to get a peek of the speedometer. Why wasn't the driver going faster?

"I'm on my way to the house," he said.

"Me too."

"You are?" He sounded surprised.

"Yeah, I have something to tell you," I said, and

swallowed a lump in my throat.

"I have something to tell you too." His words set off an alarm in my brain. It sounded like he'd made his own decision during our time away. I felt faint. What was he going to tell me?

By the time we'd turned the corner on to Fell Street, my palms were soggy. I just wanted to see James and tell him everything.

He was waiting for me outside on the sidewalk. He looked as afraid and as nervous as I felt. The cab hadn't even stopped before I pushed open the door and threw money at the driver.

"Hey." James smiled, the same way he always smiled when he hadn't seen me in a while.

"Hey." I did the same.

"It's good to see you."

"You too. Where's Cindy?" I asked. My hands were so shaky that I clutched the strap of my oversized purse, but the sweat from my palms loosened my grip.

"She'll be here soon. You said you wanted to talk about something." His face turned serious and so did mine.

"Yeah. About us. About our future." I had planned an eloquent speech, practicing it before I went to bed last night and again in the shower. In that moment, I forgot everything. My brain was mush, but my heart was bursting, so I let it talk. "I love you, James. I can't imagine loving anyone more. I do want to marry you, make a vow in front of everyone we know, and shout from the rooftops that you're mine. Forever. . . but I know you don't want

309

that."

"Marin," he interrupted, but I held my hand up to stop him from saying any more.

I took his hands in mine and felt his strong hold. "No, listen. It doesn't matter. When I was away from you, I realized that I would rather be unmarried with you than married without you. I don't need a wedding or certificate to be happy. I just want you." I couldn't stop the tears from rolling down my cheeks. I felt I was putting my heart on the line. After he said he had something to tell me, I was nervous about what he would say next.

"You mean that?" he asked, searching my eyes.

"Yes, love means taking a chance even if you're afraid. I will always be afraid to lose you, but I won't push you away anymore. I promise."

He sighed and beamed. "I'm so glad to hear you say that. I have something to show you."

He led me up the many stairs to the front door. I gave him a curious look as he pushed it open. Was there some special surprise on the other side? No, it was just the entryway. He took my hand and escorted me in.

"This is the door I'm going to walk through every day when I come home to you." James laughed. "And Marvin will rush over like he does, barking, excited to see me, and eventually our kids will do the same, but no matter who's looking for me, I'll be looking to see you."

I took in a deep breath and held it. Then, he led me into the living room near the fireplace. "This is where we'll sit and drink wine on cold nights, and over there." He pointed toward the wall. "That's where we'll curl up on the couch and watch movies together."

James walked into the dining room, pulling me along with him. "And over here, this is where we'll eat every night. You'll share your day, and I'll tell you about mine."

"Over here," James said as he walked into the kitchen and placed his hand on an empty countertop in the corner.

"This is where I'll make you coffee every morning and french toast on the weekend."

I smiled and rushed over to him. "James—"

"Wait." He held me at bay. "There's more."

James and I crept up the steps and he led me into one of the smaller bedrooms. "This will be the baby's room. The crib can go there and we can put a chair near the window so you can look out while you're nursing." He let me linger there for another moment, then I turned to him to say something.

"C'mon," he said. "I've got one more room to show you." He took my hand and we arrived in the bedroom. It was empty, except for the marks of dust that outlined the furniture that was once there. James led me to the middle.

"This is where our bed will be. The one we bought at Pottery Barn. Do you remember that night?" he asked.

I nodded, trying not to break down and cry all over him.

"This is where we'll read together before bed. Where we'll make love. Where we'll wake up to one another every day for the rest of our lives. Or until we retire and move south."

I laughed and cried. He'd painted a beautiful picture

of our life together. There was no ring, but in its place was love. And we were going to fill that entire space with it. In fact, I didn't know if that house could hold all the love we had to give.

"Thank you, for letting me take some time and for showing me this," I said.

"You know, I also realized something when you were away," he said.

"What's that?" I gazed up at him and I could feel my eyes twinkle.

"I never want to give you a reason to doubt how much I love you. And you're right. Love means taking a chance even if you're afraid you'll lose. I don't want to lose you again."

Then, James got down on one knee and pulled a ring-sized box from his pocket. I blinked once, then twice. Could it really be happening? He flipped open the box and a shiny diamond glistened inside. I felt a leap in my chest and my eyes filled with new tears, tears of happiness for a new life.

"I hope this will also be the place where we begin our new life together," he said, holding the ring box as steady as he could.

I covered my mouth and nose in my hands. This felt like a dream.

"Marin Li Johns, will you marry me?"

"Yes!" I cried.

He stood and took my face in his hands.

"Yes."

I couldn't decide whether I wanted to cry more or

smile more. So I did both.

"You sure this is what you want?" I asked after a moment, hopeful that he wouldn't change his mind.

"Without a doubt." He pushed my hair back and pulled me in for a kiss. I was reminded of the half marathon almost two years back when he had rescued me again after I fell and agreed to give me another chance. I was so grateful for that second chance, and even more grateful for this one.

He peeled my hand off his shoulder and slipped the glistening ring on my left ring finger. It was perfect. Somehow, after everything, we were engaged, really engaged with a round, cushion–cut, champagne diamond ring to prove it. I decided then and there that I'd never let anything come between us, and I'd never doubt his commitment to me.

The next day, we closed on Fell Street and the house was ours. When I returned to work as a homeowner and fiancée, there was one person I couldn't wait to share the news with.

"Hey," I said and danced into Andy's office. He looked up from his computer screen.

"What are you so happy about?" he asked.

"James and I closed on the house," I said.

"Really? Congratulations. You two patched things up?"

"We sure did. Look!" I flashed my left hand in front of his face, showing off the ring, like a proud fiancée.

"He proposed?" Andy couldn't have sounded more surprised.

My grin spread from ear to ear. I nodded like crazy.

"Oh, my God, that's amazing. Congratulations!" Andy gave me a big hug and took my hand to get a closer look at the ring. "That's beautiful."

"Thank you." I blushed.

"So I guess you got everything you wanted," he said.

"Yep, can you believe it?"

"Yeah, I can. I'm glad you finally can too."

I gave him a funny look, then remembered the other news I hadn't shared with him. "Oh, my gosh, I forgot to tell you about Telly."

"What about her?" he looked confused, but intrigued.

"She's going to have a baby," I said.

"Are you serious?" Okay, now he couldn't have sounded more surprised.

"Oh, don't worry. It's not yours."

He chuckled. "I know, Marin. You have to have sex to have a baby,"

"Ah-ha! You never slept with Telly on your date. So what did happen?" I asked, looking at him suspiciously.

"I'm not telling you. It was over a year ago."

I pursed my lips. "Are you ever going to tell me what happened between you two? Is there some waiting period that has to expire? Did she make you sign a contract or something?"

"I'll never tell, so let it go."

"Fine." I said. "I'll ask her when she's all drugged up during labor."

"I doubt that'll work, but good luck," he said.

I left him with a smile, but before I could get too far, he called me back in.

"I'm really happy for you, Marin. You're a good girl. You deserve everything you want."

"Thanks, Andy. So do you."

34

Moving On

THE SUN WARMED THE STREETS that Saturday morning in May. I met Holly, Telly, and Rachel at one of our favorite spots for brunch.

"Congrats on the new house!" Holly said as I slid next to her in the leather booth. The other girls chimed in with more congratulatory wishes.

"Thanks, guys, but I have more good news," I said.

"What's that?" Telly asked, taking a sip of her coffee, decaf I hoped. With an enormous grin, I whipped my hand out like a magician revealing something magical, because it was. "I'm engaged!"

The girls cheered and tugged my hand in every direction, each trying to get a better look than the last, fawning over the news like the best of girlfriends. They were my best girlfriends.

"What changed? I thought he didn't want to get married," Telly said. The truth was I'd never really know if it was the result of the *McQueen Method*, fear of losing me, or simply a change of heart, but in all cases, I was sure the change was genuine.

"I don't know, because I went to tell him that I wanted to be with him even if it meant we'd never be married. He was off the hook completely. The next thing I knew he was showing me through the whole house and painting a picture of what our life would be like there. When we got to the bedroom he told me that love meant taking a chance, even if you were afraid. Then he got down on one knee," I said. Holly and Rachel gazed at me all doe-eyed, even Telly looked a little awe struck. It was probably her hormones.

"He said that? That's so romantic!" Rachel squealed. Looking at all of them, I realized that all of us had taken a chance on love despite our fears. Rachel when she married David, knowing that what happened could, Holly for giving her heart to someone who lived half a world away, and Telly for taking a chance on motherhood, knowing very well that it could interfere with everything she'd worked so hard to accomplish.

"It's crazy how things change, huh?" Telly said and we all agreed. Our scrumptious breakfast platters arrived and the moment the server sat the plate in front of Telly she grimaced.

"You okay?" I asked.

She covered her mouth with the napkin. "I'll be back. Fucking pregnancy." Telly hurried to the bathroom, Holly following close behind for support. I was grateful. My breakfast did not need a side of barf.

"How are you doing?" I asked Rachel.

"I'm okay. I told David about everything."

"What did he say?"

She sighed. "He wasn't happy about it, obviously, but I think he was relieved in a way."

"Really? What now?"

"Believe it or not we agreed to forgive each other and try to move on."

"Just like that?" If only it were that simple. Hmm, maybe it could be.

She nodded and the girls were back.

"You all right there, champ?" I asked Telly.

She shot me a dirty look. "Never get pregnant."

I didn't envy her morning sickness, but as soon as James and I became husband and wife, I wanted to start a family.

"So when's the wedding?" Holly asked.

"When's you're wedding?" I smirked.

"We're thinking next spring, a wedding here, then a ceremony in Thailand."

I smiled and shot her a wink.

Rachel's fork dropped hard on her plate. "Oh, my God! Are you guys thinking what I'm thinking?" She seemed to shake with excitement while the rest of us looked confused. "Double wedding!"

"That's not a real thing." Telly frowned. I was glad she said it. Holly and I shared so much, but I was not going to share my special day with her. She deserved one of her own too.

"Well, I think it would be really cool," Rachel said under her breath as she retreated to her omelet.

"Depending on the venue, we're looking at late November or early December. I don't want to wait much longer," I said.

"What venue are you thinking?" Holly asked.

I swallowed a bite of the most delicious pancakes. I'd probably have to cut back soon if I wanted to look perfect in my wedding dress. "I'm hoping to have it at the Conservatory of Flowers."

Rachel gasped and Holly nodded her approval. "That's a great choice," Holly said.

"And all three of you are in the wedding party," I commanded in case there was any confusion. Telly sneered, as I thought she would.

"You know I'm due in mid-December, right? I'm literally gonna be all belly," Telly said.

I nodded as if I was oblivious to the point she was trying to make. She continued to glare at me. "So what, you want me to change my wedding date around your gestation period?" I smirked.

"Of course not, but do I have to be a bridesmaid?" Telly grimaced.

I shot her a wide-eye look. "Yes! I need you up there, so don't try to get out of it."

"Fine." She rolled her eyes. "Who's planning the bachelorette party?"

"No, no, no. No bachelorette party," I said.

"C'mon, Marin. It's bad enough I have to be a fat bridesmaid, at least let me do something fun." She shimmied her shoulders.

"Okay, but no strippers," I said, and she agreed, easier than I anticipated.

By midweek, all of the new furnishings had been moved into the new house and James had been working steadily to put the house together as best as he could. Meanwhile, I was packing up my apartment, sorting through items to take, leave, or giveaway. I was about to start on my bedroom when there was a knock at my door.

Telly.

"What are you doing here?" I asked.

She pushed her way through, the sound of her stilettos echoed through my nearly empty apartment.

"I came to help you pack. Remember?"

"No, but thanks. Are you sure you're up for it?"

She rolled her eyes. "I'm pregnant, not disabled."

I shrugged. "Sorry."

"What's left?" She peeked around the space.

"Just the two bedrooms. Grab a box."

We sat the boxes down and I assigned her my closet. She pulled items off the shelves with ease and tucked them in boxes. Her method was very organized, unlike mine. Who knew if I'd ever be able to pack a box or load the dishwasher the right way.

"How'd you get everything to fit so well?" I pointed to one of the boxes.

"I did a lot of moving as a kid." Telly didn't talk much about her childhood. With what little information she gave, I got the impression that things were a little unstable at Casa de la Torres. Her mother had died when she was young. That couldn't have been easy.

"Hey, how would you feel if I brought Will with me

to your wedding?" she asked.

Seeing as Will was the father of my best friend's baby, it would be best to make an effort for Telly.

"If you want him there, then I want him there."

"Really?" She looked surprised.

"Sure, why not. You're stuck with him now." I shot her a wink.

Telly looked pleased and began texting on her phone.

"Is that him?" I asked.

"Mmhmm." She stuck her phone in her pocket and resumed packing my things. A moment later, someone else knocked on the door.

"Who's that?" Telly asked.

"I dunno. I wasn't expecting anyone." We walked to the door and on the other side was a man wearing a Moving Guys uniform polo shirt.

"Are you Marin Johns?" he asked, pushing his way inside, frightening me a little.

"Yes, who are you?"

"I'm from the moving company. I understand you need some help unloading . . . your box."

Huh?

Dance music blasted behind me. I turned and Telly was grinning and dancing like a go-go girl. When I looked back, the "mover" had removed his shirt and was thrusting his groin at me like *take it baby, take it*.

"A stripper, Telly?" I raised my eyebrows.

"Yeah, girl!" She handed me some loose cash and made me sit down so the stripper could thrust his thing in my face. "Make it rain on him, Marin!"

Gross.

"Come on in, girls!" Telly shouted. Holly, Rachel, and Ginger danced into my apartment, carrying champagne, a hot pink bachelorette sash, and other party favors.

I blushed, wanting to cover my face. "What's this?"

"It's your bachelorette party!" Rachel shouted over the music.

"Wait, my wedding's not for six months," I said.

"Sorry, Marin," Telly said. "I had to throw it now, while I'm still sexy."

I pulled Telly in and kissed her cheek. "You'll always be sexy, girl!" I turned to Holly. "How could you let this happen?" I asked, laughing and pointing to the half-naked man dancing in my living room.

Holly shrugged with an innocent face.

Ginger slipped the sash over me. "Congratulations, girl! I told you." She smirked and pinched my cheek.

After the stripper left, the girls and I spent the remainder of the night drinking and packing the rest of my things for the move. Between the five of us, our lives had all recently changed in some significant ways. I was relieved to be moving forward in life alongside my best friends.

On Saturday morning, the real movers came and took all of my belongings to Fell Street. When they had removed the last box, the afternoon sun filled what was left of my apartment. As I walked through the empty space, I reminisced about the last three and half years I had spent there in my sanctuary. I'd miss it, of course. My home had been a special place. But the grief of leaving was nothing compared to the excitement of starting my new life with my soon-to-be husband in our new house. I still couldn't get my head around it, but everything that I wished for was happening.

James found me daydreaming in the bedroom.

"You ready?" he asked.

"Yeah," I smiled. He brought me in and held me for the last time in that space and kissed the top of my head. "Let's go home," he said. We walked hand in hand out of the apartment for the last time. Outside, I looked back at the building and waved goodbye to my old place and my old life.

Epilogue

Our Special Day

IT WAS SATURDAY, DECEMBER SECOND. Ginger had just finished coating my lips with color.

"Gorgeous," she said.

I looked in the mirror at my full wedding makeup, the long dark lashes, soft eye shadow, rosy cheeks, and of course, my deep crimson lips. I kissed the mirror leaving a stain on the glass.

The photographer took shots of my dress, and Holly, Rachel, and Ginger bustled around the hotel room, half dressed while Telly lay on the sofa. Her basketball shaped belly filled in her t-shirt and stretched her yoga pants as far as they could go. I scooted next to her.

"You look so pretty," she said and pouted her lip.

"Thank you. So do you," I said, looking at her perfect makeup and the beautiful waves in her long dark hair.

"Oh, please." She stretched out and ran her hands along her tummy. "I look like a balloon."

She didn't look like a balloon. Maybe like she was

hiding one under her top, but Telly had pretty much retained her stunning figure throughout the pregnancy.

"Put your dress on. It's almost time to go," I told her.

The photographer snapped a photo of us. She slowly rose from the couch, holding her lower back. "I hate that I'm going to be fat forever in your wedding photos," Telly whined.

"You're not fat, Telly," Rachel called out from the vanity in the bathroom. "You're pregnant and you're beautiful. So stop complaining. This is Marin's day."

The girls had dressed in their bridesmaid attire. Each style of the wine-colored dresses was unique to each of my friends. Rachel and Ginger carried my vintage-styled mermaid dress to me. They slipped it over my head, careful not to snag my hair or smudge my makeup. Then Rachel fastened the row of buttons in the back. I stood in front of the full-length mirror and looked at the lace covering my shoulders and down to the heart shaped neckline, then all the way to the hem on the floor. An antique broach joined the narrow satin sash below my bust.

Ginger tucked a red rose on the side of my low updo.

"Wait, don't forget this." Holly handed me the gold cuff, band-aid bracelet from James and I tightened it on my wrist.

"Thanks." We smiled at each other. The sight of her eyes shining with tears choked me up. "Don't cry," I said. "You're gonna make me cry."

"I'm so happy for you, Marin," she said, placing a

hand on my shoulder.

"Okay, that's enough. No more crying. This is a happy day." Telly handed over my bouquet of purple and red orchids, and Holly and I straightened up.

Rachel led the way outside. It was almost six o'clock and the sun had set. A cold breeze rushed through and I opened my coat to let it cool my skin. I couldn't help but sweat nervously. It was my wedding day. As we were getting in the limo, Telly crouched down and held her pregnant belly. She let out a groan.

I rushed to her side. "Are you okay?"

She stayed still for a moment and let out a deep breath. "Yeah, I'm okay."

"Are you sure?" I asked. "Do you need to go to the hospital?"

"I'm fine. It happens sometimes. I'm not due for a couple weeks anyway."

I gave Rachel and Holly nervous glances as we all piled into the car.

Ten minutes later we arrived at the Conservatory of Flowers, where James and I had one of our first dates. I'd never forget wandering around the flowers and wondering if he liked me. Turns out he did and that night he'd kissed me so perfectly that I knew it was true.

My sister-in-law Jennifer walked out to the limo, wearing a coat over her violet dress. Holly rolled down the window and she peeked in.

"All the guests have arrived and everyone's being seated," she told us.

"Is James here?" I called from deep inside the limo.

Jennifer craned to see me.

She smiled. "Yeah, he's here."

Good. This was definitely going to happen. Jennifer suggested the bridesmaids go inside and my father would be out to get me soon. While I waited alone in the car, I looked down at my band-aid cuff and slipped it off my wrist. I read the inscription.

If you should ever fall, I'll be there with a band-aid.

A few moments later, my father opened the door and slid inside.

"Hey, Dad."

"Wow, look at you," he said, voice filled with awe.

I blushed.

"My little girl is all grown up."

"Yep," I said, beaming.

He cleared his throat and lowered his eyes. "I don't think I've ever told you, but I'm very proud of you. I've always been proud of you. You've always listened to your gut, even when it wasn't easy. I know that I'm hard on you and your brother sometimes, but it's because I want the best for you both."

His words were a fresh breath of air, I breathed them in with ease. "Thank you," I said. "I've waited a long time to hear you say that."

He nodded and looked at his cell phone. "They're ready for us," he said and looked at me. "James is a good man, but are you sure this is what you want?"

"Yes," I said. "Without a shred of doubt."

"Okay, then let's get you married."

My dad hopped out of the limo and held his hand

out for me. We walked quickly into the building and one of the attendants led us to the ceremony room doors where my friends awaited us.

The attendant opened the doors and we heard the strings of the cello followed by the rest of the quartet. Pachelbel's "Canon" filled the room. Ginger started the procession, followed by Rachel then Telly, and finally Holly, who was my maid of honor.

My dad held my bouquet as I removed my coat, then handed it back. "You ready?" my dad asked.

"Ready," I whispered.

We stepped slowly inside the plant and flower filled room. A pergola lit by a thousand twinkling lights stood in the center. Inside stood James, dressed in a dark gray suit, his groomsmen, my girls, and the officiant. They all watched as my dad held me steady. If I had been on my own, I surely would have fallen on my face.

All my family and friends surrounded the Pergola, but when I looked up, my eyes met James', the same way they had the day he rescued me from that fall. The moment took my breath away. Our entire future flashed in my mind: setting up the new house; having a baby; watching our child graduate high school; celebrating the birth of our grandchildren, and finally sitting with him on a porch with whatever gray hair he had left on his head.

My hands trembled as my father handed me off to my groom. James took them, but his hands were shaking almost as much. I sucked in a deep breath, trying to hold off the tears a little longer.

The officiant began the ceremony. "We are gathered

here to join Marin Li Johns and James Christopher Young in marriage. In presenting yourselves here today, you are performing an act of faith in each other—a faith, which should grow and mature and endure. In our presence, you are now ready to pledge your love and yourselves to each other. We all rejoice in that love and in the wonder that this moment brings. You each have prepared your own vows?"

"Yes," we said in unison.

James pulled a folded piece of paper from his pocket. He cleared his throat and gave a sort of shy smile. I couldn't take my eyes from his face.

"Marin, when we first met that day in front of your office, it was like you were an angel that fell from heaven. A clumsy angel, but an angel just for me. You are the most perplexing woman I've ever met. You are also the most beautiful, warm, loving, and intriguing. Every day with you is one more day that I'm grateful to be alive. I promise to be there for you always, picking you up when you fall, finding you when you're lost, reminding you every day that you are an amazing person who deserves all the happiness in the world. I promise to contribute to that happiness throughout our long life together. You're my heart. You're my home. You're my one and only."

He slipped a white gold band on my finger.

I prayed that my mascara had not gone sliding messily down my cheeks, because there was no use fighting tears with words like his. James truly loved me and I never had anything to fear.

"I love you," I whispered through my sob.

"I love you," he said and squeezed my hands.

Then, I removed my own small paper from my dress, trying to pull myself together so I could read my words clearly.

"James," I said, looking into his misty blue eyes. "You're my hero. You've saved me time and time again, in more ways than you could ever know. When we met, I was lost and you helped me find my way back. I'm so glad because I've had the time of my life with you. I know that we can have it all as long as we have each other. Because of you, I believe in love again. You give me the greatest joy and I will spend my life trying to make you feel as incredible as you make me feel. I promise to love you with an open, honest heart because you belong with me, and I belong with you, and nothing will ever change that."

And with a simple white gold band, I made a vow.

"By the power vested in me by the state of California, I now pronounce you husband and wife. You may kiss the bride."

James took my face in his hands and pulled me in. I could feel his heart racing like my own. His warm lips touched mine and I drew deeper into him. He kissed my nose and smiled"

"We did it," I whispered in his ear.

"I know, I wish we'd done it sooner." He kissed me again.

"May I present to you Mr. and Mrs. Young!"

Our friends and family cheered as we sauntered down the aisle. I felt amazing. I was the new Mrs. Young. About halfway down the aisle, I felt something slippery under my shoe and I lost my balance. The crowd gasped. I shut my eyes tight and waited for my butt to hit the ground, but it didn't. James' arms were around me, pulling me up.

"You all right?" he asked.

I chuckled. Nothing was going to keep me down today. "Yeah, thanks to you."

"You know what I got you for a wedding gift?" he asked.

"What?" I looked at him and he smirked.

"Walking lessons." He laughed and I nudged him with my shoulder.

Afterward, our guests headed to the reception room, while James and I and the bridal party snuck off for photos. James and I were posing under the pergola when he said, "You are the most beautiful bride I've ever seen." I smiled and kissed him for what seemed like the hundredth time since we'd said I do.

At the reception, Gloria couldn't wait to congratulate us. We had barely finished our first dance when she ran up and wrapped her arms around me.

"We're so glad to have you in the family, Mrs. Young," she said.

"Thank you, Mrs. Young." I winked. Then a beautiful blonde woman snuck up behind her.

"Andrea!" James called with wide eyes. With a big smile, she wrapped her arms around her younger brother. "We didn't think you could make it."

"I wanted it to be a surprise. Are you surprised?" Andrea asked, almost giggling.

"Yes, I can't believe it." He rested his hand on the small of my back. "This is Marin, my new wife."

"Nice to meet you finally. Congratulations!" She opened her arms and embraced me with a warm hug, but I was still reeling over James calling me his wife.

"Thank you. I'm so glad you made it," I said, smiling as she walked with us to our table.

Later, James and I walked around the room separately, thanking all the guests for coming. Everyone seemed to be too shy to dance, except for Holly and Noom.

"How come you're not dancing?" I asked Telly who sat at her table with her feet up on Will's lap. He massaged her swollen ankles.

"Are you kidding? I can't dance. Those damn heels blew up my feet." Telly groaned and Will rolled his eyes.

The poor guy had had to put up with all of her gripes over the past eight months.

"I told you to wear flats," I said.

"I'm Telly Torres. I don't wear flats." She shot me a tight-lipped smile.

I sat next to her. "Are you having any fun?" I pouted my lip slightly and her attitude transformed.

"Of course I am." She smiled. "You and James are perfect together." Then she looked at Will and her smile frowned. "But I might have had more fun if somebody hadn't gotten me pregnant." She was ready for that baby to come out, and so was I. She'd been miserable the last couple of months.

Will stood with caution, careful to place her feet on the chair. "I'm going to get you some more Sprite," he said, and I gave him an apologetic look. We watched him walk to the bar and I saw Andy meet Telly's stare. They quickly turned away.

"Is it awkward having Andy here?" I asked.

"It's not awkward. Why would it be awkward? Nothing happened between us. It's totally fine." She let out a seemingly nervous chuckle.

"Mmhmm," I said.

Holly took a break from dancing and joined Telly and me. "Can you believe it," I said. "James and I are married, Telly's having a baby, and you're getting married in the spring?"

The girls nodded. "We had to grow up sometime I guess," Holly said.

"True, we're no spring chickens." I chuckled.

"Speak for yourselves. I'm still young and when this baby finally comes out, I'm going to be young *and* sexy." Telly snapped her fingers.

"We know, Tell," I said and pulled them both in for a hug. I must've held on too long because Telly shooed me away, complaining she was too hot.

I found James and my mom talking near the buffet table. "Oh, Marin, come here," my mom said, beckoning me into her arms. I lowered my body to match her height. "I'm so proud of you. You married this wonderful man." She patted James chest.

"Thanks, Mom," I said.

She looked me over, turning me from side to side. "You look beautiful, but you should've worn long sleeves or a jacket. It's so cold, you're going to get sick."

I rolled my eyes. "Mom, I'm fine. I wore a coat here. I'm not cold at all."

"No, no, no. James, give her your jacket."

James complied with my mother's orders and put his jacket over my shoulders. I could smell his cologne and I tucked my nose down to breathe it in. The jacket stayed on long enough for my mother to preoccupy herself with something else, like my niece and nephew.

Near the end, the cake was half eaten, Andy had the garter, and he had his eye on my single girlfriend who caught the bouquet. It was time for the last dance, and we got everyone to come to the floor, even Telly. She swayed with Will, while I danced with my brother and James danced with my mom.

"Can I cut in?" David asked and Michael handed me over. A couple of months after James and I moved into the house, David had come over and apologized for his earlier behavior. Since then, the four of us had hung out on a regular basis. Not all was right with David and Rachel, but they were working on it.

"I'm really happy for you guys. James is crazy about you," he said.

"Thanks. I'm glad things are starting to get back to normal."

"Normal?" He laughed. "No such thing." He spun me around and Andy grabbed my hand.

"Well, well, well. Bet you never thought we'd be dancing at a wedding," he said and raised his eyebrows.

"You're right." I smiled.

"But seriously, congratulations." He dipped me,

making me giggle, then brought me back in. "So what's the story with your friend over there?" He nodded toward Lana, the girl who was clutching my tossed bouquet.

I shook my head. "Not a chance."

"I'll take that as a challenge."

My new husband appeared next to us and Andy handed me to him. "She's all yours," Andy said. James picked me up off the ground and spun me around until I was dizzy.

"That's right. You're all mine," he said between kisses on my neck. I looked around at all the smiling faces of my dancing friends and family. The wedding had been perfect.

A few moments later, the guests began to gasp and clear the floor. The music stopped.

"What happened?" I shouted.

"My water just broke," Telly said.

"Oh, shit," Will said.

Before we knew it, the staff had rolled in a wheelchair and we took Telly out of the room. She seemed extremely calm as the rest of us panicked.

"I'll take her to the hospital," Will said.

"Wait, I need my bag. Can you go to my apartment and get my things?" she asked him.

"I'm not leaving you," he said.

"It's okay," I said. "I'll go with her to the hospital. You have time. Go get her things and meet us there."

"Marin, no! It's your wedding night," Telly demanded.

I leaned over her in the chair. "Tell, you're having a

baby. I'm not missing this for the world."

I took James' hand. "I'm sorry, but I have to go with her."

He put his palm on my cheek and kissed me. "I know. You two take the limo. I'll go help Will. We'll see you soon."

I smiled and we pushed Telly out to the limo. "I love you," I shouted to James and he echoed my words back. Telly and I climbed in and told the driver where to take us.

"Are you okay?" I asked.

"Yeah, I'm totally fine. I've read all the books. I took all the classes. I'm prepared for anything," she said with confidence and pulled out her phone.

"Who are you calling?" I asked.

"Will," she said in the phone. "Can you also bring my laptop and the files that are on the left side of my desk? It's probably going to be a long wait."

At the hospital, we made it up to the labor and delivery floor. I expected to see a busy floor with screaming women in labor, but that wasn't the case. Apparently, I watched too many movies. No, this floor was pretty quiet.

Will and James weren't far behind us and we all got Telly set up in the hospital room. The nurses got a kick out of the story, with the rest of us dressed in our wedding attire.

We waited for a couple hours, but Telly still wasn't fully dilated.

"It's late. You should go home," I told James as we stood together outside of Telly's room.

"I can stay," he said.

"I know, but you should go. When things get moving, you're not gonna want to be here anyway."

He pulled me in, glancing around. "Why don't we sneak off to one of those on-call rooms? It's our wedding night after all."

"I think that's only on TV, baby."

"You're right. It's been a long day. I'll see you at home." His lips touched mine. Soft, sweet, and tasty. I wished I could take him to a room.

"See you at home," I said. I couldn't take my eyes off him as he walked down the wide hallway. A couple of nurses did the same thing, seemingly eating him up with their eyes.

Sorry, ladies, but he was my husband. All mine.

I went back in Telly's room where she sat up, pecking away on her laptop. Manila folders and legal pads littered her bed.

"You're still working?" I asked, furrowing my brow.

"I hope you're not here to give me shit like that bastard who got me into this predicament." She barely took her eyes off the computer.

Will looked up and sighed.

"Yes, I'm talking about you," Telly said.

"I'm going to get more ice chips." Will left the room.

"Don't you want to unplug and enjoy this experience?" I sat on the stool next to her bed.

"Enjoy this experience? What do you think this is? A trip to Florence?" she snapped.

Man, she was grouchy.

"I just mean this is your baby." I softened my voice, but it didn't soften her.

"Exactly, that's why I have to finish this because once this baby's here, I have to spend all my time taking care of it instead of taking care of work. So if I could just squeeze in a couple extra hours, I'd feel a lot better."

"Okay," I said, holding my hand up. "So you're not in the mood for *Golden Girls* reruns?"

She raised an eyebrow at me. "Don't tempt me." A smile broke through her lips and mine. "Seriously, though. Just keep Will preoccupied. He's making me so crazy I've even threatened to take away his visitation rights."

"That's pretty harsh." Mean mommy.

"Desperate times, call for desperate measures." She typed away on her computer.

"Telly!"

"It's an empty threat, just keep him cool."

"We'll be lucky if he comes back the way you've been treating him," I said under my breath.

"I've seen much worse," one of the nurses told us.

I sat with her for a little while longer while she worked. Then, her contractions grew more frequent and more intense. I scooped up her computer and files and set them safely on the other side of the room.

"Holy shit this hurts!" she yelled. The nurse peeped under her blanket and a second later she announced that Telly was almost fully dilated.

"Can I see?" I asked, thinking I might as well get an idea of what this was going to be like for myself.

"No, you cannot see," Telly growled.

She was serious.

"Why not? I'm the only one who hasn't seen it."

Telly shot me a pissy look.

"You know what I mean, which reminds me, are you ever going to tell me what happened with you and Andy?"

"Marin, this isn't the time." She held her belly and screamed so loud that it made me tremble.

Uh-oh. This shit had just gotten real.

"Almost there," the nurse said. "Just hang in there."

I rushed to Telly's side. "Are you okay? I'm sorry about teasing you."

"It's okay. Can you get Will, please?" She looked so uncomfortable already that I wasn't looking forward to the next part.

"Yeah, I'll be right back." I stepped out of the room and dialed Will's cell. My shaking hands made the simple task frustrating. The phone rang and I walked the hall a little ways and found him at the end.

"It's almost time," I said. "You're going to be a father." What could be more exciting? I couldn't quite figure out the expression on Will's face. It was part emotional, part proud, and part terrified. We went back to Telly's side and waited a short time longer until she was fully dilated. The doctor was ready to deliver, giving orders to the nurses, and saying encouraging words to Telly.

Will hunkered in next to her on one side, while I was on the other. My curiosity got the best of me and I wandered over to get the full view. I blinked a couple of times not believing my eyes. It was one of those horrific, but amazing moments when you want to look away but can't. How was her vagina ever going to go back to normal size after that? Wait? How was my vagina ever going to go back to normal size when I had a baby?

I shook off the horrendous thought and went back to Telly's side.

She pushed and grunted, whining a little in between, but overall she gave birth like a champ.

"Almost done. One more push," the doctor said. Then, the sound of a teeny tiny baby crying filled the room. Telly's head fell back, while she caught her breath. "It's a boy!"

Telly looked over at Will and the two looked at each other as if they were telepathically speaking, maybe making a silent promise to be good parents to their new son.

"Oh, my God! It's a boy, Telly! You have a son." I choked on the words as my eyes filled with tears and I squeezed her hand a little more.

She glanced over at me and smiled. "I have a son."

The doctor pulled Will aside to cut the baby's cord. After that, I watched him hold his son in his arms for the first time.

"I want to see him," Telly called and Will carried the baby over, gently taking one step at a time. He placed the little one on Telly's chest and she pushed the blanket away from the baby's face to see him better.

I also snuck in a peek. He was beautiful, truly beautiful.

"Hi, baby," Telly said in a soft tone. "I'm your

mommy." She began to cry in the happy sort of way, like she knew this was going to be the best part of her life, no matter what it took from her. From here on out, she'd always be his mommy. I took a mental photo of the three of them there as a happy family, knowing the circumstances were unconventional but that the love was there.

That's when I realized that a happy life could come in many forms. Sometimes it was with a husband and a house. Sometimes it was an unexpected bundle of joy. Sometimes it was taking a chance on something or someone you loved. But in all cases it came down to courage. The courage to be honest with yourself about what you wanted, what you needed, and what you're willing to give.

I had found my happiness in an unexpected way. And I think I liked that better.

"What's his name?" one of the nurses asked.

Telly looked up and smiled. "We're calling him Leo." She held the baby a while longer then offered to let me hold him.

Finally. I beamed.

I tenderly took him from her and held him close.

"Hi, little Leo, I'm your aunt Marin." Everything about him was so little, his little face, his little nose, and his little fingers and fingernails. Suddenly I was in love and I couldn't wait to have one of my own.

Hello Reader!

I really hope you enjoyed spending time in Marin's world. If so, you'll love the rest of *The Marin Test Series*. Available now!

I hope you'll connect with me on social media. You can find me here:

Visit at www.amandaaksel.com

Like on Facebook: www.facebook.com/amandaaksel

Follow on Instagram: www.instagram.com/amandaaksel

Follow on Pinterest: www.pinterest.com/amandaaksel

XXO-Amanda

AMANDA AKSEL

Amanda Aksel loves anything that's smart, sexy, and funny. She's the author of *The Marin Test Series* and *The Londonaire Brothers Series*. You'll often find her writing novels with an adorable maltipoo on her lap, pretending to be Sara Bareilles at the piano, watching reruns of *Sex and the City*, or sprinkling a little too much feta on her salad.